CRITICAL ACCLAIM FOR
Paradise of the Blind

"Duong Thu Huong describes the problems of ordinary people and the contradictions of political reform openly. . . . *Paradise of the Blind* is a daring work of fiction."
— *The New York Times*

"We have been hearing for many years from Americans who seemed to consider the Vietnamese experience—life and war—their own. At last a woman, a Vietnamese woman, tells us Vietnamese life: the village, the city, the repression and expansion, the middle peasant, the poor peasant, the years of exquisite food and no food, working in the Soviet Union—and all beautifully told so that we can begin to understand not where *we* were for years, but where and how they—the Vietnamese—are now."
— Grace Paley

"Duong Thu Huong is a social panoramist who writes with a tight focus on individual consciousness and personal relations . . . putting into print what the people of Vietnam know, that the way things are is different from the way they are supposed to be."
— *The Nation*

"Duong Thu Huong is unmatched in her ability to capture the small details of ordinary life. Her characters are not the awesome agents of American failure in Vietnam, but ordinary men and women whose only weapon against abject poverty and political oppression is infinite endurance. I found *Paradise of the Blind* absolutely gripping and a real eye-opener. The translation is first-rate."
— Hue-Tam Ho Tai, Harvard University

"[An] extraordinary book, remarkable for its poetic beauty and insight into the soul of a people . . . *Paradise of the Blind* combines the sweep of recent Vietnamese history with insights and revelations of a deeply personal nature. . . . The novel's haunting personal drama and exotic landscapes will linger in the reader's mind for a long time."
— Robert DiAntonio, *St. Louis Post-Dispatch*

"Considering that Vietnam so absorbed the energies of an entire generation of Americans, it is remarkable how little even those of us who have been there finally know about the country and the life of its people. In *Paradise of the Blind*, Duong Thu Huong lays open the Vietnamese experience for the world as only a first-rate writer can. The novel's descriptive style is at once passionate, precise, and lyrical."   — Robert Stone

Timothy Karr

About the Author

DUONG THU HUONG, one of Vietnam's most popular writers, was born in 1947. At the age of twenty, she volunteered to lead a Communist Youth Brigade sent to the front during the Vietnam War. During China's 1979 attack on Vietnam, she also became the first woman combatant present on the front lines to chronicle the conflict. A vocal advocate of human rights and democratic political reform, Duong Thu Huong was expelled from the Vietnamese Communist Party in 1989, and was imprisoned without trial for seven months in 1991 because of her political beliefs. *Paradise of the Blind* is her fourth novel and her fourth to be effectively banned by the Vietnamese authorities; she is forbidden from traveling abroad. Duong Thu Huong lives and writes in Hanoi.

Translators PHAN HUY DUONG and NINA MCPHERSON live in France.

Paradise
OF THE
BLIND

DUONG THU HUONG

Translated from the Vietnamese by
Phan Huy Duong and Nina McPherson

Perennial
An Imprint of HarperCollinsPublishers

The translators would like to thank everyone who advised them on various aspects of the translation, most especially Keith Taylor and Patricia Pelley at Cornell University, and Kim Nguyen at the University of Washington.

Published in Vietnamese by The Women's Publishing House, Hanoi, Vietnam. English translation published by arrangement with Des Femmes (*Les Paradis Aveugles* copyright © 1991 by Des Femmes).

The first U.S. edition of this book was published in 1993 by William Morrow.

First Perennial edition published 2002.

Library of Congress Cataloging-in-Publication Data

Duong, Thu Huong.
    [Nhung thiên duòng mù. English]
    Paradise of the Blind / Duong Thu Huong; translated from the Vietnamese by Phan Huy Duong and Nina McPherson.— 1st Perennial ed.
        p. cm.
ISBN 0-06-050559-1
1. Sino-Vietnamese Conflict, 1979—Fiction. I. Title.

PL4378.9.D759 N4813 2002
895.9'2233—dc21   2002068724

08 09 RRD 20 19 18 17 16 15 14

Translator's Note

THIS NOVEL BEGINS IN THE 1980s AND IS NARRATED BY A YOUNG
Vietnamese woman, Hang, from the dormitory of the Russian
textile factory where she works. Like hundreds of thousands
of young Vietnamese men and women who came to adulthood
after the end of the Vietnam War in 1975, Hang has been
forced by her country's economic plight to cut short her education and become an "exported worker" in what was then
the Soviet Union. Most of the novel takes place in Hang's
memory as she makes the long train ride to Moscow to visit
her uncle, a Communist party cadre who has used his connec-

tions to secure a post there. Alienated and alone, Hang reflects on her childhood, on the family history she was told, on her coming of age in northern Vietnam and the events that have led her to leave her country.

Hang is an educated woman of the 1980s, but to reconstruct and ultimately escape the destiny of self-sacrifice she sees laid out for her, she must come to terms with Vietnam's recent past. Born in a northern village outside Hanoi, Hang begins by recounting the stories she was told of a revolution that would divide her family and shatter the lives of her mother and her aunt.

The historical events referred to at the beginning of the novel take place in northern Vietnam in the chaotic years just prior to, and immediately following, the surrender of the French colonial government. In 1954, Vietnam was temporarily partitioned for military regroupment at the 17th Parallel by the Geneva Accords, which officially ended almost a century of French involvement in the country. National elections to reunify the country were to be held by July of 1956, but instead, what was intended to be a temporary demarcation between north and south became a de facto political boundary. To the north of the parallel, the Vietnamese revolutionary leader Ho Chi Minh already headed the Viet Minh government in the Democratic Republic of Vietnam (established in September 1945), and in the south, an American-backed leader, Ngo Dinh Diem, became president of the newly established Republic of Vietnam (established in October 1955).

Even before Ho Chi Minh and his Viet Minh government took control of Hanoi and other major cities in 1956, they had tried to gain support for their anti-French resistance movement by launching a land reform campaign in the northern countryside. In 1953, following the example of Communist governments in China and the Soviet Union, the Viet Minh forced the redistribution of privately owned land to more than 1.5 million peasant families.

For the forty-five-year-old author of this novel, Duong

Thu Huong, the horror of the land reform campaign marked the beginning of much of her country's disillusionment with the Communist experiment. As Duong Thu Huong describes it, the land reform campaign (1953–1956)—which was inspired in part by the example of the revolutionary Chinese leader Mao Zedong—triggered a wave of violence: terrified villagers were forced to denounce their "landlord" neighbors to guerrilla "security committees"; and by 1956, tens of thousands of villagers—some of them with only a few acres of land—had been arrested. Nearly 100,000 "landlord" farmers were sentenced to forced labor camps by courts that were often composed of no more than a handful of illiterate peasants. In the chaos, many of the Communist cadres administering the land reform engaged in factional struggle, and some took advantage of their power to spare their own relatives or to seize the property of the accused for themselves. When the Viet Minh leadership realized the scale of unrest the campaign had caused, they publicly apologized for the land reform, acknowledging it as an "error" and reclassifying the peasantry in another campaign called the "Rectification of Errors." Those who survived the labor camps were sent back to their villages under orders to "forgive and forget."

The absurdities of the land reform and the other Maoist-style ideological campaigns that followed—including one in the late 1970s that arrested young people for wearing "Western imperialist" bell-bottom trousers—are reflected in the broken lives of Duong Thu Huong's characters. For Duong Thu Huong, who comes from a working-class family and was until recently a Communist party member herself, Vietnam became a schizophrenic country where a people bled white by decades of war, teetering on the edge of starvation, had suddenly to defend themselves against their own leaders, a grasping, hypocritical elite who were blind to their nation's crisis.

To follow Hang's memory is to be immersed in both the beauty and the cruelty of rural Vietnamese culture. It is to feel, as Hang does, both the strength and the suffering of

Vietnamese women in the face of the crushing weight of the Confucian cult of male authority, a legacy of more than one thousand years of Chinese rule. Whether Hang is in her village or the slums of Hanoi, as a Vietnamese woman she must confront a deeply Confucian culture of ancestor worship: where peasants still pray to altars decorated with incense, rice, and wine; where the young submit to the old; where children yield to the authority of their parents, sisters to their brothers, and wives to their husbands.

The psychological impact on the Vietnamese of the extreme poverty and widespread corruption of the postwar years is another important aspect of the novel. As was typical of many other Communist countries in the 1960s and 1970s, Vietnam's economic ruin and the extreme devaluation of its currency created a strange, parallel economy where bribery and barter were often an unavoidable part of the struggle to survive. In an economy plagued by shortages, access to housing, medical care, and material goods became, in reality, a privilege reserved for the Communist party elite. Duong Thu Huong describes Vietnam in the late 1970s, when huge numbers of Vietnamese party officials like Hang's Uncle Chinh traveled to the Soviet Union and the other East bloc "brother" countries on socialist "friendship" missions. At the time, many of them abused their positions to engage in racketeering—furtively trading their access to Vietnamese goods like textiles and foodstuffs for scarce Russian consumer products, which they could later sell back in Vietnam. For the Vietnamese, the strain of maintaining this duplicity—between the Communist rhetoric of self-sacrifice and the reality of daily life—is visible in the paranoia, the deviousness, and the humiliation Hang sees etched on the faces of her friends and relatives as they jostle each other in the daily struggle for scarce food, exit visas, and consumer goods.

To read a novel by Duong Thu Huong is also to experience the beauty of Vietnam. In our co-translation, we have tried to render the richness and sensuality of Duong Thu Huong's style by translating all but a few quintessential Vietnamese words.

We have provided a glossary of many cultural terms at the back of the book. The reader will find that the majority of these terms relate to food or rituals related to preparing and eating it. The Vietnamese reverence for food, which is reflected in many proverbs and popular sayings, is a recurrent theme in Duong Thu Huong's writing. In predominantly rural cultures like Vietnam, food is often a powerful form of human expression, a currency that, like money, is used to quantify one's love, respect, or even hatred for another human being. The Vietnamese saying "A morsel of food is like a morsel of shame" reflects the belief that to give or accept food reveals one's status in the hierarchy of the social order. When the Vietnamese offer food to those outside the family circle, whether in the form of a token gift or a lavish village banquet, the gesture can be taken as an expression of generosity or pure contempt.

Some of the subtlety of the Vietnamese language, with its myriad ways of expressing affection or respect for age and social position, is impossible to translate into English. Terms of address can be particularly confusing if translated literally, since the Vietnamese traditionally address everyone as if they were family members, often respectfully calling complete strangers "Elder Sister," "Auntie," or "Grandmother." For the sake of clarity, we have limited this form of usage to refer to actual relatives. Some readers may also be struck by the exaggerated, almost Orwellian quality of the Communist rhetoric used by some of the characters in the novel; if so, they are that much closer to the reality of the Vietnamese reader's experience. It was very much Duong Thu Huong's intention to satirize the emptiness and degradation of language as it came to be spoken by officials under the Communist regime.

—NINA MCPHERSON

Chapter ONE

[handwritten annotation: Intro of the characters — the reluctant Hang, and her hatred for her uncle]

I T WAS NINE O'CLOCK WHEN MADAME VERA HANDED ME the telegram:

————

VERY ILL. COME IMMEDIATELY.   *[handwritten: Uncle in Moscow]*

————

She looked at me and said:

"Poor little one. You really don't have much luck." She shook her enormous old head and turned to go. As she shuffled off, the smell of her cheap perfume hung in the room, sticking like glue to the yellowed, peeling walls. I just stood there shivering in my pajamas, staring at the housekeeper's buxom figure, my head spinning.

I was sick myself; for the last few days I had been racked

11

with fever. I walked with my shoulders hunched over like an old drug addict, my tiny breasts floating under a baggy shirt. The only men in our residence were real relics; they didn't even bother to stare.

Eight hundred rubles left in savings: I had already spent 450 rubles on medicine and extra food, and I had just decided to use another 50 to build up my strength so I could go back to work. This telegram felt like a curse.

"Are you crazy? What are you doing outside this early? Get back in bed. One more relapse and you'll be reduced to syrup," my roommate called. I slipped back under my sheets, pouring myself into their warmth. A feeling of happiness. It was Sunday, and we had decided to make some Vietnamese noodles for lunch. While they boiled, we stayed tucked under our covers, listening to some music that drifted down from a room just above us on the next floor. Drained by fatigue and homesickness, we strained to hear it. The window was wide open. Outside, the earth and trees were brown, not a speck of green. The sky was a lucid, icy blue.

"What does the telegram say, Hang?" asked my roommate.

"My uncle's sick."

"The one in Moscow again?"

"Yeah."

"But you've just recovered yourself."

I didn't say anything.

"Only four days of vacation left, you know. Tania just reminded me."

Still I said nothing.

"Moscow's so far. The trip will knock you out. You're as white as a woman after childbirth. Why don't you put on some makeup? It frightens me to look at you."

I kept my silence. My friend's words had stirred a dull gnawing in me, a feeling of rebellion. "I'm not going. I'm just not going, and I don't care. I really don't care."

I could already see train tracks rushing past me: mile

markers swallowed up in the distance; dense forests followed by unending fields of wheat; village after village; church spires and rooftops piercing the air; the sad, monotonous click-clack of wheels along the track; station after station drowned in fog, awash in eerie fluorescent light.

My roommate stretched and got out of bed. Dragging her long nightgown behind her, she moved toward the shelf to get a record, then reached up toward the record player she had just bought. One hundred and twenty rubles. She pulled off the cloth she used to cover it, lifted the lid, and switched it on. Then she jumped back under the sheets. The needle scratched and crackled along the record's empty tracks until it reached the song:

> *"At the end of the Red River, do you know?*
> *In the land of my birth, is another river.*
> *My heart weeps with nostalgia:*
> *Vam co Dong! Vam co Dong."*

The song echoed blue and icy through our space. Outside, the sun shone, but here, I could feel the chill of exile under my skin, in my bones. The song resonated like the thinnest thread of silver lost in the blue of the sky. I followed it and felt myself pulled back to the edge of the earth, to a familiar river and a beach of blinding white sand. A ripped sail tossed amid the waves, buffeted by the sharp, anguished cries of migratory birds as they prepared for flight.

And I saw the roof of the shack in Hanoi where my mother lived. Sheet metal patched together with tar paper. On rainy days, the roof leaked. In the heat of summer, the acrid smell of tar was overpowering, nauseating. All around, the gutters, gurgling under slabs of cement, flowed from one house to the next. Children played in this filthy black water, sailing their little white paper boats. The few mangy patches of grass were at the foot of the wall where men drunk on too much beer came to relieve themselves. The place reeked of urine. This was my street; I had grown up here.

"Hang, what are you thinking about?"

I didn't answer.

"I miss home . . . something terrible," my roommate muttered.

My friend was feeling sorry for herself. I heard her tossing about between the sheets, moaning. "It's a bitch of a life. Better to get it over with once and for all."

I stayed walled off in my silence. I don't know when I started to cry. My throat knotted in the heat, gathering the salty flavor of tears. I saw my mother's face again, the sad glow radiating from the inky depths of her eyes. Pain and infinite perseverance. I remember now, what she would say each time we were struck by misfortune:

"To live with dignity, the important thing is never to despair. You give up once, and everything gives way. They say ginger root becomes stringy, but pungent with age. Unhappiness forges a woman, makes her selfless, compassionate."

My mother had lived like this, according to proverbs and duties. She wanted me to show the same selflessness. And what had I done? My uncle, her younger brother—her only brother—had asked for my help. He was sick, and here I was, preparing to abandon him.

Madame Vera was knitting in the waiting room, using bits of yarn torn from old clothes. She was working on a shawl that could have covered her huge, bearlike back. Concentrating now on the finishing touches, she guided the needles deftly with her tiny white fingers, which looked ten years younger than her face. No one would have thought that this crude woman, with her barrellike thighs and hunched back, could knit such a delicate shawl. When she saw me, she cocked her head back slightly, peering out at me over her bifocals.

"You've decided to go to Moscow?"

"I don't have the choice, Madame Vera."

"You're still pale as a ghost."

"Yes, but he's my uncle."

She leaned toward me. "Wait a minute."

I waited impatiently. Out of politeness, I didn't dare rush her—but I was afraid I'd miss my train. She fussed over her shawl, stopping to fondle it for a moment.

"Isn't it beautiful? All from salvaged wool." Her voice quavered with pride. She scrawled my name in the register. That's what I had been waiting for, so I hurried to say goodbye.

She caught my arm, barring the door with her hand. "Wait just a moment. I'll loan you the shawl. You're going to need it tonight, my little mouse."

I said good-bye to this massive woman. She wore her heart on her sleeve and yet could be terribly nasty to us at times, flying into the murderous rages common to Russian war widows. I took the bus to the station and arrived just in time to catch the only express train for Moscow. It was five in the evening, and everything was radiant, bathed in the hazy gold of sunset: the buildings, the tree-lined streets, the woods scattered through the suburbs. Even the dresses on the young girls seemed to float more seductively. I could have watched all this forever, my spirit soothed, calmer now.

At the entrance to the train station, I brushed against a Russian woman with blond permed hair. She glared at me, and I apologized. Was my voice too soft? Hadn't she heard me? She continued on her path as if she hadn't seen me, her figure tightly molded into a red velvet blouse and black skirt. She swayed and gave off a flowery perfume as she walked straight ahead, her head tossed back. She must have been in her midtwenties, just about my age. I caught a glimpse of my own reflection in the window: a pale young woman with a lost, worried expression, stooped shoulders, and cheap maroon wool suit. A frightened human being of about eighty-two pounds.

"Don't think so much. . . ." I mumbled to myself. "Forget these complexes. Don't complicate life. Don't be so ridiculous," I continued, punishing myself with these thoughts. My cheeks burned and the hatred I felt for my uncle rose in me. I quickly boarded the train, nestled myself in a corner of the compartment, and closed my eyes.

My maternal grandfather, who died long before I was born, had practiced traditional medicine. He cured a number of gravely ill patients but didn't succeed in saving himself from a mysterious illness at the age of forty-three. Probably cancer, judging from the symptoms.

My grandmother was forty-two years old when he died. She decided never to remarry and to devote herself to their children, my mother and her younger brother, Chinh. Ten months later, a brutal typhoid fever killed her. My mother was nineteen years old. My uncle Chinh eighteen. By chance, a relative who attended the funeral took my uncle with him to join the Viet Bac underground, the anti-French resistance movement in the mountainous north. Later, my uncle joined the Liberation Army.

My mother stayed behind in the village. She worked as a street vendor, living off the sales of snacks and goods that she lugged along with her in a hamper. She used the money to tend the graves of our ancestors and to keep up my grandfather's house.

I visited that house only once. It was low and covered with tiles shaped like fish scales. There were big wooden doors and a veranda that had been perched high on layers of stone above the dampness of the ground. Attached to the main residence were three outbuildings: one for raising silkworms, one for threshing and pounding rice, and the third for storing farming tools. It was a traditional house, solidly built, but dimly lit and sinister.

One afternoon, when I was just a girl, I stood in that house, inhaling the dank, musty smell of the walls. It was the first time I had ever even seen the house and the village where my mother had been born and raised. . . . The eyes of the ghoulish sculptures carved into the wooden transoms above the doors riveted me with their mysterious gaze. A spider's web hung from the vaulted ceiling. Light flickered through cracks in the chipped, rotting tiles, flashing at me like the phosphorescent bursts that haunt cemeteries. Terrified, I rushed out into the courtyard where my mother sat chatting and sipping green tea with the other women.

"What's the matter, my child?"

"I'm scared."

"My silly chicken. Afraid in broad daylight?" she laughed, scolding me. When she smiled, I always noticed the sparkling whiteness of her teeth, aligned in perfect rows, and it made me sad. This was the last trace of her beauty, her youth, of a whole life lived for nothing, for no one.

"In the old days, when you lived here, were you ever scared?" I asked, for no particular reason.

"Of what? This is the home of our ancestors," she replied, irritation showing in her voice.

I continued, stubbornly, "But you were alone."

A neighbor seated in a corner, the same age as my mother, grinned. "She wasn't frightened. She was *bored*. That's why she couldn't wait till the end of the mourning period to marry handsome Ton."

Wild laughter rippled through the group of women, and they slapped each other on the back, cackling like a bunch of young girls. My mother flushed, as if she had been chewing betel nut.

"Who's handsome Ton?" I asked.

The neighbor snapped at me insultingly, "Your own father, you poor thing."

I ran into the garden. They had mocked me, insulted me. Me, the fatherless child, the little bitch. I hid myself to cry in the garden between an old guava tree and a spiny pineapple bush. My mother finally found me and brought me back to the house. The neighbors had left. Carambola flowers lay in ashen drifts across the bricks of the courtyard. Mother began ladling water from a bucket. She slowly filled a bronze basin. She washed my face. I sobbed for a long time. The sun glinted off the surface of the water, burning my eyes before I fell off to sleep.

At dawn, birds began to warble in the bamboo grove; the garden hummed with their singing, and a fresh breeze swept away my fears. In the distance, somewhere along the road to the village, the cry of a barley-sugar vendor rang out clear and tireless:

"Barley sugar! Who'll buy my barley sugar . . . ?"

My mother bought me two huge sticks of barley sugar. She hugged me close to her and whispered, "The handsome Ton was . . ." I was almost ten years old when I first learned about my father.

Chapter TWO

SHE TOLD ME IT HAD ALL HAPPENED LONG BEFORE I WAS born. After her parents died and her brother left for the underground, my mother lived alone, fretting and pacing through a whole year of days. The house, three main rooms and three outbuildings, was deserted but for her. It was difficult enough to clean it and scrub the floors. On top of that, there was the garden to maintain and defend from an invasion of weeds. As soon as she had weeded one corner, weeds would swallow up another. At noon, when the summer heat reached its peak, the cry of a black cuckoo bird was enough to make her jump in terror. She came and went in silence, followed only by her own shadow.

Time passed. A straw fire licking at a stoneware cooking pot filled with the daily rice. A jar of salted vegetables stinking in the corner of the house. A steamed fish pickled in its own brine. Or a hard-boiled egg on a tiny plate. A clear soup with a few sprigs of bindweed plucked from the hedge.

At night, she listened to the neighbors calling their loved ones to come eat. She listened to the to-and-fro of their lives: the sound of a pestle crushing crabs for a noodle soup, steam rising from potatoes, the crackling of young rice being roasted to make grilled sticky rice, the smell of *che* puddings for the Full-Moon Festival each month. Life was all around her, but it was a life that belonged to others. And she looked at her own little straw fire and wept.

All she could see was the misfortune that had befallen her. She was a young woman, barely twenty, and the young toughs and lecherous village chiefs sought her out like vultures. At nightfall, she would light an oil lamp, stretch out, and try to sleep until dawn. When she couldn't, she burned three incense sticks and prayed to our ancestors, imploring them to protect her in this life.

It was during this solitary year that she met my father. Ton was a schoolteacher who had just been posted to the village. He had once taught in a nearby town, but in order to care for his mother, who suffered from paralysis in one of her feet and rheumatism, he asked for a transfer.

My mother had just turned twenty. Ton was twenty-six. They say she was the most beautiful young woman in the village. My father had his charm. What's more, he had an education. Their courtship began quickly—too quickly for the taste of the village public. According to the tradition, after the death of her parents my mother should have observed a three-year mourning period during which she did not have the right to court, dress up, or join in the Buddhist festivals. When he married my mother, my father subjected himself to the contempt and mockery of the entire village:

"Ton received a Western-style education. You know, over there in France, mourning only lasts a year."

"Yes, but he isn't from the race of blue eyes and big

noses. What a shameless bunch they are, neglecting the tombs of their ancestors."

"Degenerates! Just wait and see. Misfortune comes to those who flout the ancestral laws. Their happiness won't last."

The malicious predictions came true. But not because my parents didn't get along. At first, they were very happy. That much I knew. As I listened to my mother tell of even the darkest episodes, I saw passion in her gaze: the last, fiery glow of a love that was infinite, irretrievable, the kind you live only once. . . .

Exactly one year and two months after the marriage, peace was declared throughout the country. This was all still long before my birth. The soldiers returned from the Viet Bac underground in the north. Everywhere, the forests rang out with their songs. Songs of liberation, songs of peace, songs of the rice paddies.

Happy, but anxious and numbed by her year of suffering, my mother looked forward to the return of her only brother. She hadn't had any news of him since his departure. A team of men who sold medication to the soldiers passed through our region and reported seeing him. They told her that he was well, that he had already earned his stripes and been promoted to section chief. But others told her he was sick, that his skin was as yellow as saffron, that he had had to guard horses for a transmissions battalion. They also remembered he was short of warm clothing and that they had seen him, in the bitter cold of December, shivering in a thin sweater.

My mother wept constantly, pleading with my father to go find her brother. My father made the rounds, inquiring at every army unit stationed in the area. He crisscrossed the province on his bicycle, but it was all in vain; he couldn't find a trace of my uncle. Then one day, six months after liberation, without drums or fanfare, my uncle arrived. My mother was digging up taro roots in the garden. She dropped her trowel, crumpled to the ground, and began to sob. All the relatives pleaded with her, but no one could calm her.

My father, who had just gotten home from teaching, welcomed his brother-in-law and offered to prepare him some of their best tea. But Uncle Chinh only nodded and gave a kind of grunt. There was something odd, condescending, about his behavior. My father went out into the garden, motioned to my mother to come back inside, and then left for his own mother's house.

A small garden of betel palms and a few hedges of cactus separated our house from the home of my father's mother. We would just call across from one house to the other. Grandma Nhieu, who was convalescing but could move about now, lived with Aunt Tam, my father's elder sister. My aunt was twenty-seven years old at the time and very beautiful, but since she was educated and aloof, she couldn't seem to find a husband. She worked in the rice paddies and raised silkworms.

As soon as my father had left the house, my uncle Chinh ordered my mother to sit down on a bench facing him: "Que, from now on you must not speak to, or have any further contact with, that Ton."

"'That Ton'? Why do you refer to him like this? He's now your brother-in-law."

"He's an exploiter."

"An exploiter?"

"The entire family are landlords, the mortal enemies of the peasantry. Sister, before I came back, I was asked to lead the land reform, to prepare the campaign here in this village. We just finished classifying the people in this village. Ton's family hired farm labor. According to our directives, they belong to the exploiting class. These are precisely the people we must denounce and punish."

"What does this mean?"

"It means we are going to force these criminals to kneel

in front of their peasant compatriots and confess their crimes."

"Ton's family has always lived in peace with everyone," my mother stammered. "They've never laid a finger on anyone here. You know that. Here in the village, everyone knows who's bad and who's good."

Uncle Chinh interrupted, correcting her sternly: "You must not let yourself be influenced by others, or betray your class. We must crush the landowning classes, these cruel oppressors, and return the land to the peasants. If you don't listen to me, you'll be forced out of the community and punished according to revolutionary sanctions."

My mother began to sob. "But we have always lived peacefully with the villagers. Always. Ton is so patient. When we were married, he swallowed his anger and even made friends with the same people who insulted and mocked us. I don't know how he exploits or who he . . . I've never heard of such a thing."

"No one has. But from now on, the Section for Land Reform is going to talk about it. Que, Sister, listen to me. . . ."

This exchange took place in front of close relatives. Everyone shrugged and left in silence. No one understood why my grandma Nhieu had suddenly become "an enemy of the people," "a member of the reactionary class of exploiters," just because she had inherited a few acres of rice paddy.

Her daughter, Tam, cultivated these paddies. Each season, she hired labor to help her. At sowing time, she waded into the fields herself with her seedlings. During the harvest season, she worked herself ragged, even cooking meals for the migrant workers who came from the distant Dong and So hamlets. Many families in our village lived this way. Villagers who owned a bit of land, like my aunt Tam, were the pillars of the countryside. Farming was their whole life.

In the first month of Tet, the Lunar New Year Festival drums would beat to call people to celebrate in the temple courtyard. Children scampered down the country roads, chasing each other in all directions. People formed processions, and theater troupes would compete to put on plays; everyone tried to pinch a few coins from the villagers' money belts.

The villagers watched the festivities with one eye, guarding their rice paddies and their tender green seedlings with the other. By plunging a hand into the mud, they could check the quality of their tilling, they could sense the earth's cooling or warming. In the summer, they had only to listen to the way the wind whistled through their straw roofs to divine what calamities or blessings heaven had in store for them. And, from the first crack of thunder or the first downpour, they knew whether to rush to their pickaxes and trowels near the dikes or to the vegetable patches near the river's edge.

On clear August nights, the rhythm of pestles pounding young rice rose from every courtyard in every village. The shrill jeer of women's laughter was enough to shatter these millions of white flowers. As the intoxicating fragrance of cactus floated over the gardens, the villagers studied the moon: What did it mean, this red halo, this silvery sparkle of clouds biting into the intense blue of the sky? In winter, in the deep chill of the night, they could wake in an instant, tear themselves from the warmth of their beds, and run to the cowshed to light a fire or drag a bushel of straw to the buffalo. There are always those who are conscientious and loving, who worship what they do. Devotion like this is impossible to explain. No matter, for it was this love that assured the survival of an entire way of life.

My mother never understood the tragedy that had befallen her. Like so many others at this time, she began to live in constant terror. Uncle Chinh struck hard and fast. My grandmother and my aunt were forced to prostrate themselves, heads bowed, arms crossed behind their backs, in the communal village courtyard. Facing them, behind a blaze of torches, sat the people of our village. They obeyed orders:

"Listen to our denunciation of their crimes. Then, shout

a slogan: 'Down with the landowning classes!' Raise your fist like this and scream: 'Down, down!'"

They were told that the louder they screamed, the greater their fervor and the firmer the proof of their revolutionary spirit, of the hatred they felt for the "exploiters," the landowning classes. Among these so-called "exploiters" were many well-to-do villagers, people who owned just a bit of land, who cherished their rice paddies like their own flesh. Often, they had little more than a roof, a water buffalo, and a small stock of grain to show for their labors—the fruit of this secular wisdom. All it took was one malicious remark to push them over the edge, to catapult them from the ranks of the innocent spectators into the pit of the accused. They knew that they were being stalked, that at any moment they could meet with humiliation, sorrow, even death. Their fate hung from a thread; and just as an overripe fruit hangs from a branch, they could fall at any moment.

The shouts of the villagers masked their own terror. Their screams were both a release and a sordid way of asking for grace, a baseness difficult to avoid in those troubled times.

Two peasants elevated to the status of "pillars of the land reform" led the accusations against my grandmother Nhieu and my Aunt Tam. One was a good-for-nothing who wandered from village to village in filthy army fatigues. They say he was a soldier, expelled from the French Colonial Army for drunkenness. He was tall and handsome, but very lazy. He could be trusted to perform only small household tasks like washing dishes, drying rice, turning the tobacco leaves, shooing children away from the fruit trees.

But he had had his talents. He had certainly known exactly how to amuse and flatter the village elders, prepare meals, cook chicken, and chop meat for the rich wives of the landowning villagers. He could play cards and mah-jongg with them all night. Every harvest season, he would flirt with the prettiest women among the rice pickers. The more he flirted, the more inspired he became. But he couldn't even dig a potato ditch without huffing and puffing, or finding himself up to his ears in water.

Rumor had it that he had bedded all the female officials in the village. As for the rich widows, they wouldn't have slept with him for all the gold in the world, for fear of getting pregnant. After all, without a husband around, who would there be to blame for the venom?

"Hey you, Bich, come over here." That was the way men used to speak to him, even if they were ten years younger. No one had ever addressed him with the terms of respect used in the village. Oddly, he bore a woman's given name: Ngoc Bich. No one knew whether he owed this to his parents or whether it was a nickname he had picked up in the course of his vagabond life. Also, no one knew who his parents were. He wasn't "a child of the village." He was just passing through.

"Bich, go on, tell the story."

"At your service, but which one?"

"The one about the Buddhist nun's breasts."

"Give me a drink first."

Everyone from the lecherous old village chief to the rowdy young men with their silly mustaches had known how to lure Bich with the promise of a free drink.

Suddenly promoted by Uncle Chinh to the status of "agricultural proletarian" and "pillar of the land reform," Bich became a respected figure. Now, instead of entertaining the village men with his dirty jokes, he began to preach "class consciousness," exhorting them to struggle against "the exploitative property-owning classes," to "honor the revolutionary spirit." He went from begging cups of wine on his knees to reigning over the communal roost: interrogating the accused, shouting, and insulting people. He was intoxicated with himself. His satisfaction was that of a creeping, parasitic vine.

The second "pillar" was a woman, a huge, buxom widow called Nan. The wildness of her appearance mirrored the chaos of her mind. My mother said she had once been considered rather pretty for her flabby white skin. When her husband was still alive, he beat her three days out of five for her habit of stealing food. She pilfered from her own household and her neighbors' alike: a few mushrooms here, a couple of eggs there, even a fish now and then. She could polish off plates of rice cakes with a flick of her tongue. When she squatted down in front of a snack vendor, she forgot everything: husband, child, neighbors.

Fortunately, she had brought only one daughter into the world. They said she ate so much that the fat had suffocated her ovaries, leaving her permanently sterile. If it had been otherwise, she would have reduced her children to famine.

Her husband was a soldier who had been demobilized after he fell into a pit and broke his foot. He was a well-meaning but rather oafish man who could be impulsive and mean. He spent his days puttering in the rice paddies. Every night, his hoe slung over his shoulder, he led home his water buffalo. More often than not, he found his wife asleep, having forgotten to prepare the day's rice. So he beat her with a wooden board.

Once, after the harvest, he had unloaded the rice into the granary; a month later, as if by magic, the stock of rice had shrunk by a half. At first, he was mystified. But when he secretly stood watch, he caught his own wife dipping into the rice supply to finance her snacks and sweets. He gave her a beating that almost killed her and ordered a local carpenter to build a huge chest with a cast-iron lock, which would be impossible for her to pry open.

From then on, his wife began to prowl through the village, sparing no one, not even close relatives. The villagers stopped counting the number of times when, caught red-handed, she went down on her knees to beg their forgiveness. The villagers never tired of telling one particular story about the havoc she caused with her gluttony.

It all began when Nan's relatives arrived for the ceremony of the ancestors. They saw the sticky rice steaming and the chickens butchered, but Nan was nowhere to be found. The husband ran off, breathless and sweating, to the market-place to look for her. Finally, in an alley filled with sweet vendors, he found her kneeling in front of a luscious display of cakes, an empty grocery hamper at her side. Speechless with rage, he gasped and dropped dead on the spot. People ran over, crowding around him. Only then did Nan tear her eyes away from the cakes.

To pay for the funeral, Nan sold the three outbuildings of their house. Their stock of grain was enough for both the mother and daughter until the next harvest. Still, Nan was incapable of controlling her sweet tooth, and by mid-season she had sold the last basket of rice. Incapable of working, ob-sessed with food, Nan rapidly squandered the inheritance. Soon, she had sold the house and ground, and was reduced to squatting in a hut on the outskirts of the village.

The following year, she left her daughter in the care of a relative in town. The little one departed without a tear. Once, gnawed by hunger and misery, Nan went to look for her, but the daughter managed to avoid her.

No one in the village understood why my uncle Chinh had elevated Bich and Nan, these two outcasts, to the status of "pillars of the peasantry." These two "peasants" now sat on the bench of honor, banging their fists against the table, and haranguing the villagers:

"You old bitch Nhieu, do you know who I am?"

"Yes, sir, Mr. Bich."

"And you, Tam, daughter of the cruel, deceitful land-owning classes, do you know who I am?"

"Yes, madame, you are Madame Nan."

To the left of my grandmother Nhieu and my aunt, a long line of men and women were already down on their knees, each waiting their turn. Each time the peasants shouted "Down with . . ." their victims trembled. Only my aunt Tam didn't flinch. My mother said she had the steely, impenetrable eyes of a statue.

During the second denunciation session, my grandmother and my aunt were forced to squat in a deep pit. In this position, a human being felt the full weight of helplessness. You were meant to feel cowardice, baseness, humiliation, exile. It broke even the strongest. My grandmother fell ill and died. Only my aunt Tam persevered, her nerves hard as stone.

Once, I asked my mother, "And what did my father do during this time?"

"Your father wasn't like Aunt Tam. Your father couldn't bear the humiliation," she replied sadly, her voice oddly vacant, bearing neither reproach nor admiration. She said my father had suffered from the first day Uncle Chinh came to my grandmother's house, when he wagged a finger in his face and said:

"You and Que *were* husband and wife. Now, you are a class enemy. I forbid you to see my sister. If you ever get it into your head to try, I'll have you locked up."

Uncle Chinh had barely finished his sentence, when the beating of a drum sounded outside. Young voices rose, hurling slogans like "No mercy for the landlord farmer Tran Thi Tam."

"No mercy . . ."

Uncle Chinh glared at my father and sneered, "Do you hear that? Is that clear?"

My father was silent.

Uncle Chinh yelled at him, "The section chief has just asked you a question. Are you going to answer?" My father turned ashen. Beads of sweat glistened on his temples. He still said nothing.

Just then, Aunt Tam stepped forward. "Venerable Section Chief, we accept our shame. Even without your orders, my family will never try to rise above this."

At the time, Uncle Chinh commanded the Section for Land Reform, which was sovereign and made all the laws. Aunt Tam's reply flattered his pride. So he left. But the children of the Young Pioneers Movement stayed on to carry out his orders, beat their drums, hurl his slogans, and chant:

> *"Without weakness, without hesitation,*
> *once and for all we conquer.*
> *The landowning classes will never rule again!"*

A few days passed. It was nightfall, and my aunt Tam had prepared my father's escape: "Go now, Brother. You won't be able to stand the humiliation. We have to swallow it to survive. Don't worry about me. Times will change. Heaven will reward us."

Anyone else would have demanded a thorough search, but Uncle Chinh just called for a routine investigation. "Good riddance!" he screamed at my mother. "I hope he disappears. From now on, you can live in peace. Quit your street-vending business, but keep those hampers for ripening bananas.

"The land here has been redistributed. Soon, this country is going to catch up with the Soviet Union. We'll have machines for the workers, for harvesting and threshing grain. Nobody's going to have to muck about in the mud any longer."

My mother listened to him through tears. The next morning, she grabbed her hamper and set out for the rice paddies. She pretended to chase crabs while she waited for Aunt Tam to come wash clothes. They spoke furtively at the edge of the paddy, one washing clothes, the other chasing crabs.

"Sister Tam, where is my husband?"

"Madame the Peasant, I don't know."

"I beg you. I have nothing to do with this."

"Madame, you are the sister of Chinh, the section chief. He is the law here. We are nothing."

"I beg you a hundred times, a thousand times. Please, don't torture me. Where is my husband?"

"You have a brother. You don't need a husband anymore. My brother had to leave. He would never have survived this humiliation. What difference does it make whether he's left for the mountains, the salt marshes, even the deepest jungle? Wherever he is, he'll be better than he was in this hell."

Aunt Tam heaved her hamper of wet clothes onto her shoulder and left. My mother stayed bent over the rice paddy, her arms plunged up to the elbows in mud, her face streaming with tears and sweat.

That same evening, Uncle Chinh interrogated her. "So, you just met with that bitch Tam?"

"Who told you that?"

"The guerrillas who watch you."

"I went crab fishing."

"No one keeps fishing for crabs in the same corner of the rice paddy. Stop lying."

They were both silent for a long time, and then my uncle continued, "For the last three generations, our family has lived off the sweat of their own labor . . . or through the practice of traditional medicine. The Do family never owned rice paddy, not even the tiniest patch. That is why, today, I have been promoted to chief of the village Land Reform Section. If you continue to mix with these landowners, they will denounce me to my superiors. My authority and my honor will be ruined."

"Leave me alone," my mother wailed. "I can't stand any more of this."

Uncle Chinh was furious. "Don't be so selfish. You must think of the interests of our class." With this, he left the house.

My mother moaned, pacing circles around the empty house, around the light that burned on the altar to our ancestors. She began to waste away, her eyes sinking deep into their sockets. At night, she wandered aimlessly in the garden, talking in a muffled, hysterical voice to the trunk of the old carambola tree, whispering to the cactus bushes, to the guava and the sycamore.

Did she tell them of her love for this man, the only man who ever brought her joy? At the time, she didn't know she would ever see him again. In any case, the word got around in the village: She had gone mad.

Uncle Chinh came home one day in a fury. "We're the laughingstock of the entire village. Everyone says that you've lost your senses, that you rant and rave to trees about that filthy landlord. . . ."

My mother said nothing.

"You realize that you're sabotaging my authority. You know that, don't you? No other section chief for land reform in this entire province has been as prompt, or as radical, as I have. You're undermining my efforts.

"Que. Sister. Listen to me. Haven't we always been family, won't we always be? Our parents are dead. We're alone in this world. You're all I have left. Could I care about anyone more than I care about you? Listen, you're still young. You're well mannered, pretty. You're working class. We have a house. Now we even have some rice paddy. You'll find a good match whenever you're ready.

"Think about it, choose: a future with the revolution or the life of an outcast among the enemies of the people. I'm warning you for the last time. Wake up. Face reality. In a few days, I'm going to Hanoi. I'll introduce you to my superior. During the resistance, he was captain of a transmission battalion responsible to staff headquarters."

My mother continued to stare in silence. She bundled up a few clothes and left the village that December evening. Uncle Chinh ordered a search, but no one could find her. They questioned Aunt Tam, but she denied any knowledge of my mother's whereabouts. In the end, Uncle Chinh told the villagers that my mother had contracted a kidney disease and had gone to the city for treatment. Six months later, Uncle Chinh left the village himself to join the Land Reform Section. A huge padlock condemned the door to the family house, and the key was entrusted to a close relative. Village children plugged the hole to the padlock with clay and smeared the walls with graffiti. Bamboo leaves drifted into heaps at the base of the walls, and spiderwebs hung in thick layers across the eaves.

One day, my mother resurfaced. She was emaciated, ghostlike. The skin on her face, once soft and glowing, was ashen, scored with lines. All through the night, the neighbors came to see her. Crouched down, her knees hugged tightly to her chest, my mother wept in slow, strangled sobs. Even the villagers, who were ordinarily reluctant to release their prey before they had extracted what they wanted to know, spared my mother their questions. It was partly out of pity, but mainly because they themselves were about to be swept up in a new ordeal: The "Special Section for the Rectification of Errors" had just arrived in the village.

Land reform had ripped through the village like a squall, devastating fields and rice paddies, sowing only chaos and misery in its wake. The Special Section for the Rectification of Errors was, of course, incapable of picking up the pieces, but succeeded in dispelling the sinister atmosphere that had suffocated the village. Now, each public gathering was a spontaneous concert of laughter, tears, and sighs of relief; everyone could tell of the unhappiness and the injustice they had suffered. Suddenly, you didn't have to whisper, you could even invoke the names of the innocent souls who had been massacred. In the village homes, oil lamps burned late into the night. People opened their doors again, and conversation flowed; "meetings" ran at full tilt. Now, you could scream for the punishment of the informers, apologies for tarnished honor, the settling of debts in blood. . . .

Of all of the former leaders, Uncle Chinh was the most hated. No one knew where he had gone to hide. For the villagers, the only target for their vengeance was my mother, who had stayed behind in their ancestral home. One night, a mob of villagers armed with clubs and knives surrounded the house and shouted for my mother to come out and settle her brother's debts in blood. The crowd hurled insults at her, threatening to ransack the house. Terrorized, my mother barricaded herself in her room and waited. The front door was blocked, but the mob would have knocked it down if Aunt Tam hadn't thrown herself in front of them.

"Have you all gone mad?" Her voice was icy, imperious. "Taking out your rage on this innocent woman? Does my sister-in-law deserve this? You lost your rice paddies. She lost her husband. You've gotten your rice paddies back. But who's going to return her husband?"

The mob slowly backed off. The cadres of the "Rectification Campaign" scurried over, trying to calm the people, urging them to return to their homes.

Aunt Tam called to my mother, pleading with her to open the door. When she did, the two women embraced each other without a word. This was ten years before my birth.

The train had come to a halt, the first stop of the long journey. It was a quarter to seven at night. The man next to me yawned. He closed his detective novel, stuffed it in his pocket, and glanced up at me. Rather as you would look at a kitten curled in a corner of a couch.

He muttered something unintelligible, then got up and pressed his pug nose up against the window. We had arrived in a provincial station. It was a picturesque little town, quiet, tranquil. The houses seemed to flow out of the hillside, each one different from the next, exuding a timeless softness, like the memory of an old love. The walls shone white in the feeble light of the moon. Along the roads, rows of trees swayed, filtering the golden light over the summit of the hills. A purplish haze hung over the valley below. The main road scattered into smaller roads, which snaked and then vanished into the infinite green.

The man studied the town, nodding to himself. Then he looked over at me, squinting his eyes and raising one of his eyebrows as if to say, "We have beautiful country, don't we?"

I said nothing. In this kind of situation, I didn't even try to be polite. As the train departed the station, my traveling companion fished two sandwiches out of his bag and invited me to join him. "Like a bite? Going to Moscow, are you?"

"Yes. Thanks anyway. I'm not hungry yet."

He shrugged his shoulders and smiled. His dentures were in bad shape, a patchwork of silver caps and artificial teeth. It made his smile look odd, and I tried to suppress a giggle. The man chewed noisily, and after a few bites, he paused, pulled a Japanese-made radio/cassette player out of his bag, and perched it on the table. He turned it on, and the familiar voice of the singer Pugatnova crackled out. "This won't bother you, I hope?" My traveling companion said, glancing over at me.

"No, it's pleasant. Thank you."

The traveler slumped back against his seat. He listened to the music, munching his bread. He had a contented air about him. I had stopped paying attention to him, the train, and the passing stations: The voice of the singer enthralled me. Ever since I had moved to this country to be an "exported worker," her music was one of the few pleasures that made me forget my homesickness.

I had heard the singer for the first time in the room of a Ph.D. student in Kiev, the uncle of a friend who lived in my residence. My friend, who was older, more mature, and more self-possessed than I, lived a passionate life, juggling half a dozen lovers at a time without remembering a single one of them.

"There's no place for a man's face in my dreams," she put it. Nevertheless, men adored her. Women, often envious, whispered that she used a witchcraft learned from the Gypsies. She had a wild, sensual kind of beauty. Weak-willed men couldn't resist this inferno. She reduced them to ash. I liked her. And I liked her frankness. She was honest, even with herself, and she always sided with the underdog.

I met her in the middle of winter, just after I'd arrived in Russia. I was distant, melancholy. We "exported workers" had shut ourselves away in our boxlike rooms, savoring our homesickness, fermenting in our own sadness. On holidays, we would always try to go out for walks, just to escape the monotony of our four walls, to hear an unfamiliar voice, or meet a new face among our compatriots.

Once, my friend took me to Kiev. She had an uncle there who studied electromechanics. The campus was clogged with the intense, furtive traffic of black marketeers, who rumbled about in trucks and liked to move huge shipping crates of imported goods at all hours. It was impossible to find your way in this labyrinth. Fortunately, I knew a bit of Russian, so we could do some shopping. My friend said, "Old academics are stingy. We'd better take our own provisions."

Her uncle, now over forty, had the look of an intellectual. When we arrived, he was plucking hairs off a pig's foot, the cheap kind sold to people eager to save money. He stuffed it in a casserole when we arrived. My friend snickered when she discovered it. "Come on, you don't have to hide it. Everyone knows how you are. You older people, you always go through the same circus to save face."

Her uncle flushed and sneaked a glance in my direction. Probably finding me a bit nervous, a bit provincial, he regained his composure and beamed at me.

"Here, you can put the pig's foot away," said his niece. "I've brought you some beef, and a chicken that's ready to be cooked. It's first-rate, imported from Hungary. You start preparing the meal with Hang. I've got an errand to do at a friend's house." Without waiting for me to answer, she dumped the provisions on the table, washed her hands, and threw on her coat. "You stay here, Hang, I'll be back in a minute."

I didn't have much of a choice, so I started preparing the

meal with her uncle. An hour passed, then two, then three. The uncle urged me to start eating. Snow had begun to fall in long, oblique drifts. A net of gray clouds hung over the city and the trees, leafless now, seemed to trace frantic skeletons in the night. A shadow darted through them. It must have been a crow.

I had my face glued to the window when my friend's uncle called over to me, "Let's have a bit of wine to warm us up." I was puzzled, but before I could reply, he had produced a bottle from the linen chest. He kneeled and pulled out a wooden box filled with porcelain and crystal glasses. He poured the wine and offered me a glass. "Drink up, it'll warm you. The snow's still falling. God, it's cold."

"Thanks, but I can't drink alcohol."

"Don't worry. This wine is very light. Anyway, in this cold, even the strongest liquor won't have much effect."

He pushed the glass to my lips. I felt uneasy, but out of respect I swallowed a mouthful. "Have another sip. Another sip and you'll feel the warmth of it."

He seemed to be almost imploring, and he forced me to drink the whole glass in one gulp. A tongue of fire licked through my body, and my eyes blurred. My friend's uncle emptied his glass too. Another glass and then another. Odd, why did he drink after the meal? The man sat sprawled in his chair, giggling idiotically. Suddenly, he bounded across the room and grabbed me. "Darling, darling . . . come over here, darling."

His breath stank of alcohol, and his thick, fleshy lips smacked open grotesquely. He dug his fingers, pincerlike, into my shoulders. I felt rage rising in me. I was lucid now. I saw every hair of his thinning mustache, the wart on his nostril, the oily sweat glistening on his flaming cheeks.

"Let me go. I'm going to scream." My voice was low and firm. I forced myself to stare him in the face, and I pushed his head back with my hand so I could take a hard look at him.

"It's nothing, darling . . . it's nothing."

He babbled something, his lips opening and closing idiotically. At that moment, he looked like the mask of the Earth Spirit we made back home to amuse children at the midautumn Moon Festival. I didn't feel fear anymore. Only disgust. Loathing.

He must have seen it in my gaze, because he pulled back and forced a smile. "The snow . . . it's cold out . . . so cold."

A banging sound at the door; it was my friend. She looked us over and smiled.

"You too, Uncle? Aren't you ashamed?"

Her uncle seemed to shrink, and he slumped onto the bed, his arms flailing. The flabby muscles in his face had fallen slack. He looked like an old man of sixty. My friend opened the chest and poured herself a glass of water. "So you don't spare anyone, not even my own friend?"

The uncle stood with his shoulders hunched over. He didn't dare reply. But my friend went on, "Go on, go find a bed next door. Tonight we're sleeping here. From now on, watch it."

The uncle rolled out the bed and brought out a down comforter and a pillow. "Here, I washed them last week." Then, ashamed, he went out.

My friend latched the door, spread out the sheets and the covers, and said, "Don't be sad. . . . That's life. I suppose there are a few good folks. But what's the use of moping about it? How about some music? Listen to this."

Outside, the snow was falling. The air shimmered as the snowflakes pierced the night with a thousand needlelike points. Like a tide held back too long, a wave of sadness, a feeling of humiliation and homesickness, washed over me.

My friend put on a pair of blue pajamas and went off to rummage in her pile of old records. As the light faded, the drifts of white flakes formed a mirage. The singer's voice quivered out of nowhere. At first, I couldn't make out the words. It was as if thunder had shaken the space. Like a sudden downpour, a vision of endless mountain ranges, dense forest, fields set ablaze, nature unleashed. I felt dizzy. This strange flash of consciousness receded, and I was engulfed, plunged into eddy after eddy of sounds, each one softer, more tender. The song finished. Another followed. I couldn't remember anything, only songs one after another, in a blur. My friend got up and turned the record over. I wasn't listening anymore. I was thinking about the woman singing. She must have suffered, seen her hopes snuffed out, her passions ground to ash.

She too must have known this weariness, this despair. Like us, she must have had to reinvent hope and a yearning for life. The song crackled forth like the wing of a bird lost in the limitless blue of space, like a spark from an inferno.

I listened in silence. The evening's repugnant scene flashed through my mind. The music had come from that bastard's room. So this was life, this strange muddle, this flower plucked from a swamp.

Now, the voice had come to me again, on a train leaving for Moscow. The mile markers swept past me in a blur. Out the window, a forest of white poplars quivered softly: color of velvet, color of tenderness. It was then that I understood why the voice had enchanted me. Like a call, it beckoned me to a kind of love—to revolt, the most essential force in human existence. I wrapped my arms around myself and huddled in a corner of the compartment. If only my mother could feel this revolt, if only her heart could gather a spark from this inferno.

Chapter THREE

MY MOTHER COULDN'T LIVE IN THE VILLAGE ANY longer. No one had the guts to hate her, but her very presence seemed to brew a kind of rancor. Brother and sister resembled each other like two drops of water: the same bearing, the same silhouette, the same curve of the mouth, those eyebrows, the ring of their laugh. That voice.

The ancestral home held nothing but bitter memories. Following Uncle Chinh's orders, my mother sold her street-vending business. The pair of wicker hampers she had used to transport food moldered in a corner of the house, serving their new function: ripening bananas. My mother fretted for a week, then mortgaged the house to a relative, packed up her belongings, and left her village for Hanoi.

Ten years later, I was born in a brick hut, under a roof patched together out of tar, tiles, and rusty sheet metal. Our street was on the edge of Hanoi in a working-class slum. Every day, at the crack of dawn, street vendors swarmed around the houses to hawk their homemade snacks: sticky rice, fried dumplings, steamed rice cakes, spring rolls, snail and crab soups, and other delicacies. Their charcoal and husk fires crackled and sputtered, and the aroma of onions, crispy dumplings, and red chilies fried in oil filled the air, their fragrances overpowering the stench of the garbage, the open sewers, the walls reeking of rancid urine. Little by little, these intoxicating smells floated about and were drowned out by the creaking of the hampers we carried, lost amid the vendors' cries:

"Sticky rice, who wants sticky rice . . . ?"

"I've got cakes. Taste my delicious cakes."

Each vendor had her own song, with its own trills and low rumblings. In our neighborhood alone, there were seven different sticky-rice vendors. You could recognize each one immediately by the lilt of her voice. Their dawn cries were the first music of my childhood.

Each morning, my mother scurried about, tidying her display of foodstuffs and snacks. She piled them up helter-skelter in her hamper until it brimmed over with a bit of everything: dried bamboo shoots, rice crisps, and wheat crackers, Chinese cellophane noodles and Vietnamese vermicelli, soybeans, red beans, black beans, peanuts, raw sesame seeds, shelled sesame seeds. Some days she even stocked preserved fruit and star anise. After she put the finishing touches on all this, she woke me with a thump on my back.

"My child, eat your rice before you have to leave for school. I've left the key to the house in the hole in the wall."

Then she was off. I slid out of bed. A warped bronze bowl was perched on the table. Beside it, a bowl of pickled cabbage and a platter of fried silkworms. Sometimes, there was also a bowl of taro root marinated in soy sauce or a small dried fish that she had grilled for me. Winter and summer, year in and year out, the dishes were always the same. We kept the rice warm in a small earthenware jar wrapped in straw. Next to the tea tray, there was always a little packet of candy: sugary flour balls or toffee sticks flavored with green tea.

"How about some more of those green-tea toffees? I'll buy some for you tomorrow."

"Mr. Tao flavors his flour candies with ginger. Can't you taste it?"

Mother would bend over me, murmuring these things. She looked at me tenderly, with a sort of admiration in her gaze. It frightened me. The other women in our neighborhood never looked at their children this way.

One winter morning, I couldn't have been much more than eight years old, I woke up to a cold spell that could have frozen over the earth. The water in my basin had to be stirred with a knife. Mother had already left for the market. Tet was approaching, and everyone was out trying to sell their goods. For street vendors, this was the only time of the year they could count on bringing in a bit of extra money.

When I woke up, I found my cotton jacket stuffed behind my pillow. It was still warm. Mother had heated it near the fire before she left for the market. I put it on, wolfed down my rice, and scampered over to the neighbor's house. She was still sound asleep, and her elderly father, an addicted water-pipe smoker, was slumped, shivering, on a corner of their low table.

When he caught sight of me, he wagged his pipe at me: "Get home immediately! It's madness for you to be out in this cold. Do you want to catch pneumonia?"

I wandered back into the street. The wind swirled the rotten leaves around me in eddies. I spotted Madame Mieu's white dog, shivering slightly, dragging its withered tail on the cobblestones. He groped his way forward, searching with his cloudy old eyes, sniffing about painfully with his crumpled old nose.

"Hey, Fuzzy White, want to take a walk with me?"

The old dog gave me a look of disdain, ignoring my question. Just then, Madame Mieu's son, a cripple, started to sing:

"Hail autumn and its procession of dead leaves,
The rows of barren poplars stand silent on the hillside."

Day after day, his falsetto voice spilled into the streets, mixing with the city sounds, the clicking of bamboo poles the street vendors carried.

I felt like crying. Little Thu jumped out from behind me: "Wanna play?" I didn't reply. No one in our neighborhood would play with her. She was mean and lied shamelessly. More than once she had been the instigator of one of our mischievous little games, but each time we got caught, she managed to point the finger at us and disappear. The little girl blocked my path: "Come and play with me."

I hesitated. Thu rolled her eyes at me wickedly. "No one will know. My mother won't be back until noon. There's a party at her office today." I was torn, but the idea of going back to our empty house made me anxious. Thu read my thoughts and tugged at my sleeve.

"Come on. Come down to the dike and watch the sampans with me. It'll be fun. We can even catch some crickets if we try hard enough."

I gave in, following her along the streets of Hanoi. We crossed onto the dike at the edge of the Red River. The trees, heavy with purplish flowers, drooped low in the heat. Daisies peeped over the tall grasses, and from time to time, a passion flower unfurled to reveal its lantern-shaped fruit. Out on the river, sailboats sliced through the water. The sampan drivers, their bronze faces glistening, hung over the edges of their barges, clutched their rudders, and chanted to keep the rhythm.

On the far bank, the rivermen sang as they put a boat out to sail. We raced down the length of the sand beach, lurching and stumbling like drunks. Tireless, we chased after dragonflies, darted after the dusty gold wings of the June bugs. Thu gathered ripe fruits in the hem of her dress and then almost choked herself trying to eat them, never once offering me any. I listened in silence to the distant echo of the fishermen singing.

Suddenly, someone yelled from the dike. "Thu, Thu . . ."

In the distance, a woman was running, her dark silhouette advanced toward us along the edge of the dike. Thu ducked, dragging me along with her into a cornfield. Her mother continued to holler for her: "Thu, Thu . . ."

The woman's voice was rasping and angry. We held our breath. Thu lay flat on her stomach in a ditch, and she held me down with her. Only after her mother was far away, back on the sand beach where the men were putting the boat out to sail, did we stand up.

"Let's get home. Fast."

We scampered through the fields filled with corn and red pumpkins, finally arriving at the first road on the way home. "Pretend we were playing ticktacktoe. Let's go to the fortune-teller's courtyard," Thu whispered, pulling me into the first alley of our neighborhood. A blind man who lived off fortune-telling had made his home there in a tiny brick house. They said his wife had built it for him seventeen years earlier, before she ran off with another man. The house was tiny, but clean and well equipped. It looked out onto a large courtyard covered with chestnut-colored tiles and bordered by walls choked with vines and climbing flowers. There was a little strip of land planted all year round with peach and plum, and a few pomegranate trees. People who had heard of the blind man's reputation traveled from all over to come here and sat in the courtyard, waiting their turn. The neighborhood children liked to meet here too; they scuttled about, playing ball and jump rope.

Thu made me sit down and thrust my hand into a pile of brick dust she had gathered. "Quick. Draw the squares before my mother gets here."

Frantic, I drew a board in the dust. Meanwhile, Thu scrambled about, filling the pockets of her dress with pebbles. She had just finished divvying up the pebbles between us when her mother appeared.

"Where were you? Where?"

The little girl lifted her head. "We've been playing games."

Thu's mother's eyes narrowed to slits, and her mouth screwed up; she was livid. She grabbed the girl by her hair. "I came by here before going to look for you by the river. Now, where were you? Just where did you hide yourself?"

"I was playing." Her lips pursed in an odd quiver, and she started to whimper.

Her mother yanked Thu's hair, forcing her to stand up. Then she spat out her words again one by one: "Where . . . were . . . you. If you want to save your hide, you tell me now. You keep lying, and you're going to get punished. So. Where were you?"

Thu was white, her eyes wide with fear. She started to sniff and then bawl.

"Hang made me do it. She took me to the river . . . to catch crickets . . . to pick some corn to roast."

The woman turned on me, her huge, bulging eyes blank and glassy, her lips pursed into a taut white line. She stared me down, silently; the contempt in her eyes pinned me to the spot. I trembled and felt my knees go weak. I clenched my fists and stuffed them into the pockets of my dress, forcing myself to meet her gaze. My throat knotted. She looked me over the way she would a monkey in a zoo. But she restrained her anger just long enough to scream at me, "You little bitch. I forbid you to come near my daughter or my courtyard, you little bitch without roots. This time, I'm going to spare your little runt face. Next time, don't expect my pity."

She grabbed her daughter's hand and dragged her off. I stood in the courtyard still swirling with dead leaves. The north wind was whistling in gusts through the sky, and I felt, as I would never feel again, the weight of my fatherless fate. Madame Mieu's old dog shuffled by, dragging his tail on the cobblestones, sniffing here and there absently. Even he was probably less miserable, less lonely, I thought. The old blind man called to me, "Hang, little Hang, come here. I want to talk to you."

I felt lost, and my eyes smarted with tears. "Hang, come over here." I ran into the icy wind. Gray clouds drifted in the urban sky, and the last of the migratory birds rose in a slow skyward arc. Was this all it was, my life, just this lump in my throat?

I ran for a long time. Finally, exhausted, I stopped to watch the mud-red waves of the river breaking on the sand. In the distance, a small sailboat bobbed and drifted along, its flag made out of a string of rags flapping in the wind.

That night, as I lay in bed, I felt my mother's tears wet my forehead.

"Don't cry, child, don't cry anymore now."

"But I must have a father. Somebody . . . must be."

"Please, don't ask me any more questions."

"They all have a father, even if he's dead or blind. Tell me. Tell me who my father is."

"Don't ask me these questions, please. At least we will always be together, you and I. Someday we'll be happy, but please, don't ask these questions again."

My mother's tears numbed me. And once again, I yielded to her. The image of my father would remain in shadow.

*   *   *

A year later, on a similar winter day, a man came to our house. Very tall, but a bit stooped, with a square jaw, jet-black eyes, and a lively smile. "This is Uncle Chinh, my brother," said my mother.

Eager to please, I welcomed him. He looked so much like my mother that I instantly felt close to him. "Should I prepare a meal, Mother? Do you want me to go buy some meat?"

"I'm going to start cooking the rice," my mother replied. "You go to the Chinese butcher. Get us a pound of the honey-eyed pork, a pound of roast goose, and some pickled shallots."

Uncle Chinh frowned. "Why all this fuss?"

"We haven't seen each other for almost ten years," my mother said softly. She sent me off to the bedroom to look for her hamper. "How old is she now?" I heard my uncle Chinh ask her.

"Almost nine and a half."

"She's the spitting image of her father."

My mother said nothing. My uncle paused for a long time before he spoke. "You come from the working classes. You don't have to worry about the stigma of a bad family background. Forget him. You should have remarried a long time ago."

I heard my mother's voice crack as she replied, "His family was reclassified as middle peasantry during the Rectification Campaign. But let's not talk about the past."

I went out, a hamper under my arm. They both went oddly silent.

"Mother, should I get some vegetables and bean curd too?"

My mother shook her head. "That'll be enough."

She lowered her eyes abruptly and I saw tears wet the knees of her pants.

That evening, after dinner, my mother invited the neighbors over to meet her brother. Our neighbors were simple people, living day to day off small businesses, peddling goods from wagons they pulled behind them on makeshift bicycle "cabs," which we called cyclos. They were all mute with respect when they learned that my uncle Chinh was a cadre responsible for ideological education in the northern province of Quang Ninh.

In their eyes, teachers of "ideology" practiced a noble profession, far superior to all others. They were regarded as deeply learned men and women, dispensers of enlightenment and precious thoughts that no money could buy. Also, my uncle had privileged access to many confidential foreign and state documents, and his conversation enthralled everyone. People listened in rapt attention as he spoke excitedly about the progress of the "Three Great Revolutionary Fronts," about an "International Struggle" between capitalism and communism, about mass strikes polarizing the capitalist world, about a labor movement that had challenged the queen of England. He spoke of the "Great Leaders" of "National Liberation" in Africa, of Indian tribes struggling for recognition by a "Neo-imperialist, materialist civilization."

The neighbors didn't leave for their homes until far into the night. My mother was radiant, her face beaming with pride. She arranged cups and glasses, served up plates of delicacies, and cleared off cigarette stubs as proudly as if it had been a wedding banquet. Then she laid out a clean rush mat with fresh covers and strung up the mosquito net for Uncle Chinh.

"We sleep just fine in the hammock. You rest, dear Brother. The journey was a long one, I'm sure."

"There's no urgency. Put the little one to bed. We have to talk."

My mother sent me off to bed. She made chrysanthemum tea and set it aside to steep. "How would you like me to make you a lotus-seed pudding? When Mother and Father were still alive, we made them every year for Tet and the Festival of the Fifteenth Day."

"I don't remember. I was too little."

"But I was born in the year of the Boar and you under the sign of the Water Buffalo. You're only two years younger than I am. How could you forget?"

After a long silence, Uncle Chinh said, "True. But I was busy with affairs of state."

My mother sighed. Then she spoke again, a hint of reproach in her voice. "And for the past nine years, you never once thought to ask about me, to make contact? I could have died, and no one would have even gathered my ashes."

"I've already explained," Uncle Chinh grumbled. "I was very busy. Not on my own behalf. Government business. There were the seminars, all the committee meetings. After the National Front, I had to organize the unions. I never had a single day of rest. Soon we'll launch a campaign to publicize the latest Central Committee resolutions. I won't finish before Tet."

They went silent. I heard Uncle Chinh pour himself a cup of tea, sip it noisily, and then set it down on the aluminum tray with a click. Another silence. All of a sudden, my mother raised her voice.

"Why did you never even bother to organize the memorial ceremonies in honor of our parents? After all these years."

Uncle Chinh sighed. "My God, you're difficult! They died when we were young. They've been dead for years. Why bring this up now?"

"But they're our parents," said my mother, her voice choked with bitterness. "Dead or alive, we have no others. You were all they had to continue the family line."

"Come on, let's drop this nonsense," Uncle Chinh replied curtly. "We live in a materialist age. No one cares about all this ancestor worship. After death, there's nothing."

A silence fell over the house, broken only by the sound of my mother's crying. It was Uncle Chinh who finally spoke. "By the way, what are you living on at the moment?"

"Haven't you seen the hampers? Back when I was in the

49

village, my street-vending business was all I had. You ordered me to sell it. Those two big hampers ended up rotting with the bananas. I was in no shape to keep up the garden. I had to mortgage the house and come to live here in Hanoi. At first, I worked in a textile mill. Then my friends helped find me a stall at the market. I had nothing. No savings. I sold vegetables, a few pieces of fruit, a handful of bamboo shoots, vermicelli, rice-stick noodles, that sort of thing. After a while, I put some money aside. Then I was able to sell sugar, beans, spices, and cereals."

"In short, you're a businesswoman." My uncle's voice was stern and cutting.

My mother stopped speaking, but my uncle raised his voice, haranguing her:

"In our society, there are only two respectable types of people: the proletariat—the avant-garde of our society, the beacon of the revolution—and the peasantry, faithful ally of the proletariat in its struggle for the construction of socialism. The rest is nothing. The merchants, the petty tradespeople, they're only exploiters. You cannot remain with these parasites."

My mother was panicked. "But what am I supposed to live on? Who is going to feed my daughter?"

"I'll find a place for you at the factory," Uncle Chinh said coldly. "You'll start as an apprentice. Then, after you learn a profession, I'll see to it that you find work in any factory you like—the March Eighth Textile Mill, the Yen Phu Electrical Factory, the Luong Yen Shelling and Husking Factory . . ."

My mother started to whimper and plead. "Please, I beg you. How can I learn a profession at my age? My hair will go white before I learn anything. What will I do then? Retire?"

"The truth is, you're too scared to work. You're addicted to this world of small traders. Take my advice. Sooner or later, the party will launch a radical campaign against these parasites. Distance yourself now, rejoin the workers."

My mother tried to defend herself. "It took the government less than two years to 'reform' the 'petty bourgeoisie. As for the rest of us, aren't we still slaving away? We street vendors only have time to eat late at night, after work, by the light of an oil lamp. Who could we possibly exploit? These last few years, I can't even earn enough to buy pencils and notebooks for Hang. There was even a time when I had to build a bonfire, every night, by the side of the road, and sell roast corn to make ends meet."

"Stop," Uncle Chinh cut her off. "You don't need to rail on any longer. Small traders like you *are* bourgeoisie. But our country will achieve socialism directly, without passing through the stage of capitalism. The bourgeoisie is the enemy of the revolution, and we will smash it, yank it out at the root."

I heard my mother sigh. "Chinh, Brother, forgive me," she said wearily. "I never did get much of an education, so I don't reason very well. But you will, at least, allow me to provide food and education for my own daughter?"

"It is precisely *because* I worry about Hang's future that I want you to work in a factory. In the new society, children of the proletariat will have all sorts of advantages. They'll be able to develop their talents. In the Soviet Union, the writers and musicians of genius, the professors, doctors, and scientists—they all come from the ranks of the proletariat."

My mother didn't reply.

"I am a cadre responsible for educating the masses. I cannot have a lousy street vendor for a sister."

My mother took a sip of tea and said weakly, "I'm tired. If you'll excuse me, I think I'll try and get some sleep. I'll think about this later."

Uncle Chinh yielded, softening his voice. "Yes. But I have one more thing to discuss with you. My wife and I have asked for a transfer here to the capital. She's one of the leaders of the Communist Youth League, so they've allocated us an apartment. But we're going to need some money to fix it up, furnish it. . . ."

My mother cut in. "I've already mortgaged our parents' house. The act of sale won't be legal until it is entirely paid off. Your share of the money is intact. When do you need it?"

"Right away. The sooner the better."

"Will you go to the village yourself to claim it, or would you prefer I do it?"

"I don't know when I'll find the time. I'm so busy."

"Fine. I'll arrange to be free next week."

A week later, my mother took me with her to the village to get the money, but also so I could see the relatives and our old neighbors. The bus dropped us off at the county township. From there, you had to walk eight miles to the river. On the way, I asked my mother if we could stop to visit a peasant market perched on a hill, about five hundred yards from the road. A lush green grove of mango trees and banyans wove a canopy of foliage over our heads. Under this natural sunshade, the market people had set up primitive stalls, fixed them to the ground with a few stakes, and pitched roofs thatched with sugarcane leaves or crushed reeds. Behind the market stood a small pagoda, its whitewashed walls blotchy and covered with mildew, its roof eaten away by lichens.

On a little knoll in front of the market, a dyer and his wife were wringing out lengths of silk that they fished out of their vats with a bamboo pole. A dense, steamy vapor rose from the silk, which was the startling, iridescent white of lotus flowers. Slung over a pole next to the silk were long strips of fabric—blue-black, sienna, and mahogany—the traditional, favorite colors peasants have always loved. Seated cross-legged in front of the dyer was an old man in dirty clothes. He was kneading a floury paste that he molded with his fingers into a wondrous array of figurines: pigs, chickens, buffalo, generals, queens, pawns, tanks. The old man lined up the rainbow-colored statuettes along a wooden plank perched on four bricks.

"Come on over, come admire my French music troupe," shouted the old man. He had just finished sculpting a miniature trumpet out of the paste, and now he pretended to blow into it. Children swarmed around him, fascinated, watching his Adam's apple bob up and down in his throat.

"Come, come and see my French musical instruments."

His display was irresistible. My mother bought me a dozen of his statuettes and a rainbow-colored trumpet. I arranged my new treasures in a box in front of the envious eyes of the other children. Then my mother took me to see the traveling bazaar. I saw her gaze longingly at the tiny wooden boxes fitted with glass lids, some no bigger than the palm of a man's hand. You could see everything inside those boxes: rainbow-colored marbles, Chinese handkerchiefs embroidered with brightly colored butterfly and bird motifs, thread, imported sewing needles, steel pens, mothballs, shell necklaces, and fake pearls.

"Once, I had a stand in a traveling bazaar like this," said my mother wistfully. "It was in the commune market."

The younger women among the vendors had plucked their eyebrows to arch over their eyes like crescent moons. Squatted down behind their stalls, they shelled periwinkles. The smell of fermented fish sauce and ginger permeated the air.

Next to the peasant market, you could find both expensive delicacies and a mouthwatering variety of delicious, cheap street food. Here, they made tiny sticky-rice cakes and hemp cakes small as jackfruit pits and wrapped in five or seven layers of banana leaves. Next to the crab-noodle and snail-soup stands, a cabbage-soup vendor hawked his specialty: steamed river spinach. Behind him, another vendor sold roast corn basted with honey. Yet another man made sweet *che* puddings from mashed rice seedlings seasoned with five-spice curry and fried a special type of doughnut twisted into the shape of a caterpillar.

With a single coin, you could buy twelve of these doughnuts, no bigger than a baby's little finger. To make them, you mashed cold cooked rice, left over from a meal, and mixed it with sticky rice. Two volumes of flour to two scoops of rice. Then you rolled out the paste, pummeling it and kneading it into the shape of a caterpillar, the kind that nests in heads of lettuce. Thrown into a pot of boiling oil, these stringy cakes turned golden brown. When they floated, light and crispy, to the surface, they were ready.

A couple of blind singers lumbered over to the stall of a vendor who sold sweet potatoes, boiled water chestnuts, and water-lily seeds. The husband had a strange, ugly vein bulging on his neck and wore a pair of black-rimmed glasses; he strummed a Chinese two-string violin while his wife sang.

When my mother asked if I wanted something to eat, I just shook my head. In truth, I was starting to feel hungry. But somehow, I didn't feel like eating just then. I watched two women nearby devouring big bowls of rice noodles with shrimp sauce, their faces hidden beneath their conical straw sun hats. All I could see were their hands bobbing up and down, plunging their chopsticks into their bowls, lifting them to their faces.

We threaded our way through the alleys of market stalls, pursued by the wail of the blind singers behind us. Just hearing their song reminded me of the vein on that blind man's neck, swollen huge as a chopstick, and the sweat that ran down his drawn, sooty forehead.

"Mother, let's go to the pagoda." I grabbed her hand, pulling her along behind me toward the gate to the pagoda. A wonderful, hoary old banyan tree guarded the entrance, its huge trunk flanked by six smaller ones. The secondary trunks were clusters of roots that had fallen from the tree's branches and drilled their way into the earth. Now large and tough as the main trunk, they laced together like vaulted gateways. I imagined them as doors to a palace built to commemorate some mysterious, ancient feat.

I sat down at the foot of the banyan tree and snuggled up to my mother. The ash-gray roots of the banyan swung in front of my eyes. They seemed to stick to me like suckers on the tentacles of an immense octopus, tearing me from the arms of my mother. I wanted to scream. But my voice was drowned in my sleepy throat, and the roots of the banyan swung me softly in a cradle of moss-green leaves. A breeze caressed me as I floated, drifted up into the gateway to the sky. Heavy clouds streaked with silver barred my way, but in their midst, two immense pillars framed a huge door before disappearing into rainbow-colored clouds.

Dragons writhed and slithered around the pillars in a dance. The doors were two huge sheets of copper, dazzling, shiny as mirrors. One was closed, the other ajar, inviting. Behind these doors, a green space spread out mysterious, incandescent, as if it masked thousands and thousands of stars.

"Dearest, wake up, wake up."

I opened my eyes. My mother started to laugh.

"Poor kitten, you were sound asleep."

Her pearl-white teeth glistened, but her beauty and her youth had already faded. From sorrow. For nothing. For no one.

"Child, you really should eat a little something. I'm starting to get hungry."

I got up, leaving behind the banyan tree with its suffocating foliage and its mythical door to heaven. The Buddhist nuns were selling food: sticky-rice cakes with green mung beans, plump squares of bean curd. One of the nuns was shooing away flies with her fan. We sampled the bean curd, washing it down with some ginger-flavored "poor man's tea." The sun faded over the crest of the mountains, and its rays, still flickering, gave off the heat of a brick furnace.

"It's still hot. Let's hurry before it gets colder," said my mother. With one hand clutching her package, the other clutching me, she started to walk.

It was a very unusual winter day, balmy, without a trace of wind. Our path wound and cut through rice paddies and hamlets, a grassy field with an old cotton tree, a cemetery cluttered with public benches and a huge gate hung with a five-point star and a plaque inscribed THE FATHERLAND IS THANKFUL. There was also a huge, stagnant pond, its surface dotted with wilted lotus stems.

"Hurry up. Or hold on to my neck, and I'll carry you."

"I can walk."

"We've still got a few miles from here to the river."

"Don't worry. I'll make it."

I broke into a sprint, passing my mother. I waited just long enough for her to catch up with me and then started running again. That was how we got to the river's edge before dusk.

The bank sloped down to the water's edge. Rubbish floated in the water, catching in eddies and spinning around the dead carcasses of waterflies. Mother washed my hands and feet, and we sat down on a rock to wait for the ferry. A cool wind picked up, blowing off the surface of the river, chilling us. I wrapped my arms around my mother's neck.

"Where is Father?"

She looked at me, surprised, and then imploring. "Please, don't ask me these questions."

But I insisted. "Where is my father? Why won't you tell me?"

She took my hand in silence. Dusk was falling, casting its dark shadow in a pool at the foot of the mountains. A cloud of smoke dispersed into the air, blurring the edges of objects. I knew I was torturing her, but I couldn't stop myself. I couldn't imagine what a father was, what a father could be.

But there was the solitude of this place, the bite of the evening wind, this mist that hung between the sky and the water, and I shuddered. I felt desolate. My mother, too, looked fragile, abandoned. I needed another presence, another shoulder to lean on in this life.

The wind howled violently, racing up and down the high-tension cables. My mother sat crouched down in silence. Just then, a sailboat approached the bank, pitching from side to side.

"Get in quickly if you want to cross. This is the last run." The boatman's voice echoed brutally. The passengers on the boat got up in a rush.

"Let's go, my child."

We hurtled down the steep bank, sending an avalanche of pebbles sliding into the water. I tripped once and almost fell. When all the passengers had disembarked, the boatman let us on deck. A woman, stooped under the weight of a huge basket of potatoes slung on her back, came running down the dike, and she cried out to us, "Wait for me, wait for me!"

The boatman waited, leaning on his perch as the woman heaved her basket of potatoes onto the barge. She pulled off the veil covering her head and mopped the sweat off her forehead.

"Thank God! What luck. I'd die if I missed this crossing."

Her face and neck were flushed, dripping with sweat, and her upper arms were as brawny as a stonemason's. But her bones stuck out at funny angles, as if she had rheumatoid arthritis, and her shoulders were thin and shrunken. It seemed incredible to me that she could support the weight of the potatoes at the extremities of her thin bamboo pole.

A second cry came from the bank:

"Ho, boatman . . . wait for me."

The man had the look of a traveling salesman. He wore khaki yellow pants and had knotted his ripped plaid shirt around his hips. He was clutching a dusty old suitcase, and he wore clunky old officer's shoes with thick soles, crudely stitched. As he jumped onto the bridge, the sampan tipped to one side under his weight.

"Oh my, he's a heavy one, isn't he?" cackled the woman with the baskets of potatoes.

Fuming, the new passenger turned on her, rolling his eyes. "Yeah, what's it to you?"

The poor woman gaped at him, dumbfounded. She sneaked an embarrassed glance in our direction, stammering, "Well, all I meant was . . ."

The man reeled around and glared at her again. He had a wide, coarse face with big ruddy cheekbones. His primitive features were softened by a small, pretty mouth with full, finely traced lips. The contrast was unnerving: this sensual, feline mouth in the middle of a butcher's face. A vicious glow animated his beady eyes, which glinted around bloodshot whites and fixed pupils. He stung the woman with another murderous look. "Shut up!"

His violent outburst stunned us. My mother and I, the other passengers, and the poor woman with the potatoes, we all sat without speaking, staring down at the leaky floor of the barge. A wooden ladle lay bobbing in a puddle of water. The old boatman gazed absently at the other side of the river. He propped the oar against his bent knee, fiddling with a few hairs on his beard. The wind whistled through the ripped sail, and the sampan pitched and tossed. The bleached-out carcasses of dragonflies floated on the surface of the waves like a handful of jasmine flowers and then vanished, sucked under in a whirlpool of mud. On the other bank, we heard someone humming a song. "Let's go," shouted the boatman.

Suddenly, he leaned back at an angle from his perch, pushing the boat off from the shore with his oar. Lapping, watery sounds echoed in the silence of dusk as the boat's stern broke through the circles on the violet surface of the river. A chill mist evaporated off the water, and I huddled against my mother. As the boat drifted toward the other bank, the sail puffed out, flapping in the wind. The mast creaked so noisily I thought it would fall and crush me.

When we reached the middle of the river, we heard a

young woman call from the bank, "Boatman, ho, boatman!"

Her cry bounced off the surface of the river. The sky shifted, extinguishing the last cloud aglow with the rays of the dying sun. On the distant bank, curls of smoke fused with the clouds, erasing the horizon line.

The water suddenly turned silvery, opaque and mysterious under its mantle of cinders. Waves shimmered like mercury, and the line of the riverbank receded, fading in the darkness. Already, the opposite shore was taking shape.

That night, I dreamed that I was being beaten. I didn't know what for or by whom. I wailed into my pillow for a long time. It was the humiliation, the feeling of injustice, that had haunted me since the neighbors had mocked me. Perhaps it was the sight of my suffering that made my mother change her mind, made her tell me about her husband, about the father I never knew; and for the first time, I saw him clearly.

Chapter FOUR

U NABLE TO BEAR THE INJUSTICE OR THE HUMILIATION, my father fled the village. He left with only his sister's meager savings. At first, he sought refuge in the home of an old friend, a man who had once taught in the same high school in the county capital. This man was the son of a family that had devoted itself to the city's fish-sauce business for more than three generations. But by the time my father arrived, his friend had already fled to Lao Cai. His family was suspected of sheltering members of the Nationalist party, and had all been put under surveillance.

At the entrance to the town was a huge village green, which doubled as a racecourse on festival days. At the time, it had been converted into a makeshift kangaroo court, where the landlords, the scapegoat "model tyrants" from the surrounding villages and communes, were dragged before a jury of peasants to be denounced and judged. The glow of bonfires lit up the sky, eerie curls of smoke illuminating the night.

The air echoed with the sounds of fury: Drums beat, bugles sounded the charge, mobs shrieked, and guerrilla patrols crisscrossed the roads, bayonets glinting at the tips of their rifles. The guerrillas kept their weapons cocked, threatening, ready to do battle. Their bayonets reflected in the gleam of their eyes as they glared suspiciously at every passerby. NO LANDLORD WILL SLIP THROUGH OUR NET: That was the new slogan, scrawled in lurid colors across the roads. Whomever they stopped shuddered under the violence of their gaze, this blind hatred that needed no basis, no justification.

The landlord family that had sheltered my father was terrified. They were the parents of one of my father's former students. But in those days they knew that the mere presence of a stranger in their house was a perfect excuse for their enemies to whip up the vengeance of the envious few: "relations with landowning classes," "fleeing Nationalists," "suspicious attitude," "sabotaging the revolution."

"Master, leave quickly, we beg you. We know this is ungracious. But take pity on us," they said, slipping a tiny paper packet into the palm of my father's hand. The couple closed the door and retreated into the house. My father called out to them, to return the packet, but the door remained closed.

A moment later, the shrill voice of a schoolboy whispered through the keyhole, "Master, keep the packet. You'll need it to survive. My parents have asked me to tell you this. . . ."

The child was panting, breathless with fear. My father heard him run off, his footsteps echoing across the inner courtyard of the house. He stuffed the packet into his pocket and headed for the main road. Night was falling. The squads of guerrilla soldiers hadn't yet begun their patrols. As he neared the town bus stop, he saw a man asleep on a bench, his conical straw hat angled to hide his face. But as my father approached, the man suddenly pulled up the brim and addressed him:

"Don't be afraid, Master. You taught the children in this town. Me, I peddled a cyclo to feed my wife and kids. Times have changed. Bastards fish shamelessly in muddied waters, but honest people are powerless. All we can do is keep our hands clean."

"Thanks. I don't know where to run anymore. I had a friend here, a colleague named Tuan. . . ."

"Yes, Master Tuan, son of the house of Van Van. He's fled. I drove him myself last month to the bus station for the city," said the man, gesturing to an old bicycle-drawn "taxi."

Both men went silent. A patrol had appeared at the other end of the station.

The cyclo driver whispered to my father, "Get in fast. I'm going to drive you. If you stay here, they'll ask for your papers. You're going to have problems."

My father got into the cyclo seat, and the driver mounted the bicycle in front, pedaling slowly along the edge of the fields.

When they arrived at the main road, the driver said, "I know you fled the countryside. But here too everything has gone mad, upside down. You won't be safe. Your old school is still open. But there aren't many of the old schoolteachers left. Well, as the wise men say, nothing lasts forever. Perhaps the time for exile has come for you."

All my father could say was "Thank you." The driver continued to pedal the length of the main road. At an intersection, he turned to speak to my father.

"What's your rising sign?"

"Wood."

The cyclo driver muttered to himself, "Water engenders wood and nourishes it. I'll drive you to the river. You'll find a ferryman there. For five and a half coins, he'll take you to the end of the line. You'll be there in three days."

He straightened his back and then threw the weight of

his body down on the pedals. The cyclo veered southwest. Eight miles on, they arrived at Con Village and the bank of the river. The cyclo stopped to let my father off. It was about nine-thirty in the evening. The sky was teeming with stars. The barges stood motionless, silent, as if they were asleep. My father rummaged in his pocket for a bill.

The driver took it and said, "I accept this money, Master, to put your heart at ease. But now I entrust it to you. Keep it for my funeral. When the grass has grown green around my grave, burn some fake gold, a few packets of paper money, a few sticks of incense. Scatter flowers so my soul will remember their fragrance. Go. May luck be with you. May you find some peace."

He placed the bill in the palm of my father's hand and then mounted his cyclo. My father watched the man pedal off until he disappeared into the night.

A call rose from the river's edge. "Hey, you, aren't you going to board?"

Aboard the sampan, someone brought out a storm lamp from the cabin and perched it on the bridge. A peasant woman, her hair bound up in a turban of black gauze, lifted her head. My father scaled down the bank.

"Where do you want to go?"

My father stammered a reply that had nothing to do with the question: "I'm a teacher."

"Where?" the woman snapped back.

"At the communal school."

"Do you want to go upstream or downstream?"

"It doesn't matter."

An impatient male voice boomed from inside the boat cabin, "What do you want?"

After a pause, the woman grumbled, "He's probably a rich peasant or a landlord fleeing his village. Does he have his papers?"

My father replied, "I'm a schoolteacher. Here's my identity card."

The woman with the turban pushed it aside with the back of her hand.

"Who gives a damn . . . will it be upstream or downstream?"

"Upstream."

"Twenty coins."

My father sighed, impatient. "My God, all I have, really all I have is twenty-six coins. This trip usually only costs five and a half."

The woman grumbled back at him, "Who cares what the usual price is? Take it or leave it."

My father must have hesitated for a long time, because the woman lowered her voice and said, "Look, I'll give a two-coin discount. Just give me eighteen, but get on board."

My father didn't hesitate. He counted out eighteen coins into the sampan owner's hand and crawled down into the hull. A white-haired old man and a fourteen-year-old boy sat squatted in the middle of a sack of dried potatoes. The sampan owner motioned to my father to sit near them and then shouted up to her husband, "Go. Upstream."

The husband moved like a shadow toward the prow and grabbed the oars. The sampan sliced through the water and turned, tracing a half-circle on the shimmering, moonlit surface of the lake.

For three days and nights, they ascended the river. On the third night, the old man and the young boy got off. They left to search for a farm that belonged to a relative who lived there raising canaries, livestock, and growing various cereals. My father went ashore, the next evening at the hour of the shepherd's star.

The place was deserted. There were only two rooftops as far as the eye could see; one sheltered a food vendor and the other his half-wit wife, who drove a buffalo wagon.

They were a couple who had taken refuge here during the days of the anti-French resistance. They had no children. Undoubtedly, some implacable hatred toward their relatives had driven them to this backwater, where they had built their huts on an uninhabited bank. During the day, they made dozens of sticky-rice cakes for the travelers who passed through. At night, they wove wicker baskets to sell at the local farmers' market. During the jackfruit season, the wife peeled the fruits and filled huge baskets with them before drying and storing the pieces in a jar.

My father stayed with these people for two weeks. They were hospitable but stingy. After he had spent his last eight coins, my father didn't allow himself to join them for their meals, even if it was just a bit of rice mixed with potato and grilled sesame seeds. All the while, his hosts remained taciturn, inscrutable. They almost never spoke. They baked their cakes, opened their shop, cooked rice, served and sold, sliced wicker strips and wove their baskets in silence, like two automatons pacing in the shadows. They rarely looked at each other.

My father had a strange feeling that they must have been linked by some crime that had kept them there, far from their village. Their shadowy past seemed to be both a bond and a yawning chasm between them, wedding their destinies but sundering their souls. Their life together was poisonous.

This lugubrious atmosphere spooked my father. He gave his best suit to the merchant as a gift and then left without a coin on him. It was only then that he unfolded the tiny packet that the parents of his former student had given him; it contained a golden chain.

"Your destiny is linked to wood; water nourishes wood. Follow the river."

Remembering the cyclo driver's words, my father traveled further up the river, arriving in a Muong minority region. The first village was tiny, and its people subsisted off slash-and-burn agriculture. The second Muong village had a highly developed economy with a very refined tradition of linen weaving. These villagers also planted fruit trees, raised livestock, and engaged in logging and other trades. In this village, my father's gold chain had immense value, and it permitted him to break out of his nomadic, hand-to-mouth existence. He married again and became the son-in-law of the village vice president.

My father taught Vietnamese and the rudiments of science to the children of the wealthy families. In addition to their traditional gongs, the Muong villagers had a guitar and two mandolins. My father played both these instruments. Naturally, he became a kind of honored sage in their eyes, an artist revered by everyone in the village. He had a son within the first year and another the following year.

His past life, with all its ordeals, had receded, but it lay dormant under the swamp grasses like an insistent nightmare. Even so, the years of mud and stench, the dregs of that past, seemed to settle and dissolve under the depths.

The years went by. At the beginning of the sixth year, a traveling salesman appeared. He sold a bit of everything: dried fish, herbal concoctions for coughs, special Hang Bac candies from Hanoi.

"Come buy my delicacies, get off your backsides and come have a look," he shouted. His voice was mischievous, full of charm and humor. After one phrase in Vietnamese, he would shout a different one in Muong dialect. Warming to this man's humor, my father invited him to his house. Suddenly, he recognized the man as someone he had seen in a neighboring village, separated from his own by only a small canal.

My father treated the man as a guest of honor, serving him chicken steamed in wine at every meal. On the second day of his visit, they killed a kid goat. The man was delighted and even began to prepare the specialty dishes himself: a minced roast, a fragrant herb salad flavored with roasted rice powder, black soy sauce, and fresh ginger root. It was a true country feast. On the third day, the village hunters offered them a gift: a large goat thigh. The traveling salesman had never seen such delicacies. He was overjoyed, and he talked himself hoarse, telling his whole repertoire of bawdy stories. The young people in the village wept with mirth.

Late into the night, when all the guests had gone home, he stopped his joking. In the low, sober voice of someone who has led an errant life, he told my father of the events that had befallen his village: the Land Reform Movement, the Rectification Campaign, the Collectivization Campaign. He knew Aunt Tam. He also knew my mother.

My father learned through the man that my mother had mortgaged the house to leave for the city. And the past started to live and stir again inside him. He felt his heart race. Suddenly, the ease and tranquillity of his life in the Muong village could no longer hold him.

The following week, he left with the traveling salesman, descending the river on a wooden raft. From his birthplace in the village to the city, he followed my mother's traces to her tiny back-alley home on the outskirts of Hanoi.

My mother was still young and beautiful, but she looked at no one, smiled at no one. Like ashes rising under the caress of a slight wind, their love rose again, melting the years of separation, the yearning, the emptiness, the hatred, the humiliation of an entire lifetime of bitterness, of two lives almost snuffed out, buffeted by a series of absurd, incomprehensible events. All this, fused in the space of an instant, quivering through every pore of their bodies, transported them. All this, here, under the leaky roof of this pathetic hovel, in this place where my parents had lived and loved each other, where I had come into the world.

Sirens blaring. The train came to a halt, throwing me forward. My traveling companion caught me and smiled, the silver caps of his teeth glinting. Pugatnova's voice rang out one last time and then faded. The man switched off the cassette player and put it back in his bag. He stretched, yawned a few times, and spread his long legs across the train seat.

Outside, the sky darkened to violet. Rows of poplars traced white lines in the night. A few storax trees draped their hairy branches over the wooden fences. Here and there, I saw mounds of earth covered with silvery gray flowers. In the sad, uncertain half-light of the evening, I could just make out an old house with a pointed roof and a chimney. The sight of the house stirred something in me: a vision of a former life, my own, that of my parents, of my friends, of my country; a past to which each of us is linked, inextricably, by the ties of blood and race.

The train pulled out of the station, but the old house at the edge of the lake continued to haunt me. I remembered an old swamp bathed in the fiery light of sunset, back there, in her village, the night my mother took me to visit our relatives.

Hg & Que visit Aunt Tam, who, against all adversity, struggled & achieved wealth. Hang & Que learn that Ton died from connection outside following an argument with his unhappy wife (who had married during the time he was away from Que. He could not bear the shame.

Chapter FIVE

Flashback to present. Recalls a pilgrimage to Con Son in North. the fear of such beauty. Then recalls as Tam gives Hang golden earrings and she tells how that she will support her education & success.

EVEN THOUGH WE LIVED IN HANOI, WHEN WE VISITED the village, my mother still observed all the rituals. After you returned from a faraway place, you had to offer small gifts to everyone and recount your travels. So we brought gifts, and my mother told of our life in the city. As for me, my duty was to greet everyone in a quiet voice, answer questions obediently, and remember the details of the family hierarchy, so as not to offend anyone. Anyone younger than I was to call me "Auntie," and I was told to address any older woman, even those twenty to thirty years older, as "Elder Sister." All this made me feel jittery, on edge.

Only the path to the village was somehow reassuring and precious to me. On our first morning back, when I was barely awake, I set off to stalk the *chich choe* bird, following its shrill song. I went hunting for ripe guavas, the kind that fell when the birds pecked at them.

I hid myself in the shadow between a thicket of rushes and the trunk of the old carambola tree to watch a chameleon climb up its branches, its skin turning from ruddy brown to leafy green. The cactus bushes gave off a musky perfume, especially toward midday, when the sun set the air ablaze.

"Who wants barley sugar? Who wants to swap chicken feathers, duck feathers, for my nice barley sugar? Does anyone want to turn in broken mirrors, old cooking pots for my barley sugar?"

The street vendor's cry rang out, echoing through the hamlets until it was lost in the rustle of bamboo. As she trudged past us, a straw hat hiding her face, I stared at her blackened, dusty feet.

"Mother, when you were little, was there always someone like this?"

"Mmh. She's dead now. This one is her daughter."

I was mesmerized by her huge, splayed feet. They were scored with tiny cracks, encrusted with gray patches of dead skin. Decades before her, another woman, just like her, had crisscrossed the same village, plodded along with the same feet.

"Mother?"

I grabbed the hem of my mother's dress, too frightened to speak. My mother bent down toward me:

"Yes?"

"No, nothing," I stammered. I didn't dare ask her if, in another ten years, I would live her life, this life. The thought made me shiver.

My mother smiled, her radiant, useless smile. "Silly. You're starting to talk to yourself. Come on, let's go to the courtyard. Aunt Tam is back from the South, and she's invited us over."

My mother bathed and washed me carefully and then dressed me up in one of my best outfits: a white blouse embroidered with a swallow and a pair of Western-style pants with a belt made out of imported Chinese fabric. Compared to average peasant's clothing, this was luxury.

Just a few hundred yards separated our house from Aunt Tam's. We found the gate open for us. Inside, an old woman who was seated, slicing bamboo into strips, looked up. "Come in, please, Madame Tam is expecting you."

She scrutinized me as one would look over a precious vase before buying it. "My goodness, like they say, each basket tips toward her owner! She's the mirror image of her father. Madame Tam's going to love her."

Mother started to laugh, her eyes twinkling.

"Thank you, madame."

She led us into a vast courtyard covered with tiles, each decorated with a painting of a different aromatic herb, like the mint and basil we ate with fried spring rolls. Unlike other courtyards in the village, which were often made of brick or cement and scrubbed down for drying rice, this one had an air of refinement and opulence. To the left stood a spacious, modern house painted with a pale yellow wash made from lime. The house opened onto a huge wooden veranda covered with a flat roof. On the right, a hedge of flowers and a grove of betel palms bordered a fruit garden.

Here and there, you could see the reddish glow of oranges and kaki fruit. Several outbuildings stretched out behind the house, a bit to the left of the main building. Between the outbuildings and the garden was a well, sheltered by a sheet-metal roof. The cord of a pulley rested on the edge of the well. Everything was clean, well ordered. It had all been coldly, rigorously studied in great detail. A potted ginseng bush, set in a vase, had been placed in the center.

The main door swung open, and a woman walked quickly across the courtyard. "Is this her?"

Her voice was stern, rasping. I felt my heartbeat quicken. Two huge eyes stared at me. Her dried lips twitched as she spoke.

"Is this her, Sister Que?"

"Yes, it's her," said my mother. Then she ordered me, "Greet your aunt."

I didn't dare meet her eyes.

Aunt Tam suddenly dropped to her knees, bringing her face toward mine. She fingered my hair and ran her hands over my temples and face, caressing the shape of my shoulders as if she was looking for something. She had tiny, claw-like hands, gnarled and coarse. Her eyes glittered, and as they searched my face, I felt as if she left no eyelash or freckle unexamined.

This voraciousness put me ill at ease. I knew she was my blood, the link to my father. This was the love that had been buried, impossible to imagine.

I stood very still, letting her touch me, caress me. Her wizened face, which ordinarily must have been quite severe, was ecstatic, reverent. "She's a drop of his blood. My niece," she murmured.

The tears in her eyes welled over and streamed in rivulets down her cheeks. I dropped my eyes to avoid staring; those cheeks so brown, so ravaged by the sun that they seemed to be dusted with ash.

All of a sudden, Aunt Tam raised herself. "Come on, let's go in."

She walked briskly in front of us. Her silhouette was thin and graceful. Her face had gone sullen, and she pursed her lips together in a tight line.

I stared, fascinated by the thick calluses and cracks that scored the skin of her feet. Horrible deep, ugly furrows separated the soles of her feet into flaky layers. Time and back-breaking work in the fields had ravaged them. At the same time, they were dainty feet, thin and elegant. Rich now, she could afford to wear imported plastic sandals from Thailand, a luxury in this village. Still, they could never hide her past.

"Please, have a seat at the table. I'm going to get some wine."

Her voice was the unmistakable, imperious voice of the
eldest. We entered through a room on the left. A low, impos-
ing table of amboyna wood sat next to the wall, its grainy
black surface shining like polished buffalo horn. Flowers and
leaves carved out of mother-of-pearl had been embedded and
lacquered into the wood around the sides of the table. At each
of the four corners, bunches of grapes pieced together from
the pearly insides of snail shells reflected the colors of the
rainbow.

The table was so beautiful that I hesitated to sit down. I
could imagine it belonging to the museum collection. As if
she read my thoughts, Aunt Tam urged us on:

"Please, do sit down."

I was seized with fear. What witchcraft had allowed her
to read my thoughts with her back turned to me?

She walked toward the altar to the ancestors in the center
of the room. Brightly polished copper vases of all sizes, porcelain Buddhas, and candelabras glinted in the light of red candles burning on both sides of the altar. An enormous plate
heaped with five kinds of fruit formed a centerpiece. Behind
it were offerings of cakes and wines and a vase filled with
fragrant white orchids.

Aunt Tam pondered her choice among bottles of lemon,
orange, plum, and coffee brandy.

"We'll have some of this sweet sticky-rice liqueur. I distilled this one myself. Hang will have a drink with us."

She put the other bottles away and opened the door to
the room to the right of us with a key. A second later, she
reappeared with a huge glass jar filled with a clear, viscous
liquid. She set the jar down on a little table, pulled out an
empty glass bottle, and proceeded to fill it through a funnel.

Her task complete, she nodded to my mother. "Sister
Que, please, let's eat."

My mother lifted the domed wicker cover used to cover
the bronze platter. It was a feast worthy of a Tet banquet:
steamed chicken, fried chicken, pork pâté, cinnamon pâté,

spring rolls seasoned with rice powder, spicy cold salads, asparagus, vermicelli, and sautéed side dishes.

My mother let out a cry of amazement. "Why such a banquet? Who are we expecting?"

"Who would I be waiting for? There's only the three of us. Madame Dua ate before we made the offerings to the ancestors. She can't stand hunger."

She had an almost imperceptible smile on her lips. I thought I detected a trace of contempt. Pulling up the hem of her black silk pants, she knelt at the low table. "Please start."

My mother counted out chopsticks for us. Aunt Tam poured the wine into tiny porcelain cups the size of a water buffalo's eye. Our ancestors used to drink lotus tea in them at dawn.

"Today, because you have brought the child back to this house, I have prepared offerings to the ancestors, and to Ton's spirit." Raising her glass, she continued, "May these deceased souls taste this sweetness, may they protect and favor Hang's destiny."

I felt confused. I had never imagined that I could have such importance for others. Aunt Tam caught my eye and pointed to the altar.

"You should have prayed to the ancestors and to the spirit of your father. But I had an early start. Anyway, you're still young, so I prayed for you. In a few years, when you mature, remember this and fulfill your duties."

"Yes, my aunt."

Satisfied, she continued, "You realize how happy this makes me. That your father and I will not have lived in vain. I've lost so much, suffered so much in this world. But I don't regret this life. Come, lift your glass now."

I raised my glass. The thick alcohol glinted a deep red, like blood, in the glow of sunset. A wave of fear, a dense sugary perfume, a burning sensation, sharp and intoxicating. I felt as if I were drinking to some solemn, merciless vow, some sacred, primitive rite.

You could hear the villagers returning from the rice fields, coaxing their water buffalo up the paths to their hamlets, women bickering with each other, scolding their children.

Evening sounds filled the air: rice being rinsed, swishing rhythmically in rush baskets; women beating laundry on rocks at the edge of the pond; children shrieking and tussling with each other in the water.

You could smell the evening smells melting into one: straw fires burning, bean shells mixed with young rice roasting, the pungent stench of fresh buffalo dung, guavas ripening in the garden. Everything blurred, vanishing into the half-light of dusk. Night settled like dust over the roads, cloaking the hamlet in a lazy softness. The shrill, irritating noises muted now, settling like silt to the bottom of a lake. The bamboo groves swayed, lulling the earth in their eternal, harmonious whisper.

The indestructible purity of a countryside at peace. This was a world apart, like a great lake. Even a tempest could only ripple its surface, stirring up a bit of weed or algae here and there. Then all would return to an ancient swamp, to the yapping of toads at dusk, to the sawing rasp of insects in the night, the thud of buffalo footsteps and the sound of men, at dawn, in the rice fields.

"Come, let's have tea out in the courtyard. It's cooler there. Sister Que, bring that thermos. You, Hang, you take the teapot and the cups."

Aunt Tam carried two mahogany stools. I saw the muscles and veins in her arms ripple. But she walked down the steps slowly, gingerly; the feet of the two stools didn't even brush the ground until she placed them in the center of the courtyard. Few men could have matched her strength. With a delicate, unhurried gesture, she swept a strand of hair off her face and seated herself.

"I scented the tea with jasmine flower. You remember that jasmine bush at the foot of the wall? The tea for your wedding was scented with that same jasmine."

"It's still alive? After all this time?"

Aunt Tam pursed her lips together. You couldn't tell whether it was to smile or to mock. "I replanted it the same year I rebuilt this house."

"It's been five years . . . let's see. Hasn't it? Yes, five years.

"Five years and two and a half months."

She poured the tea, and the scent of jasmine perfumed the air, mixing with the odor of palm fronds and roses. She crossed her arms before she spoke.

"Remember now: During the land reform, they cut this house into two. Bich took possession of one half, the other went to Nan. They evicted me. I had to take refuge in a hut next to the temple. They left me only a few acres of wasteland: no buffalo, no cow, no wagon. The few dozen coins I had been able to save, I gave to Ton.

"When I couldn't sleep, I would just stare at those devastated rice fields and weep. Sometimes, I considered suicide. As if by coincidence, I had to walk past the old well at the gate to the temple five or six times a day. The water was so clear. It was as if it were beckoning to me. I would stare at my reflection and tell myself, 'I could end my suffering. But it would be too cowardly. They'll just come and laugh on my grave. I've got to survive. To see *their* undoing and to win this chess game with heaven.'

"I still had two ankle-length silk *ao dai*. They were the yellowy color of chicken fat. I never wore them. Sold them one day at the market for two baskets of potatoes. Since I had no rice, the potatoes gave me the energy to work. I sowed other people's rice paddies from dawn to dusk in exchange for help with plowing. I bartered five hours of my labor for one hour of theirs. After the sowing, I would till the earth until the mud was as fine as cake flour. In my fields, the rice seedlings grew thick and bushy. Then I had to find fertilizer. If you're ready to sweat, you can turn even the most barren land into a good rice paddy.

"While I waited for the rice to ripen, I worked as hired labor for one of my aunts. My aunt knew how to make vermicelli noodles out of riverweed. Remember? In this village, they only eat riverweed in times of scarcity. But it was amazing; no one could deny it: Ground riverweed made a flour that we could whiten. Then we made pancakes out of it, cutting the dried pancakes into fine strips, a long, clear vermicelli that was absolutely delicious. At first, I nearly wore myself out at the grindstone to make the flour, to get that very fine consistency. But little by little, I mastered how to sift it and bleach it, how to roll out the pancakes and cut them. I bought two big pots and pounds and pounds of duckweed with my salary.

"After a week of experimenting, I invented a machine that ground the duckweed by crank. I did everything, every step of it, myself, and when I sold the noodles at the village market, I made quite a tidy sum. At the time, the duckweed cost me next to nothing, so I bought two tons. Filled the house up with it. There wasn't a corner left to hang my hammock in, so I slept on a mat in the temple courtyard.

"I kept every penny I earned in my belt and slept with a knife under my neck. Stretched out like that, I slept until dawn. I was never afraid anymore. And after I had made those two tons of duckweed into noodles, I had enough to buy a real machine, to save me time cutting the noodles. In those days, there were only three of these machines in the whole township. The bleach for the flour was cheap. So was the labor. I hired people to do the noodle business while I worked in the rice paddies. My paddy was the nicest in the village.

"At the end of the harvest, 'the Team for the Rectification of Errors' arrived. I was reclassified as a 'middle peasant.' They returned the house and my five acres of good paddy. After more than a year of absence, I went home. Before the land reform, I had a mother, a brother. Now, I was alone. Before, the house had been spacious and clean. Now, it looked like a neglected grave. Bich and Nan had cut the main room in two with a bamboo partition. They pilfered bricks from the kitchen and the walls and sold them to buy food. Inside the house, they each made their own cooking fire between three broken bricks. Cinders and smoke and mosquitoes swirled above their beds. Chickens and geese ran wild all over the house. The floor was caked in their excrement. The tiles in the courtyard had vanished. They had sold them piece by piece, at the last minute, before they were forced to return the house.

"I cleaned and scrubbed for three days straight. Then I set up my own noodle-and-chip business. My help had all left me, so I worked alone. At the third dawn watch, I was still up working. At the fifth, I was already out of bed. At first, the lack of sleep drove me mad. Then I got used to it. My eyes never shut.

"I never wanted to make a fortune. My mother always said I loved the work, not the money. Remember? When a pause in fieldwork left us a bit of free time, I would go to visit the pagodas; I never missed a festival day. It was my only pleasure, going to those big pagoda festivals at Huong and Thay, the festival of Giong Village. . . . Whatever the distance, I always found a way of getting there.

"But from then on, I had one obsession: to get rich. The festivals, the ceremonies, even Tet—they didn't exist for me anymore. I didn't even hear the boom of the theater drum rocking the temple, or the people rushing to see performances by artists on tour from Hanoi. I worked constantly. Through the heat and the freezing cold, I sowed the rice paddies, worked in the garden, planted trees, made the noodles. I never stopped. Even a rock would have crumbled. In five years, I never once fell sick. Strange species we are. . . ."

She paused. Her eyes flickered like embers in the soft light of dusk. My mother poured her some tea. They drank in small sips, without speaking.

This was only the calm at the eye of the storm. A flash of lightning welled up from the depths of my aunt's eyes.

She stared at something, somewhere beyond the dark shadows of the palm trees and the hedge of flowers, and then pushed her teacup back on the tray abruptly.

"Someday I'll be even richer. This ancestral house will be renovated. It's going to be even more opulent than before. I'll show people. Even if I have to tear this body of mine apart. Look—I rebuilt this house. Replanted the flower hedge. The palms. This jasmine bush. The old guava orchard is covered with orange and kaki trees again. People come all the way from Hanoi to try and buy up my entire harvest. I had the floor of this house built on three layers of stone. Raised it higher than any other in this village. And the ceramic tiling inside, it's of the finest quality. I had it shipped from Hanoi. The mahogany living-room furniture, I bought it off the deputy director of the plantations in the next village.

"People say I'm extravagant. I tell them, 'Yes, that's right, and I'm offering this to myself in memory of all my suffering.' After I repaired the house and the courtyard, I asked some bronze craftsmen to make me copies of the family heirlooms which once decorated the family altar and which Bich and Nan stole from me. They hawked all the antiques, most of them for just a bottle of wine or a few pounds of meat.

"It's like that old proverb goes: 'A rich man loves to work, a poor man loves to eat.' In the end, they were reduced to misery. That's what happens when you can't miss a meal to flood the rice paddies, when you can't stay awake at night to get a field just right. . . .

"Bich wandered off to the east hamlet, and he's still moldering away there. Nan lives on the edge of the village. I'll take you to see her tomorrow. She's just a sack of meat and filthy rags. She hides from the rain under pieces of nylon. She doesn't have the energy to repair her own roof. They aren't even worthy of my contempt. . . . The real offender is your brother, Chinh. Where is he now?"

"He's at Quang Ninh. I hear he's preparing to leave for Hanoi," my mother stammered.

"So he still visits you?"

"He came to see me for the first time in nine years last month. He needed his share of the mortgage."

"He wouldn't dare show his face in this village. I guess he's afraid that his victims will dish it right back to him."

"He was obeying orders," my mother ventured, feebly.

"Didn't the leaders themselves admit their errors by launching the Rectification Campaign? Why are you still defending him?" Aunt Tam lowered her voice: "Do you know how your husband died?"

"Two months after I gave birth, I heard that he had come down with malaria, that they weren't able to transfer him to the village in time," my mother replied.

Aunt Tam cut her off brutally. "That's it. Sickness, death. A nice story; it fools everybody. At first, I didn't know what to think, so I believed it. Last year, when I went to the neighboring village to arrange for the repair of the table, I met a street vendor, the same man who visited the Muong village where Ton lived. When Ton first came back, it was I who gave him your address in Hanoi. While you were preparing to give birth, Ton left for the Muong village. He thought he could get permission from his Muong wife to come to town and help you himself with the child. But the woman refused. They probably quarreled. She must have insulted him, accused him of ingratitude. He's my younger brother. I know him. He could stand hunger, thirst, even cold. But not shame. One morning he went out into the forest. Hunters found his body washed up at the edge of a river two days later. The street vendor had come to the village the same day for his funeral."

Aunt Tam went silent. My mother's head had dropped to her chest. She fumbled helplessly in her pocket. When she couldn't find her handkerchief, she wiped her tears on the sleeve of her *ao dai*.

Aunt Tam went on, "If your brother hadn't persecuted him, would he have had to hide in that village, in exile? Would he have died so horribly? No, I won't stand for it. You cannot continue to absolve my brother's assassin."

My mother sobbed for a long time before she could say anything. "Please, I'm begging you. We have to bury this hatred."

My aunt made no reply. She gazed fixedly at the orangerie. The outline of the trees blurred with the night until all you could see was a muddle of heavy shadows. A firefly flashed, tracing a circle in the somber grove, and then disappeared. Then Aunt Tam began to laugh, a forced, rasping laugh.

"That would be too easy! And my mother who died calling for her son. I can still see her eyes, how they refused to shut. And everything that . . ."

Her voice choked and wore out. Her eyes shone bloodshot, and above her angular, sun-ravaged cheeks, her forehead was scored with a welter of lines. I stared at her brittle, faded brown hair streaked with white.

A shooting star careened across the sky, ripping into the horizon. A firefly flashed out of the shadows, swirled for a moment, and vanished. Wave after wave of the heady scent of wild roses infused the air like an invisible tide, smothering all in tension and fear.

I stayed in the shadow, motionless, silent, not daring to breathe. I felt the jerky, hot breathing of the woman beside me. Her blood flowed in my veins. She was a lost replica of my father. This past had poisoned life for her, taking with it all joy, all warmth, all maternal feeling, all the happiness the world might have offered her. Aunt Tam was living her vengeance now, crushing everything that blocked her way.

My neighbor yawned loudly, not bothering to hide his mouth with his hand. His eyes fluttered, and he fell asleep on the edge of the seat, his head propped against his pea jacket. The train rumbled through an anonymous town: a few streets, a bridge, a thin stream, a swaying thicket of grasses, before it was sucked past us into the night. The last lights sputtered out. On both sides of the train, the earth, luminous in the clarity of starlight, stretched out like a discolored ocean, an expanse of sadness.

All the landscapes here began like this. On my first winter day in Russia, I had stayed awake for six hours, just to watch my first snowfall. It was freezing, but I stayed glued to the window, watching these strange flowers flood the earth with their icy whiteness. Light sparked off them in blinding shards, frail and luminous as a childhood dream. This beauty pierced my soul like sorrow. Extremes have always wounded me.

I had experienced the exact same sensation as a girl. My mother had taken me on a pilgrimage to Con Son, in the north. On the way back, the road passed through the "Burned Beach." I dozed off in her arms. Suddenly, the car stopped, and I heard her say, "Wake up, Hang, we're here."

I rubbed my eyes and opened them: The Along Bay stretched before us in all its splendor, the serenity of the sea dissolving into the fog. Not a ripple, or sail, not a murmur of leaves, not even a lapping sound. An infinite silence in the infinite greenness of the water. The rocks, mirrored in the water, looked to me like slabs of Chinese ink, shrouding riddles of history, marvelous legends, and lost treasure in their shadows. The caves stood guard like wary eyes, each one closing over a thousand faces—tortured witnesses, lost heroes, murdered men and women of genius, pirates.

Clouds floated like puffs of jade along the horizon, a line broken jagged by solitary rocks. I gazed at the horizon for a long time, this endless jade-colored necklace fallen to earth. Color of clouds at dawn. Color of young leaves tinted with smoke, filtered through the dawning sun, an exquisite green that would only exist once, in one place in the universe. I'll never know why this beauty was so painful to me.

The snow fell to an unfamiliar, foreign earth. Beauty knows no frontiers, seduces without discrimination. The snow spilled onto the earth as if the sky had welled over with flowers. I had already been in Russia for several years, but I still stared at the snow.

Behind me, a voice squeaked, "Who stole the sewing machine under my bed?"

I jumped and wheeled around. We lived four in a room then. The girl glared at each of us in turn, frantic. I stood in front of the window. My two other roommates were still snuggled under their bed covers. They uncovered them hurriedly, just enough to poke their noses out. "What do you mean? What sewing machine?"

"The sixty-nine-ruble sewing machine. My nephew from Karkov lent it to me yesterday when you went to get bread."

"How would we know?"

"Look, there are only four of us here. . . . So . . . well." She flushed and went silent. Perhaps out of concern, perhaps out of anger, I said, "Yesterday, we made those rice noodles. We ate them together. Then you had guests here in the afternoon while we went out for groceries and then to the circus. We weren't back here for dinner until nine-thirty. How could we have known that you had a sewing machine, or where you stashed it?"

She blushed even deeper, and scrambled to explain. "I'm sure I put it under the bed. I even checked the contents of the sewing box. I covered it myself with that violet fabric, the same one we liked to use as a tablecloth."

One of my roommates was furious. "Who cares whether it was white or violet? Is that any of our business?"

Her red face turned livid now, and her hands started to

shake. "Stop torturing me. You're the only ones here. How could it have disappeared? Do you think it sprouted wings?"

The other two girls threw off their covers and sat up in bed. "So you're accusing us of theft, is that it?"

Their eyes flashed angrily.

She panicked and paced about, stammering, "No, no it's not that I suspect you. . . . But the sewing machine, I put it here. . . ."

Her nostrils quivered. She wiped her tears with the back of her hand, pulling it across the bridge of her nose. Suddenly, I felt overcome by a kind of pity. I turned to my two friends and snapped at them, "Calm down. Let's not make a scene. The people in the next room can hear us. Get up and get dressed and we'll search. This apartment isn't exactly a palace. It'll take us half an hour to search it, including the shed."

My friends, anxious not to annoy me any further, threw on their bathrobes, and we started to search under the furniture. Then the kitchen. Not more than ten minutes later, one of them shouted, "Found it!"

She pulled it out from the lowest and widest drawer of the chest. We used the chest as a kind of pantry for our noodles, rice, potatoes, onions, garlic, and other spices. Undoubtedly, the girl had pulled the sewing machine out from under the bed to put it in her baggage but hid it temporarily in the drawer. Then she had forgotten it.

In my neighborhood in Hanoi, I had a neighbor afflicted with the same mania. From time to time, you could hear her husband curse her, after he found a package of moldy tea stuffed under a pile of clothes, or a pound of sugar in a tin of noodles. Other times, it would be a packet of preserved lotus saved from one Tet to another in half-rotted boxes. The habit of misery had twisted these people, driving them to this paranoia. What had once been diligence turned to desperation.

"And this, what's this?" my roommate shrieked, threatening the other young girl with a metal bar. "Look, will you! Open your eyes . . . this is it, isn't it?"

The girl stood next to the table, motionless, her arms limp, her eyes glued to the floor. Her flat pug nose looked even flatter. A woman can be ugly, I thought, but if she's a coward, she becomes hideous. How do you explain paranoia in a twenty-one-year-old girl? I tried to calm my friend. "Stop it, please."

She spun around and hissed at me, "It's revolting. I won't stand for it. It's your fault, Hang. We never wanted her in this room. You had to go and . . ."

I grabbed her wrist. "No shouting. In any case, it's over."

My friend threw the sewing machine on the table and sat down, fuming. The young girl was still standing in the same place, picking at the scaly green paint of the table with her fingernail. Tears trickled down her flat cheeks, pooling at the tip of her nose. She had a low forehead, and a thick strand of hair had fallen over her left temple, setting her face off balance. A birthmark nestled between her eyebrows. We had all lived together for two years, but this was the first time I had ever really looked at her.

We retreated to the bedroom, leaving her there in the kitchen with her machine, with the packages of noodles and rice. One of my roommates slid back under her bed covers. The other started to brush her hair, getting ready to go out. It was still snowing outside. The storm, this torrent of pure beauty, continued to flood the earth. Outside my window, a sense of perfection still permeated the air. But I felt lost.

I wandered back to my desk: a half-finished book, a few hair curlers, some spidery black lines on a piece of white paper. I stared at those black lines, unable to make out the words. I understood something, perhaps for the first time: In every life, there must come a moment when what is most sacred, most noble, in us evaporates into thin air. In a flash of lucidity, the values we have honored and cherished reveal themselves in all their poverty and vulgarity, as they had to this girl. From this moment, no one is spared.

During our stay in the village, my mother observed custom and went to visit everyone. It took a week before the man who bought our house could convince his family to give him the sum required. My mother took the money and signed the act of sale.

The next morning, at dawn, we returned to Hanoi. Aunt Tam wanted to accompany us to the ferry pier. She had gotten up in the middle of the night to prepare the sticky rice and the chicken and pork. When she appeared with a bamboo basket brimming with provisions from Lang Son's shop, my mother was embarrassed: "Please, you really don't have to go to all the trouble. It's a long way to the pier."

"Not as long as the one I used to have to walk during the Land Reform, on my way to work."

"But the house, all the chores . . ."

"I've been up since the third dawn watch. Don't worry about me."

And she took me by the hand. It was still dark out, and the branches, heavy with dew, brushed against my hair. Without a word, Aunt Tam handed the basket of provisions to my mother and hauled me onto her back. I tried to argue with her. "Please, Aunt, I can walk myself."

"Hush. You're going to get scratched by all these branches. It could even get infected."

Her imperious voice terrified me. She carried me this way, piggyback, all the way to the main road. When she let me down, I let out a sigh of relief and dashed ahead, afraid she would force me back up again onto her emaciated back. I sensed, rising from within her, a love repressed, buried under years of hatred and revenge.

I saw it in the looks she gave me, in her abrupt, excessive tenderness, in her voice. And it scared me. Perhaps I was too young to be the object of such a love; somehow, it seemed abnormal, too violent, too implacable. As much as I loved my aunt, I avoided her when I could.

"Careful, Hang. You're going to fall. Don't run, the road is full of potholes and bumps. Come here, give me your hand."

She clasped my hand greedily, the way a child clutches the coin her mother gives her on the way to school. My mother understood. Aunt Tam watched her from the corner of her eye.

When she was out of earshot, Aunt Tam whispered, "You're the last drop of blood in my family. The house, the altar to the ancestors, the rice paddies, the garden, I'm keeping them for you, do you understand?"

"Yes, my aunt."

"A long time ago, your grandfather was a schoolteacher in this village. Everyone knew and admired him. Your father was also a decent, gifted man. By the age of twelve, he read French fluently. You must study conscientiously so you will never dishonor their memory. Do you hear me?"

"Yes, my aunt."

"You still don't understand the injustice your father endured. Remember it. One day, you will."

"Yes."

"Write me every month to tell me how you're doing, your studies and your health. I can provide for all your needs: food, clothing, medication. You will have everything you want to succeed. These days, lots of women are successful. Did you know that?"

"Yes, my aunt."

"Madame But's daughter, from the Duong village, she got her diploma in Poland. And you too, you're going to have to travel all that way to the university. I'll buy you a French Peugeot bicycle. If you succeed in going abroad to study, I'll buy you a house in Hanoi. Do you hear me?"

"Yes, my aunt."

Crouching down, she pulled a small package from her pocket and said, "Wait, look at this." She unfurled the packet and, from within it, took a triangle of black silk that looked as if it had been salvaged from an old pair of women's silk pajama pants. Inside, on a pillow of immaculate cotton, lay a pair of tiny, antique earrings set with two pendants of precious stones. At the time, I wore two tiny red plastic studs my mother had given me. Aunt Tam took them off and put the gold earrings in their place. She fished another parcel out of her shirt pocket: a pair of rings wrapped in a ball of wool.

"You can wear them."

"I don't want to wear them. I'd be afraid to."

"Of what? I'm giving them to you."

"But . . . back home, in Hanoi, kids who wear gold are attacked."

"Wear them until you get there. Your mother will put them away later. It's a trust I've been saving for you alone. I have many other things for you as well."

She stepped back to inspect me. The jewelry was unbefitting a nine-year-old girl, but Aunt Tam had the gaze of a painter before a portrait. These jewels had been locked in their hiding place since the day of their purchase. I should have been delighted; instead, I was paralyzed with fear. I touched my earlobe, tracing the sharp edges of the lozenge-shaped stone. I pulled my hand back and stuffed it in my pocket. I felt chilled, numb. I didn't know why, but there was something sinister about all this finery, like throwing flower petals on an abandoned grave.

We took our seats on the barge. Aunt Tam stood on the riverbank for a long time, following us with her eyes. She didn't leave until the barge reached the middle of the river. In the dawn light, her shadow stood out, a stroke of ink on an old landscape painting.

To the east, the clouds glowed like the color of plum blossoms before fusing into a radiant yellow. A swarm of flies

[handwritten margin note: Wealth to be returned and poured down upon in peasantry society]

88

and bees swirled in the air over the corpse of a drowned cat. A fetid odor hung in the air.

As we pulled ashore, the sun rose. The boatman set up the wooden gangplank and shouted, "Steady, steady. There's no need to push and shove. What are you all running for?"

A group of passengers were trampling each other in their impatience to get off the barge. We were lucky; as soon as we stepped ashore, we found two cyclo drivers lazing about on the shore. They must have been about forty years old, since they still wore the old brown uniforms and chatted to each other as they smoked their cigarettes. They agreed to take us to the bus station for a small sum, and we arrived just in time for the second departure. We were only three hours from Hanoi. By early afternoon, we would be home.

Chapter SIX

H EY, SOMEONE CAME LOOKING FOR YOU ALMOST EV-
ery day," called the bean-soup vendor, her old
voice carrying through the rush curtain of her shop. My
mother shouted thanks, unlocked the door, and immediately
began to tidy the house. I went off to see my friends: Khang,
with the harelip, little Kim, Quyen . . . and Madame Mieu's
dog. He was sleeping, curled across the legs of the cripple. As
always, the cripple was seated in his cloth chair. From time
to time, he tossed aside the book he was reading, rolled his
eyes skyward, and belted out his song:

"*Hail autumn and its procession of dead leaves . . .*"

I scampered off, running until I was dizzy and out of

breath. My mother had finished tidying the house and preparing our meal. "Wash up and we'll eat. Tonight, we're going to have a visitor."

I was puzzled. "How do you know?"

"Uncle Chinh came by to see us last week, when I wasn't in. A neighbor just told me. He must have some problem."

I couldn't stop myself. "He's coming for the money. That's all."

"Who said that?"

"Aunt Tam."

She said nothing, tossed the grocery basket in a corner and started to serve the steamed rice. She had also made my favorite dish, a pork-filet soup with lily buds. I polished off three bowls of rice and another bowl of the crispy rice crust from the bottom of the pot. Full, I drifted off to sleep. I slept for a long time, and I awoke to the clock striking three o'clock. Each chime echoed inside me, and I closed my eyes, lulled by this familiar music. From the street, the cripple's chant rose again:

> "Already the fog covers the house on the hill
> The one I am waiting for has yet to come. . . ."

I tried to remember a man I never knew: Father. To me, my childhood seemed like a ball kicked across the road, aimless, without any purpose. Streets, streets, nothing but dirty, sooty streets. The wind howled down from the north, and dark clouds clotted the sky, blocking the horizon. The air here was oppressive, clogged with factory fumes and the dust of unending convoys. Fuzzy White barked at the moon, and I finally shooed him away.

(I saw Fuzzy White years later, when he was very old with just a few hairs clinging to his ragged tail. He wandered, half-blind, didn't even recognize me anymore. Each time I called to him, he raised his clammy nose in the air, sniffing, his bald head cocked to one side. Perhaps he whiffed something of the aroma of our shared past. But it had been too long. He didn't have the courage to love anymore, this childhood friend.)

He continued barking. I could almost feel him nudge his nose, smooth and wet, against my skin.

"Father." A cry lingering in the air, floating through the three rooms of this house like an invisible dust. I swallowed my tears and went out without bothering to lock the door. Anyway, my mother wasn't far off. I wandered through the streets, my checkered scarf wound around my neck. All the doors were locked. I walked toward the old blind soothsayer's hut. His courtyard was deserted, strewn with flowers from his peach and plum trees. The dead leaves swirled and rustled from one corner of the courtyard to the other. The old man was crouched on his bed, his arms grasping his knees. "Who's there?"

"It's me, old man."

"Ah, it's little Hang from Mother Que's. Come chat with me."

I was drained and didn't feel like chatting with anyone. "I can't. I've got to go to the market."

As I ran off, I kicked up a swirl of dead leaves. I ran for a long time, in no particular direction. I ended up at the mouth of a sewer. The water sloshed toward the gutter through an old grate that was clogged with trash: a toothbrush, the remains of a comb, a duck egg, a tomato skin, a custard-apple pit, a sugarcane husk, chicken innards, the label off a wine bottle, a torn bank note. I took a long bamboo pole and forced myself to free each object, trying to guess its origin: there were pumpkin and watermelon seeds, the sucked-out remains of a wedding banque; a swatch of fabric embroidered with sequins, the shreds of an artist's smock; children's excrement floating next to burned-out light bulbs. A hand seized my shoulder roughly. "Hang!"

I looked up into Uncle Chinh's face.

"How dare you play in this filth?" he snapped at me.

Still straddling his bicycle, he grabbed my hand and pulled me up toward him. As I looked up at him, I realized just how much he resembled my mother. He sat me on the back of his bicycle, perched on the iron clip used to transport groceries, and brought me back to the house. My mother was busy roasting tea. She had probably come home immediately after my departure. Next to the fire, steam rose from a wicker hamper filled with pounds of tea. Seeing Uncle Chinh, she put down her chopsticks and dumped the tea leaves into the sorting basket. "Come in, Brother."

My uncle propped his bicycle near the door and locked it carefully before entering the house. Even before taking a seat, he said, "I came by many times, these last few days."

"The neighbors told me. Hang, pass me the package of lotus tea, there, on the shelf."

"Never mind. I drink enough tea at the office. Do you have the money?"

"Relax. Have a sip of tea. Warm up a bit. I've already collected the money and signed the act of sale." My mother served the tea and then disappeared into her room. She returned with a wad of bank notes. "Here's your share."

Uncle Chinh fiddled with the packet, turning it over and over in his hands.

My mother understood. "There's no need to count it. I received it yesterday, and I've already counted it. The people are relatives. They wouldn't dare try anything dishonest."

My uncle sipped his tea in silence for a moment, then said, "I've found you a job, a post as an apprentice clerk in the offices of the Red River Food Factory. Go over there early tomorrow, and you can start."

My mother stared at him, incredulous. When she digested his words, she was indignant. "My God, how could you be so inconsiderate? I need time to think."

My uncle was annoyed. "What more is there to explain? I've already told you everything. Why do you keep going down blind alleys when so many other roads are open to you?"

My mother pleaded. "At my age, hanging about in an office! When could I ever hope to have a real profession? And with a miserable salary like that, how could I provide for Hang?"

"Working as a street vendor is hopeless. Listen to me. It only permits you to make ends met. You must think about rejoining the ranks of the proletariat. It's a guaranteed future, even as an apprentice. That's clear. Now, what do you choose?"

My mother lowered her head, but a second later, she was shaking it, her voice imploring. "I can't. Let me think about it. I can't make a decision like this just like that."

Exasperated, my uncle let out a deep sigh. "Do as you like. If you're miserable later, it won't be my fault. I've done my duty by you."

My mother was shaking. "Thank you, Brother. Don't be angry. The fact is that . . ."

"The fact is that you can't see further than the tip of your nose. You don't have the courage to face the future. If Hang finds herself an outcast, on the fringe of society, you'll have only yourself to blame."

My mother just stood there. She looked so unhappy that I ran to her side:

"Stop torturing my mother."

My uncle rolled his eyes at me. "My concern, all these worries I have, are for you, for your future, for your life, understand?"

He wrapped the money in a leather cloth and hung it from the handlebars of the bicycle. Then he clicked open the lock and pedaled off. My mother shuffled after him, not daring to speak, even to say good-bye. He finally turned the corner of our street and pedaled out of sight. She came back into the house and slumped into a chair, her head bowed. Her eyes were brimming with tears.

"What's the matter?" I asked her.

"He's all I have left of our family. It's finished."

"It's not your fault."

She lifted her head. "After our parents died, I should have raised him, paid for his studies. I wasn't up to the task. I neglected my duties as the eldest."

The atmosphere in the house that evening was funereal. My mother collapsed on her bed, her back turned to the wall in silence. How could someone lie motionless for so long? I arranged my school notebooks and left to go play ticktacktoe with my friend Khang. A few weeks later, I overheard my mother talking to her only real friend, a matronly neighbor we called Neighbor Vi. "He wants to disown me. I'm neither a member of the proletariat nor a real laboring peasant. It reflects badly on him."

"In what way?"

"For his career. He says that if I had been a party member with ten years of seniority, he could have gotten his promotion last year. One of his colleagues is less competent than he is, but the sister has been a militant since 1945 and works at the Central Commission for the Women's Union. So the man was named deputy last year." My mother let out a deep sigh.

Vi just stood there, mute, for a long time. Then she burst out, "Why mourn? Who chooses his birth? If we could choose the world we were born into, would we be stupid enough, you and I, to pass up the lot of the winners, the powerful ones? Who would choose the life we lead, peddling at the markets, dragging hampers around from dawn to dusk?"

My mother spoke softly. "Without Hang, I could risk taking a lousy job like that. It wouldn't be a real profession, but at least I would be a worker. If I were alone, you could throw me in a swamp, and I'd survive. Unfortunately, there's Hang to think of."

"My brother is a worker at the Yen Phu Factory, and my sister works at the Minh Khai Textile Factory. They haven't disowned me," said Neighbor Vi. "I live an honest life. I don't steal, don't cheat, and I don't hurt my neighbors."

"Of course. It's true. But each family has its own way. Chinh has always been difficult, but then he is the only male heir. We've always bent to his will," my mother explained.

"God, he's a real little tyrant, that brother of yours! And they call that revolutionary? My family is poor. Five brothers and sisters. But no one tries to boss anyone around. Whenever one of us has troubles, the others are close by. Everyone pitches in. When one of the children gets married, the whole family saves up. One of us buys the clothes, somebody else gets the firecrackers, another the betel nuts. Everyone takes turns, even for the Grave-Sweeping Festival. In my house, family duties are light. Your story makes me shiver. Of course, when blood runs thick, the heart seizes up. And there should be solidarity between brothers and sisters. But within reason, within the limits of human feeling!"

"But I've never had an education. He's a state functionary. He understands more than I do," said my mother.

"Well, I'm ignorant too," Neighbor Vi huffed. "I live as my parents lived, my feet on the ground. Higher virtues? Let's think about those when your belly's full. Nobody can fast the whole Year of the Pig in hopes of some sumptuous feast in the Year of the Dog. . . ." At this point in her speech, she paused. "Damn! My bean pudding's burning. You can smell it from here."

She scurried over to the courtyard. Even I could smell the scent of the burning beans. Ten minutes later, she was back, a plate of cakes in her hand: "Taste some of my *che*. It's a real devil to prepare. It tastes just as it should—like a coconut cake grilled over a fire."

It was chilly out. The *che* steamed as it thickened, taking on the consistency of a cake. Sesame seeds glinted on the crust. My mother stared at it admiringly and said, "This is a real treat. Could you save us a portion of the *che* you make for Tet?"

"Sure, it'll be my gift. Ten plates. You'll be able to feast on it for three days, even with all your guests."

When Neighbor Vi left, my mother seemed preoccupied.

From then on, until Tet, Uncle Chinh didn't come by the house anymore. On the twenty-eighth day of the last month before New Year's, Neighbor Vi closed up her shop and spent the whole night washing the rice and beans, cutting the pork and the banana leaves for the New Year's cakes. At dawn, she put a huge, simmering pot of *che* on the fire and dished out ten plates of it for us.

"Just get the plates back to me when you can. I'm not even going to face washing dishes during the three festival days."

She had rosy cheeks, and despite all her wrinkles she looked radiant. We carried the plates back to the house. Just as we arrived, we glimpsed a woman near the altar, her back turned to the door. A thin, flat back under an *ao dai* the color of freshly tilled earth.

My mother called out, "Aunt Tam . . . Did you just get here?"

Aunt Tam reached out and took the platters of *che* from my mother's hands. "Where were you two? Out getting groceries?"

"It's a gift. From our neighbor. I'm too lazy to make this," said my mother.

Seeing me laden with gifts, Aunt Tam shook her head. "What's all this? Are you begging now? It's Tet. Why didn't you prepare these yourselves and stay at home, in peace?"

Irritated, she held me by the arm and began straightening my hair, sniffing it suspiciously. Fortunately, my mother had washed it with a fragrant herbal rinse for me just that morning. Aunt Tam commented approvingly.

"The teeth and the hair are a person's dignity. We

should wash the hair regularly with concoctions made of fragrant herbs, so it will stay smooth and supple."

It was impossible to tell whether she was lecturing me or my mother. She opened the two grocery hampers that she had set down by one of the legs of the table. They were brimming with provisions, huge quantities of everything. There were pounds and pounds of pâtés, made of cinnamon and pork tendon. They must have been cooked just the previous evening, since green traces of banana-leaf wrappers still stuck to their rinds. There was Thanh's green tea, Bac's special five-spice mixture, Thai Binh's spicy cakes—all top-quality brands—jasmine tea, aglaiata flower tea, candied lotus seeds, butter cookies, croquettes, hemp cakes and cakes stained pink with rose-apple juice and smoked over a rice-husk fire. An athlete would have had trouble lifting those hampers.

My mother was stunned and embarrassed. "I can't accept all this. I've got enough to celebrate Tet already. This is too much. How could we eat it all?"

Aunt Tam replied coldly, "I'm not giving this food to you. This is my offering to my brother's memory. It's all for Hang. She can offer the food to her teachers, her friends, *anyone* she likes."

It was my turn to be petrified now. I didn't know what to say. This gift was a catastrophe for me. Aunt Tam lifted me into her arms.

"I started the preparations two weeks ago. I hear you received honors at school for your grades this semester. Is it true?"

"Yes, my aunt."

"Why didn't you tell me?"

"I was too busy. Last month, the school launched a big campaign to clean up trash."

"What nonsense! Can't they stop torturing our children? In the village, the Bung family's girl had to go gather bits of barbed wire to make some money. She ripped open her foot and got tetanus. Killed her. From now on, you must not pick up any glass or paper. It's very dangerous. The Tran family depends on you, and you alone."

She opened a pin she used to fasten her blouse pocket. Under her earth-brown wool *ao dai*, she wore a white, embroidered blouse.

"Take this money. Give them whatever they need, but don't pick up any more trash."

It was a thick wad of bills the likes of which no one would ever give to a child. I was shaking now. How could I take the money of a woman who had never known motherhood, or a man's love, who had camped out on tree roots for a whole winter, slept with a knife under her neck? She had saved this money, note by note. This was her revenge, her only answer to existence.

She curled the fingers of my hands around the bills. "Take it."

I tried to refuse, circling my arms around her neck. "I really can't. Dearest Aunt, I'm too young to spend this money. Keep it, please."

She scolded me. "No. I told you to take it. You must obey. Don't fuss with me. What is this money compared to your life? As long as I'm alive, as long as these hands are capable of working . . ."

I looked at her gnarled, sinewy hands, listened to the rasp in her voice.

"As long as these hands can work, there will always be money. Don't worry. I know how to get by. I can earn three times the value of rice harvest with one of my tomato crops. With one of my mandarin-orange harvests, I made enough to buy you a gold necklace. I've already ordered it. The pendant is heart-shaped and it weighs a gram and a half, and the chain the same. When you turn sixteen, you'll wear it."

Her eyes flashed at me, as if the vision of my future liberated her from her suffering and humiliation. I couldn't find words to speak to her anymore, so I turned away.

Her voice cracked with emotion as she spoke, as she

stacked the bills in a drawer and instructed my mother to clean the altar. She shook off the dust with a red cloth we used to cover the portraits of my maternal grandparents and placed another portrait, framed in glass, by their side. It was a portrait of my father cut out of a family photo taken just before he left for school. He had the tender gaze of a very young man, with the same features as Aunt Tam, a bit blurry because the photo had been enlarged.

She ordered me to bring a fresh bowl of rice to hold the incense sticks; then she spread the offerings on the altar and sent my mother off to the market.

"Bring back a big bunch of those white peonies and the violets. Those were his favorite flowers."

Satisfied with her work, she stepped back to admire the altar. I had never seen an altar as splendid as the one she created for my father that New Year. Candles blazed. Firecrackers snapped, echoing in the distance. People shuffled in and out of our gate bearing ridiculous New Year's offerings: a branch of flowering peach in one hand, a mandarin-orange flower in the other.

I went outside, propped myself against the door, and lit a sparkler. I watched it flicker in my hand. With the money Aunt Tam had given me, I could buy myself a whole paper house of firecrackers. But for me, there was no joy. Even the air here seemed to shiver with faded voices and unfulfilled promises.

I tossed the sparkler into the stream and headed for the street. I walked for a long time before stumbling on an abandoned shack. It belonged to a barber who had gone to celebrate Tet in his village. He didn't have a permit to live in our neighborhood, so he squatted in hiding in this shack. An ugly little footstool made of wood stood in the middle of the room, tufts of hair scattered around it. I slipped in through the door, left ajar, and sat down on the stool. I watched the people file past. The idea of going back to the house made me sad. I couldn't stand the sight of my aunt and my mother preparing me a sumptuous feast: the red and white candles, the sticks and crowns of incense, the flowers, the rich New Year's delicacies, the monotonous prayers. To me, it was all an extravagant, postponed form of regret, a yearning for their lost paradise.

Spring came and went. Summer passed. Uncle Chinh disappeared from our life, and somehow, in his absence, my mother stopped feeling like an outcast. I studied hard and wrote Aunt Tam a progress report every month. I was a different person now. I submitted to a different world, a new authority: the glory of the Tran family, my father and grandfather.

Aunt Tam personified this fate. My letters were just a few lines; hers were always four pages of tightly scrawled hand. And it was through these letters to me, in which she recounted the vicissitudes of her existence, that she mended the broken narrative of her life. I would hear all the stories. There was the night of the full moon she had just spent in the Pheo pagoda, listening to the old Buddhist nun praying. She described the feeling of lightness that had washed over her on the way back. There was the old guava plant in the orangerie, next to the flower hedge. One day, termites had puffed up the earth around the tree, setting off a flurry of rumors in the village. So she had summoned the old blind soothsayer, and he predicted fame and fortune for the Tran family. Because the lucky star fell in the female yin cycle, the soothsayer had predicted that success would come from a woman. They had had a superb mandarin-orange harvest, and she had hidden a bunch of them, under sand, to preserve and send to me, orange by orange. She lavished advice and encouragement on me, letter after letter.

That same autumn, my mother repaired the wall in the kitchen. I suggested we sell the earrings Aunt Tam had given me so we could replace the sheet-metal-and-tar roof, but she refused.

"We can't cut into the capital that Aunt Tam gave you."

"But that's what I want."

"You can't dispose of them like that."

"She gave them to me."

"That's not the problem. She gave them to you to wear, not to sell."

"But I'm too young to wear jewelry, and we're going to rot under this roof."

My mother sighed. After a long pause, she said, "Your father is dead. You don't know what it's like for me, that I can't even provide a decent roof for us. I can't face them anymore—your aunt Tam, our family, the neighbors. Please. Give me time."

Since Aunt Tam had come into our life, Mother had stopped doting on me and calling me her "dear child." She had become distant and reserved. Still, we led the same life under the same roof, this island where my parents had loved each other. I was born of a love neither legitimate nor illegitimate. I had grown up without a name, as an anonymous weed grows between the cracks of a wall.

In the summer, the tar-covered roof gave off an acrid, poisonous smell in the heat. In autumn, the drumming of the rain was like the monotony of sadness itself. I can still see this roof, with its welter of gray and black spots, like strips of rags used to patch up an old shirt.

Toward the end of winter, a tavern opened up on the main road. The young toughs adopted it as their hangout, spent their time shuttling between this beer hall and the state brewery. Food vendors flocked to the street to hawk their snacks, their grilled or boiled peanuts, green papaya salads, and calves' feet. And little by little, the shop filled up with a new breed of wealthier clients, the cyclo drivers from the provinces, the used-motorcycle-and-bicycle salesmen. Food stalls sprung up selling dog-meat dishes, grilled sausage, dried squid and fish, beef marinated in vinegar and red-hot chilies. The street reeled with these tantalizing aromas. Drunks lurched and staggered, relieving themselves against the walls. The buildings were streaked with streams of rancid urine. On hot days, the stench was overpowering.

Day by day, the street became more and more bustling, breathing life into the nearby market, where food vendors could now reap huge profits. My mother and her friends had visions of getting rich overnight. My mother started to rake in the money. She had already used all the profits to buy metal rods and several thousand bricks. After Tet, she planned to raise the house on stone slabs and build a roof over the terrace. All she had to do was buy the cement and hire the workers.

"Give me until Tet," she promised, beaming at me. She had her confidence back now and no longer felt inferior to her sister-in-law. Still, I couldn't understand her stubbornness, and I used to plead with her not to worry so much.

"After Tet, we'll have a new roof. No more leaks, no more heat. And all without Aunt Tam's earrings," she said.

She grinned just thinking about it. But she never did have much luck. One evening, when I came home from high school, I found her packing up her wares.

"Why are you home so early?"

"Wash your face and get changed. Uncle Chinh is very sick. We don't know whether he'll live through it. Hurry now."

She rushed into her bedroom to change. I'd never seen her so frantic. I got ready in a flash. At the end of the street, we hailed a cyclo. It was rush hour, and the streets were teeming with them.

It took us half an hour to get to the hospital. The gate swarmed with people arriving, departing, bringing provisions, taking away dirty laundry. A man of about fifty with a belly and an absent look guarded the entry. Cautious, as always, my mother didn't have the nerve to ignore him, so she presented herself to the guard post, showed her identity card, and asked for permission to visit her brother. The guard squinted at us out of the corner of one eye, peering at heaven or hell out of the other. He asked us a series of odd questions in a suspicious voice and then, finally, he decreed sternly, "Wait here, your case will be examined at a later date."

It was always the same, this decree, this reply that punctuated our daily rhythm. The next day, exasperated, I tugged at the hem of my mother's *ao dai*. The man was buried in his newspaper.

"This time let's go in without asking, Mother," I whispered.

My mother was jittery. "But what if they catch us?"

I was just irritated. "What are you scared of? We aren't thieves."

I took her hand and pulled her along with me. After we reached an inner courtyard, we had to wander and search, one by one, through four buildings before we found Uncle Chinh's room. His roommate, an old man, told us, "You've come too late. He was discharged yesterday evening."

After a moment of confusion, my mother succeeded in articulating something. "You mean Do Quoc Chinh?"

"Yes. That was his name. The nurse called him by name every day when it was time for the shots."

"But they told me he was seriously ill, that his chances were very slim," my mother insisted.

The old man smiled. "It must have been the fainting. They imagined he was on the verge of death. But in fact, it's nothing. Just a bit of hypertension. It's very common with party cadres: poor nutrition, hunger, lack of protein. All you need is a quart of blood from this place. Perks you right up."

My mother gaped at him, bewildered. He shook his head. "Why would I lie to you? Go on now. You'll find him at home."

"Thank you, sir."

We walked out right under the nose of the old guard.

He dropped his newspaper for a minute, staring at us through bleary eyes. We pushed and elbowed our way through a crowd of street vendors who were pressed up against the exit to the hospital. My mother fumbled in her pocket and pulled out an old, crumpled calendar. She pored over it, trying to decipher Uncle Chinh's address: "Cyclo!"

A brawny young man with a crew cut pedaled toward us. "Where are you going?"

"To Communal Residence K."

"Two bills. That okay?"

"Okay."

"Well, there's a lady who knows her mind. Jump in."

The driver pedaled like a maniac. Fortunately, the streets were empty. Through the trees, I could see the green mirror of Tuyen Quang Lake. A beefy woman in a yellow dress passed us, cackling away, as another middle-aged woman, straddled on the back of a Honda, tried to race past her. Amused, the driver hooted at them.

We arrived at the guard post about an hour later. It was made of wood, much like the boxes built for traffic police in Hanoi. But instead of being painted white or green, it was a yellowish brown, like a roach's wing. It gave me a queasy feeling. Inside, a spidery-looking old man with a bald head coughed regularly as he watched people pass by. "Do Quoc Chinh. Yeah, he's here. Just saw him go by with his eldest son. Let's see your papers."

"I have my identity card."

He hesitated a moment, then gave us an officious wave of his hand: "Okay, okay. No need. Go ahead."

We walked down a long, paved alleyway about three yards wide, flanked on both sides by enormous wooden crates. They were all marked FRAGILE and stenciled here and there with the symbols for an umbrella, or a wineglass. They were container crates of pinewood, relics of the international aid sent during the time of the anti-American resistance. The ink on the crates had faded, and the wood was worm-eaten.

At the end of the street, we took the alley to the left. Rows of one-story houses lined the street like classes of schoolchildren preparing for a parade. They were exactly the same: the same model, the same roach-colored walls. There was something crude and frightening about it all. All the windows were brightly lit, and you could look right in and see people eating their dinner. My mother squinted, trying to make out the address again: "Number fifty-six, Alley G."

We followed the alleyways. Uncle Chinh's was the last, at the edge of the neighborhood, built up against the wall of a factory, probably a printing press. You could hear the machines clanging and screeching on the other side of the wall.

We caught them in the middle of a meal, seated around the dinner table. There were two boys and a woman with a coarse, pockmarked face. The oldest one must have been about seven years old and the youngest, three. They were as thin as reeds. Uncle Chinh looked shrunken; his yellowish cheekbones protruded, and his nose was as pointy and sharp as a sugarcane leaf. He was wearing an old, washed-out blue cotton Mao jacket over his pajamas.

"Brother Chinh!" My mother yelled from the sidewalk. They turned their heads in our direction, but they were blinded by the light and probably didn't see us.

"Brother Chinh," she shouted again, and without waiting any longer, she dragged me with her into the house. "They told me you were critically ill. We looked all over the hospital before I found out you had been discharged yesterday."

Uncle Chinh rose from the table and turned stiffly toward the woman with the pockmarked face.

"Thanh, this is my sister, Que."

Then he introduced her. "My wife. She's a cadre in the school for the Communist Youth League."

My aunt acknowledged my mother with a grunt. My mother hadn't even had time to greet her when the woman rapped one of the boys on the head with her chopstick.

"Eat. I forbid you to speak at meals."

I looked over at my mother. Somehow, she looked ashamed. Her body seemed to have shrunk, her shoulders retracting under the stern, interrogating gaze of her sister-in-law. My aunt was probably used to bullying her students at the Communist Youth League School. My mother never felt comfortable calling her Thanh, so we always referred to her as "Aunt Chinh." Her icy gaze took in my mother's velour scarf, her beige wool jacket with its shiny gold buttons, the plastic food hamper, her neatly hemmed Western pants. You could read the reproach in my aunt's eyes: My mother's clothes betrayed her as leading the life of a small businesswoman. In an instant, she was weighed on the scale of social values.

My uncle poured boiling water into the teapot. But the tea was pale and weak. They must have used leaves from the day before.

"Please, drink some."

My mother demurred. "Please, don't let us disturb you. Finish eating." She eyed the two boys tenderly. "Are these my nephews?"

"Yes. Go on now, Tuan, Tu, greet your aunt."

"Hello, Aunt," they chimed in one voice.

"My goodness, they're so well behaved. What grade are you in now, Tuan?" My mother fawned over the two boys.

The little one stared at her wide-eyed.

"Answer your aunt," Uncle Chinh snapped.

"I'm in third grade."

Tuan ducked his head and lunged with his chopsticks toward a platter of onions and roast silkworms. The younger boy started to bawl. Like lightning, the mother hit the eldest over the head with one of her chopsticks. "Watch it, Tuan."

In fact, whether it was conscious or not, the elder boy had been nibbling at the little one's portion. Tuan rubbed his head in silence. I examined the platter: There were three portions, each with fifteen silkworms. Next to them, there was a platter of river spinach and a tiny bowl filled with a bit of minced meat. No doubt this was the "special nutritional supplement" reserved for my sick uncle. Uncle Chinh gulped down the last of his bowl of rice and started to sip the tea. Aunt Chinh rose from the table and took her cup over to the desk. She emptied it in one gulp, seated herself, and began to write.

"My wife has to prepare lectures for tomorrow. She's one of the most respected cadres at the school. Her family is one hundred percent working class and she's already accumulated eleven years seniority in the party," said my uncle, pride showing in his voice.

"Oh really," murmured my mother, lowering her head. Uncle Chinh started to clean his teeth.

"I'm still on leave. But it's not serious. You mustn't go to any trouble. It's not easy to get into this residence. We're all families of cadres here."

I heard my mother swallow. After a moment's pause, she raised her head. "But . . . they told me you were weak from lack of protein."

"Nonsense. I was just overworked. Too much to do."

He spoke in a haughty tone. My mother couldn't seem to find anything more to say, so she picked up her straw hat and her hamper and got up to leave. "Well, I guess I'll be going then."

"Yes, take Hang on back," he said, nodding his head in agreement. Then, turning toward his wife: "Thanh, Sister Que is going."

The woman glanced up. "Good-bye, Sister."

These were the only words she exchanged with us. Then she buried herself in a thick, glossy white book. I could just make out, at the top of the page, *I.V. Lenin. Volume 13*.

"Say good-bye to your aunt, children."

"Good-bye, Aunt," echoed the two boys, bobbing their necks, swanlike, in our direction.

Uncle Chinh saw us off to the end of Alley G. We left

the residence by following the path bordered with container crates. My mother walked with her head down and her back hunched over. She was crying. She had the look of someone condemned for something.

"Let's never come back here, Mother."

"He's my brother. You can't deny blood ties." She wiped her nose and eyes.

"You'll come without me, then. I'm never setting foot here again."

She said nothing, her shoulders heaving slightly, and remained silent until we reached the road. I took my hat and hailed a cyclo to take us back to our dusty suburb. From each house along the way, sad, monotonous songs from the popular theater spilled onto the streets. Voices layered over each other. A *pho* soup vendor clicked sticks of bamboo together to attract his customers. The air was fragrant with the aroma of the anise- and ginger-flavored beef soup. I grabbed my mother's shirt. "I'm hungry, Mother."

She was flustered. "Oh, how could I forget? We haven't eaten anything since noon."

We ate squatting down on the edge of the sidewalk, at the corner of our street. As we finished the meal, my mother felt ill. "Quick, come quickly!" she said, dashing toward the house. As I ran after her, she suddenly bent over the mouth of the sewer and vomited. "Hang, go get Neighbor Vi."

I ran to her house and banged on her door. "Neighbor Vi, Neighbor Vi, my mother's sick." She was busy eating watermelon seeds, cracking them with her teeth, but when she heard me, she dumped them on the bed and rushed over to our house, her four children in tow.

Neighbor Vi lifted my mother in her arms and carried her into the house. Then she began to massage her. She burned the ends of absinthe twigs, pricking the sensitive points in my mother's body with their cauterized tips. She massaged my mother's head with a balm, yanking at tufts of her hair in tiny, well-placed jerks. My mother regained consciousness and looked up at her. "Did I catch a chill?"

"It's the cold. The hunger, all the worries. It's serious. You have to take care of yourself."

My mother squeezed the neighbor's hand, trying to speak between sobs. "My poor Hang."

She couldn't see me. I had hidden in the shadow behind Neighbor Vi, in the middle of the four kids. I could just see her face, her bleary eyes. I couldn't stand the pity of others. I went out and squatted down in the shadow of a creeper vine that had climbed over the wall of Neighbor Vi's house. For several years now, everyone in the neighborhood had grown this plant. It was a beautiful wild creeper with an intense, lush green foliage. Sometimes it was covered with dazzling saffron-colored blooms, their color a mixture of blood, fire, and sunset.

I stayed there, crouched down, listening to the hum of their conversation. The pungent, stinging smell of the balm and the burned absinthe hung in the air. Suddenly, I spotted an animal slinking toward me. Probably some stray dog, or Neighbor Tin's cat come back to end his vagabond existence. It came closer. When it reached the lamp, I recognized Fuzzy White.

I murmured his name, my voice strange and floating, like someone else's. "Fuzzy White. Come on. Come here." The dog shook a flea-bitten ear. He probably hadn't recognized my voice. He lumbered toward me on shaky paws, and then retraced his steps. In the lamplight, his silhouette looked like a crumpled rag abandoned on the cobblestones.

And then the cripple began to bellow. He lived, year in and year out, stretched out on that bed of coarse linen. Some days, he wanted to get married, to learn a profession. Some days, he wanted to drown himself in a well. In the end, he ticked out his life reading and rereading the same spy novels, teasing children, being taunted by the young toughs, listening to absurd stories, dreaming of paradise, and, from time to time, just screaming:

"*Hail autumn and its procession of dead leaves,
The rows of barren poplars stand silent on the
hillside.*"

Neighbor Vi finally took her kids home, and as she
walked by, she mussed my hair. "Your mother's better. Go
back and get some sleep."

I pulled the latch to our door and let myself in. I
stretched out on the bed. Mother was asleep. I could still see
her bleary eyes, and in her sadness it seemed to me I glimpsed
a vision of my own future. Like the last, sharp rays of sunlight, there is something prescient about the final thoughts of
a human being drifting off to sleep.

The next morning, my mother was still feverish. When
I brought her a bowl of rice, she gave my hand a squeeze.
"I'll eat, but you must promise me something."

"Eat. Quickly. You need your strength. I'll promise you
anything you want."

Her jet-black eyes sparkled for an instant.

"You love me?"

"What a question. Eat. Before it gets cold. Neighbor Vi
used more than a half-bowl of cactus and scallions to
make it."

She looked me in the eye, staring at me, dead level. "I'll
eat. I'll get better. But you must go see your uncle Chinh."
I didn't answer, but I must have raised an eyebrow or cringed.

"He's all the family I have left. He's so unhappy. Needs
so much." She went on, indignant. "And your poor cousins
. . . they looked so straggly, like potato vines."

I thought to myself, Mother, why don't you just say
what you mean: "My two nephews, my two little drops of
Do blood." At bottom, she was just like Aunt Tam. These
were the only two loving women I had in my life. I said nothing. My solitude had taught me the value of silence. Besides,
I had long since lost my childhood innocence. So I answered
her calmly, "Okay, but eat something first."

I lifted a bowl of rice gruel to her lips. She held my hand back, looking at me imploringly, like someone asking for a last request, a final prayer before throwing herself into a fire. "Don't ever stop loving me, promise?"

I nodded, and her face lit up. When she had finished the gruel and swallowed the medicine, she asked me to bring her the hamper. She took it from me and pulled out a tiny drawstring satchel made of black silk, and from that, a wad of bank notes. As she counted them out, she instructed me, "Buy two pounds of pork and cinnamon pâté and two pounds of pork filet. Bring these to your uncle. Your aunt can make some dried meat with the filet, and the little ones can eat the pâtés. Tell them it's my gift to Tuan and Tu."

I took the money. She continued to rattle off instructions to me: "Buy the pâtés on Cotton Tree Street and the filet from old lady Heo. Tell her to give us the best piece.

"That's all. Get changed quickly and go. . . . And you mustn't tell them that I'm sick." Her instructions complete, she relaxed, slumped back on the bed, and pulled the covers over herself.

I left on my bicycle, pedaling furiously all the way to Cotton Tree Street. By the time I had found everything my mother had ordered, it was still only ten o'clock, so I went off to play at a friend's house. At eleven-thirty, I got back on my bicycle and pedaled to the Commune K Residence, clutching my student identity card tightly inside my pocket. Fortunately, the entry was guarded by a plump, easygoing woman. She was busy slicing cabbage into fine strips for pickling, so she waved me by without even checking my papers. I cycled directly to Uncle Chinh's place. His two boys were busy playing in front of the doorway, stirring up the dirt between two broken tiles with a spoon-sized plastic shovel and plastic teacup for a bucket. When they saw me, they yelled, "Ma, we've got a visitor."

Aunt Chinh was busy tidying up, and she snapped at them, "What visitor?" My mother's imploring eyes flashed before me. I bowed slightly to my aunt. Her eyes swept over me and then looked away. "Your uncle isn't here."

"My mother asked me to bring this to Tuan and . . ."

She glanced around furtively and spoke to me in a low voice. "Come in, come in quickly."

I pulled the heavy hamper off the handlebars of my bicycle and lugged it into the house. She closed the door with a slam and said, "Sit down, my niece." But I stood near the door.

"My mother asked me to bring this food to Tuan and Tu. Here . . ."

I pulled off the layer of newspaper my mother had used to cover the basket and set the groceries on the table: two huge rolls of roast pork and cinnamon pâté rolled in banana leaves, and two pounds of pork filet. She looked troubled and stammered, "This is incredible. . . ." Her eyes darted warily from the window, to the door, out the window again, as if someone were watching her. I took the empty hamper back from her and said good-bye.

She clasped my hands, speaking to me in a worried voice. "I don't understand. Wait, just a moment. Your uncle won't be long." When I looked at her pockmarked face, I felt an immense fatigue. I didn't have the energy to get back on the bicycle, so I sat down. The two boys peeked through the door. "Out! Go play outside!" she snapped at them.

The violence in her voice made me jump. I could read the fear in her eyes. I felt trapped. I gripped the arms of the sofa as I watched the kids dart about in the street like rats. She slammed the door and began to stock the food away in a cupboard near the bedroom. She looked frantic, like someone who steals compulsively. From outside, a booming voice: "Why is the door locked?"

It was Uncle Chinh. He pushed his way through the door, but when he saw me, the expression on his face fell. "I told you, I've recovered. Why did she send you here again?"

"To see how we were," said Aunt Chinh.

"My mother thought my cousins looked thin, so she asked me to bring them some food," I added.

He winced, his forehead flushing in anger. "Yes, they are naturally thin. Not all skinny people are starving." After a silence, he went on, "Even if we don't always eat our fill, this is the common lot. This is still a poor country."

"I don't know. . . . I just did what my mother told me to do," I stammered. Without waiting for a reply, I got up and picked up the hamper. Aunt Chinh stepped between me and her husband, her voice soft, accommodating.

"He's speaking generally, of course. In any case, it was very kind of your mother . . ."

I didn't answer. I just left. When I arrived home, my mother called out to me from her room. "Is that you, Hang?" She looked me over impatiently.

"Well, it's done. I brought them everything."

Her eyes twinkled. She barraged me with questions.

"So he's back at work?"

"How are Tuan and Tu?"

"Did they remember you?"

"Were they happy to see you?"

Suddenly, my mother clucked her tongue in irritation. "How forgetful of me. I wanted you to buy some of those sticky-rice cakes for the little ones. They're delicious with the cinnamon-pork pâté. With their lousy salaries, your cousins must not get that kind of thing very often."

I said nothing, paralyzed by my own anger. I wasn't envious of these cousins, but I couldn't bring myself to like them, let alone their parents. I turned to the wall, swearing to myself. "And after all that, she wanted to hide her own sickness, a lot they cared."

Fortunately, my mother hadn't heard me, and she asked me, "What's the matter, Hang?"

"Nothing, Mother. I was cursing the damn ants. They're swarming around the sugar canister."

Two days later, over Neighbor Vi's protests, my mother

went back to the market, hunched under the weight of her bamboo shoulder pole and her hampers.

"Don't worry. I've got my strength back. These hampers are as light as goose feathers to me," she said.

I realized she had a mission now, a new source of happiness: to serve the needs of my little cousins. How intoxicating it can be, self-sacrifice. Every night, I watched her count out her money, breathing noisily, whispering sums between her teeth. Soon, she added tomatoes and bamboo shoots to her business. Neighbor Vi noticed too. "Your mother is too greedy. The body's resistance has limits. If she keeps running around like this, one of these days she's going to crack. An elephant wouldn't be able to bear this pressure, let alone a human being."

It was vacation time, and I had gone for a walk near the riverbank with some of my high school friends. These walks always filled us with wonder. I brought matches for a bonfire, and as we watched the flames licking at the dead branches, we talked dreamily of fleeing to a desert island, of a life in the wild. The wind howled, and the aroma of roasting corn, wild daisies, pumpkins, and herbs swirled in the air like perfume. Our "Chief," a deaf girl named Hanh, cast a tall, spindly silhouette as she led the three of us across the cornfield. Before leaving on a foray with the other girls, she ordered me to stand guard for her and gather some dried branches.

I shook my head. "No, I'm not staying by myself."

She screwed up her eyebrows at me. "Sissy. Don't you dare move from here." I had to obey her, but I watched the fire halfheartedly, gathering only a few branches. A half hour later, the other girls were back, their shirts bulging with ears of corn. Nothing will ever equal the taste of that roasted corn.

It was dark before we headed back. The street lamps had already been turned on. Voices echoed from my house. I couldn't make out the words, but I could see people shaking their heads. They were neighbors, friends of my mother's from the market. They drifted home one by one as I approached. My mother was seated alone now, on the edge of her bed. She muttered my name absently. I moved toward her.

"What's the matter, Mother? Are you sick?"

I reached out to stroke her forehead. It was icy. The veins at the sides of her temples were swollen, pulsing. She spoke in a thin, choked voice:

"I lost everything. In a second. For a bowl of soup. I've lost everything. All my savings for the last two weeks."

I stared at her in disbelief. "What? What do you mean? I thought the other women always brought you something to eat at the stall?"

Ordinarily, the spice vendors at the market set up their hampers side by side in long aisle. At mealtimes, people brought them rice, a bowl of chicken, duck or snail soup. How could they have pickpocketed her wallet? This was even stranger because women from the same aisle usually protected each other. Avoiding my gaze, she murmured, "I'd gone to get a bowl of red bean soup."

So that was it. To save a few coins, she had left her stall to buy a bowl of red bean soup she could sweeten with her own cheap brown sugar. The robbers had taken advantage of her negligence and stripped her of everything she had. It was the height of Tet, the peak season for the market women; everyone was hustling to sell, to buy; no one had noticed. But then, no one would have been so careless.

My mother kept muttering to herself, "It's fate. What can I do?"

"Rest. I'll make you some soup."

"As you like. I'll eat whatever there is. This bitter taste in my mouth feels like lime."

I boiled up a rice soup for her with a bit of pork, seasoning it with onion and black pepper. I had only a small bowl myself and then went out to buy an ear of grilled corn down the street. The corn vendor, an old woman hunched over a charcoal fire, tended the coals patiently. Sparks flew up in a spray of fire. The older, dried-out kernels popped open, unfurling into enormous white blooms.

"Give me one of those nice yellow ones."

She looked up. "Are you Que's girl? My, you've grown. Such nice rosy cheeks. Look at those eyes, like black agate. They'll marry you off in no time."

It was then that I remembered. When I was little, my mother had also sold grilled corn under a street lamp like this. She too had counted out tiny, crumpled bills smudged with charcoal to raise me. The old woman rotated a long, slender ear of corn with nice, regular kernels. She basted it, turning it from side to side over the coals. "Here you go. It's the best one."

I paid her and bit into it, savoring the chewy flesh of the corn as it stuck to my gums. The smell of that roasted corn, the spray of sparks, all this kindled another memory in me, of another winter night. The street lamps floated, lost in fog as I drifted off into my thoughts.

Suddenly, a young man grabbed me by the waist. "Hey, honey," he laughed. "Oh, what cute lips. Smile, so I can look at you. . . . What are you, thirteen? They used to get married at that age. You know, like the song: 'At thirteen I was married, at eighteen I already had five kids under my arm.' Hey, there's nothing to blush about."

I struggled loose. He must have been about twenty, handsome, with a finely etched mustache. He stank of beer. He folded me in his arms, spinning me as if I were a wooden doll. He laughed again as he let me go. "Ah, a girl afraid of losing her virtue? Poor little pretty one."

I ran toward the house, still clutching my ear of hot corn. My mother had woken up. She was staring absently at a tiny calendar.

"Why aren't you asleep?"

She peered out at the sky. "Tomorrow is the eighth day

of Tet. Neighbor Vi already honored her household gods yesterday. I was so busy with my stall that I forgot. . . ."

She heaved another sigh. "It's fate."

I tried to console her. "What's happened has happened. Get some sleep." She folded up the calendar, mumbling to herself, "There's so much to do."

"We're alone. A few New Year's cakes will be fine. Don't exhaust yourself for so little."

She shook her head. "It's not that simple."

I could read her mind. She had other duties now, other responsibilities. Sacrifices, sweet sacrifices . . .

The next morning, I woke up late. It was chilly out. As I put on my clogs, I heard voices in the courtyard. I ran to the door to have a look and saw two brawny young men shouldering heavy iron bars. My mother had sold the bars cheap to Mr. Tao, who lived near the main road. He was getting ready to build a second story on his house and wanted to finish it all before the Tet celebrations were over. He smiled, visibly pleased with this windfall. He directed his sons with loud shouts, baring four gold-capped teeth. My mother slung her bamboo pole over her shoulder and prepared to leave for the market. She instructed me, "Tonight, make dinner a bit earlier. We've got things to do."

By four o'clock, I had finished everything. Marinated fish, pickled cabbage, a few slices of fresh bean curd. We had always lived simply.

My mother came back with two brimming hampers, her bamboo shoulder pole curved into an arch under their weight. When she had unwrapped all the merchandise, I realized she had bought everything needed for a magnificent Tet banquet: pork pâtés, meat, lard, sticky rice, dried green mung beans, peanuts, bamboo shoots, vermicelli, rice-flour pancake wrappers, pork rind. She was beaming.

"Let heaven be stingy with us. Let's kiss good-bye to a

year of bad luck. When our good fortune returns, I'll repair that damn roof once and for all."

It was only 5:27 when we finished dinner. "At this hour, Uncle Chinh must just be preparing dinner," my mother reflected. "We still have time."

I left to go see a friend who lived nearby. A half hour later, when I came home, my mother had tidied up, and a huge rush basket was waiting near the door. We hurried into a cyclo and set off toward Communal Residence K.

At Uncle Chinh's house, they were just sitting down to eat. Here, everyone ate later than the city's other inhabitants. Aunt Chinh was chopping a salted eggplant into thin strips, seasoning it with garlic and sugar. On the same dinner tray was a plate of sautéed cabbage and a few thin slices of fish marinating in a bowl of fish sauce. The two boys were hitting their chopsticks against the dinner tray, waiting for the signal to begin. Uncle Chinh looked up from his newspaper.

"Ah, it's you, Sister Que." He grimaced. "I told you not to worry. You're always complicating everything."

Apologetic, my mother replied, "It's just that . . . they're so skinny. I brought them some goodies."

"What nonsense," my uncle grumbled. "I keep telling you, they're naturally frail. In our day, wasn't I as well?"

"In our day" . . . These words alone were enough to evoke their shared family past, and my mother's eyes started to shine. She looked both moved and needy, like a faithful dog heeling at the scent of its master.

"Oh, you weren't so bad. Nothing like the skinniness of Tuan and Tu here."

Smiling, the woman with the pockmarked face moved forward with her platter of eggplant. "Sister Que, please share our meal." Then, remembering my presence, she added, "And you too, my niece."

My mother was overjoyed. She beamed at Aunt Chinh, her face breaking into a grin.

"We've already eaten, thanks. Please feed the children.

Here are some gifts for Tuan and Tu," she said, opening the hamper. Aunt Chinh immediately rushed to close the door and draw the curtains over the window. The curtains, made from imported Chinese fabric, were decorated with huge flowers splashed against a garish red background. My mother spread out the groceries. It was a feast for at least eight people. Her sister-in-law's eyes widened against her pale face. Her gaze was meek, vacillating. Uncle Chinh wheeled around. "This isn't necessary, really, why all this waste?" But his voice was unconvincing and toneless, directed at no one in particular.

The two boys let out a squeal; they had never seen such opulence. Aunt Chinh busied herself stashing the provisions out of sight, in the cupboard, on the buffet. I could hear the clatter of dishes in the other room; no doubt the anarchy caused by the subversive, unplanned invasion of our provisions. The clock at the neighbor's chimed seven o'clock. Uncle Chinh announced, "Come now, Thanh, give the children something to eat."

"Coming," she called, reappearing with a plate of pâté sliced as thin as a cat's tongue. She gestured to the closed windows. "So they won't see." I suddenly understood why, when I brought out the gifts, she had shot me the anxious look of a shoplifter. This was the way they lived here, vigilant, spying on each other, each keeping watch over his neighbor. One mouthful too many, and the others might turn you in as a potential threat to the collective. The two boys had stopped hitting the sides of their bowls with their chopsticks and sat motionless, their eyes glued to the platter of pâté. Their mother began to divy up the platter. After hesitating for a moment, my mother got up the nerve to speak her mind. "Give them a few more pieces."

"Absolutely not," Aunt Chinh snapped back, "in this house, everything must be organized, disciplined."

Then she plunged her chopsticks into the plate of cabbage, chewing loudly. "If you'll excuse me . . ."

I wanted to leave. My mother gazed adoringly at the heirs to the Do family lineage. They were munching away, appreciative. She watched them, fascinated. Aunt Chinh broke in, "When my husband got his share of the house sale, I told him to buy a television. But he didn't listen to me. After we bought the furniture, he put it all in a savings account. Now, all we have left are pieces of paper."

Uncle Chinh shot her a threatening look. "Thanh, how dare you talk like that?" She composed herself, sulking in silence.

My mother tried to smooth things over. "Who could have predicted this? Many older people were cheated as well."

Uncle Chinh broke in, furious. "Sister, we're talking about entrusting money to the State Bank. How can you even suggest that . . . ?"

My mother stuttered: "I-I was just talking off the top of my head . . . for the last two years, the currency has lost more than ten times its value. You put in two ounces of gold, and you're left with just enough to buy a few packets of MSG powder."

"Gold. Money." My uncle cut her off. "What do you take me for, a street vendor? Talking about money like this!"

My mother shut up, lowering her head. I had just gotten my nerve up to take her home when someone knocked at the door.

"Chief, are you there?" It was a cheery, youthful voice. Without waiting for a reply, a young man walked in. "Ha-ha, eating late, chief?"

My uncle put down his bowl and chopsticks and strode toward the living room. "Have a seat." Spotting the visitor, my mother pulled me toward the bed. The young man winked and nodded to us reassuringly.

"Please . . . this is a democracy."

He was about twenty, very slight, with a thick head of hair and almond-shaped eyes. When he laughed, there was something charming and roguish about him. Over his jeans, he wore a blue shirt flecked with black. Tanned and ruddy-cheeked, he glowed with health. As my uncle poured him some weak tea, he said, "Chief, are you using those leaves the third or fourth time?"

Uncle Chinh set down the teacup officiously and said, "So, what would you like to discuss?"

"Here you are," said the young man, pulling a notebook out of the back pocket of his jeans. "At your service, chief. We have a workers' delegation from the southern provinces coming to visit us for Tet. In their honor, we decided to celebrate the memory of the poet Do Chieu."

"Who is this Do Chieu?"

"Why, the most famous of the early patriotic twentieth-century poets, the soul of resistance in the hearts of our southern compatriots!"

"Show me your proposal." Uncle Chinh spread the paper across the table, put on his spectacles, and started to pore over it. The young man waited patiently, glancing furtively at a picture of a female dancer that had been tacked to the wall. After a long silence, Uncle Chinh looked up and said in a stern voice, "The answer is no."

The young man jumped. "What do you mean?"

Uncle Chinh frowned. "What kind of a patriot is he, anyway? . . . What does this lament mean? . . . Listen to this." He bent over, tracing the text with his finger:

"On the banks of River Nghe, the foam scatters,
On the banks of River Dong Nai the clouds are tinted
with smoke.

"Where do you find the spirit of the front line, of permanent attack? Do Chieu or not, the answer is no, absolutely not."

The young man stammered, "Chief, these were the dark years of the resistance. Hoang Dieu had just committed suicide. Truong Cong Dinh had been decapitated. Tens of thousands of soldiers had been massacred, exiled. . . . Under such conditions . . .''

"I know. . . .'' said Uncle Chinh, flipping his hand in the air dismissively. ''I know . . . but whatever the situation is, a revolutionary must never yield to tenderness or despair. This Do Chieu is not a revolutionary. Listen to this, here . . .

> "Phan and Lam sold the country;
> the court despised the people. . . .

"This is terrible, terrible. This verse is even more dangerous than the preceding one. Are you insinuating that the Central Committee is like the imperial court?''

The young man flushed a drunken red and a vein in his neck pulsed. ''But, chief, during the anti-American resistance, the southern soldiers left for the front singing Do Chieu's verses. Anyone who has even a bit of education and understands the South knows that Do Chieu is irreplaceable for our compatriots.''

Now it was Uncle Chinh's turn to blush. He stared the boy down with his myopic gaze. ''Irreplaceable? . . . So you are saying that Do Chieu is more important than the Party in the soul of the Vietnamese people? Is that it?''

Uncle Chinh waved his hand in the air like a sword, as if he were intending to cut off someone's neck. The young man paled, and sweat trickled down his forehead. Uncle Chinh droned on, ''The party has absolute prestige in the hearts of the people, today and always. No one compares to the party, no one can challenge its place.''

The young man clammed up, bowing his head. My uncle quieted down too, like a rooster who has just humiliated his adversary. He continued, but in a calmer voice, ''The party has led the people to victory, a huge victory. It has made us humanity's conscience, the flame of the liberation of oppressed people everywhere. Of the three great international revolutionary trends, we are the touchstone, the standard. You must commit yourself to this truth."

"Yes, chief, I'll make a note of it."

"We ideological cadres, we are the guardians of revolutionary purity. We must be vigilant, on guard for all signs of weakness, declining morale, decadence. . . ."

"Chief, when will the ceremony take place?"

"I'll give it some thought."

"But there are only two days left to send out the invitations, hang the posters, decorate the party hall, invite speakers, artists. . . ."

"Oh . . . really?" Uncle Chinh blinked, taking off his glasses. "Well, maybe this Do Chieu character really isn't that dangerous. Why don't we ever hear about him in the newspapers? Why didn't you propose some poems by To Huu? He's always a sure bet when it comes to revolutionary poetry."

"Chief, Do Chieu is a poet from the beginning of the century, and a historical . . ."

"Wait a minute." Uncle Chinh bent over, scoured the lines of small characters on the proposal and began to read aloud: "According to *The Great History of the Dai Viet* . . . Who wrote this book?"

"*The Great History of the Dai Viet*. That's by . . ."

Uncle Chinh let out a short cry, thumping his forehead in glee. "Ah! Yes. Of course. I remember now . . . *The Great History of the Dai Viet* by Le Quy Don. He's famous, born in Thai Binh. . . ."

The young man smiled surreptitiously, his lips bending into a smirk. Uncle Chinh shook his head, delighted with himself and his erudition.

"Well, in that case . . . Fine. I give my permission." He folded the paper and returned it to the young man. "Careful. Don't forget to invite the committees responsible for ideology at all levels. Remember the departments, the directors, the institutes—so that it will all be perfectly organized."

"Yes, chief." The young man said a quick good-bye and left rather abruptly.

I turned to my mother. "I'm going home."

My mother gathered her bags and said good-bye to everyone. This time, Aunt Chinh walked us all the way to the entry to the residence, to the guard post painted roach brown. But every time she bumped into one of her colleagues, she would rush a few feet ahead of us. Or she would bend down for no reason, pretending to look for a stone in her shoe, so we would pass her.

I didn't understand this family. I had no desire ever to return to this place. From then on, my mother went alone.

A year passed. Once, in conversation, my mother started to complain to Neighbor Vi:

"She refuses to walk alongside me. I don't understand. Do I look like a thief or an assassin?"

"Are you surprised? It's like an army barracks," said Neighbor Vi.

My mother looked at her, uncomprehending. She continued to debone the tiny birds she was preparing to marinate in fish sauce. "What do you mean?"

"The life they lead is like army life. Everyone has to conform. The house, the clothes, the food. These people are incapable of tolerating even the slightest difference. So you see, a little bit more money, a nicer bowl . . . it's dramatic for them. Listen to my advice. Wear the same clothes as your sister-in-law. Then see if she doesn't change her attitude. I'll give you my neck to chop if it isn't true."

My mother laughed. But a few days later she sewed herself exactly the same suit her sister-in-law wore. She put it on every time she visited Commune Residence K. When she returned, she seemed more cheerful, more relaxed.

My mother had exhausted her savings for Uncle Chinh's Tet dinner. At home, all we had were a few New Year's cakes and a pound of pork pâté. On the twenty-ninth of the month, Aunt Tam came to visit. Madame Dua accompanied her with a hamper full of cakes, pâtés, and meat. It was a feast: She also brought oranges, grapefruits, kaki fruit. She even brought a bantam rooster and six young hens.

"I'm offering you the rooster for the end-of-the-year parties. As for the young hens, these are for you, Hang. You'll have to steam them. Now that you're a teenager, you must eat right, round out a bit."

She walked toward the family altar, lifted up the red cloth coverslip, and gazed at the photo of my father for a moment. Then she called for Madame Dua.

"I asked a neighbor to look after the house for the day. I've got to be back tonight, so there's no need to prepare a meal. I've got money, and I'll eat something on the way back."

She gathered me in her arms, stroking my hair.

"The older you get, the more you look like your father. Really, to each plant its own little slug. No doubt about it." She sniffed my hair. It was her little habit, to ferret through my hair looking for lice.

"Smells good. It's clean. Don't ever go and perm your hair, child."

"Yes, my aunt."

"Well, I've got to be going. Don't forget to write."

"Yes, my aunt."

I had grabbed the edge of her *ao dai*. I accompanied her to the main road and hailed a cyclo for her. Her wool scarf seemed to float in the dusty air as I watched her cyclo disappear from sight.

On my return, I found my mother in the middle of the room, decorating the ancestors' altar. I knew she had been counting on Aunt Tam to offer me the Tet banquet. That suited her just fine, since it left her free to put her savings toward her brother's family.

"It's just splendid, our Tet. Thank your lucky star." She

kissed me. I couldn't stand the indignity of it, and I turned away.

How could my mother accept this humiliation? Why did she lower herself in front of my uncle and his pockmarked wife, before their children? Why did she love people who enslaved her?

The cripple had started to howl again, his chant a sinister echo amid the joy and the bustle of those festival days.

The beauty of the duckweed flowers in the midst of the dirty, murky waters is symbolic of how Hans clings to hope and beauty, even in a world of greed, stupidity war and famine.

Chapter SEVEN

H EY, LITTLE ONE . . ."

There were two taps on my shoulder, and I awoke with a jolt. I had let myself go, drifting off with my memories.

My traveling companion chuckled, his silver teeth gleaming in the half-light. "Don't you have something to cover yourself?"

I realized that I had nestled myself against his shoulder, and I blushed, apologetic.

The man shook his head. "Don't worry about it. I can lend you my wool jacket."

"Thanks anyway, I've got something."

I undid my knapsack and took out Madame Vera's shawl. My companion shrugged and let out a whistle of admiration. Madame Vera was right: It was freezing at night. Her wool shawl was like a nest, and I burrowed myself in its warmth, thinking of the lonely woman who had lent it to me.

I felt fine. The train shuttled along, monotonous. Beyond the window was a landscape awash in fog, like a painting by an unknown artist I had met on the banks of the Crimea. He was an Englishman who seemed to carry the fog of his country with him everywhere. Fog invaded his paintings like an obsession, dissolving all colors in a blur. He must have showed me hundreds of paintings, oils and pastels. Judging from the dates, he had traveled farther and farther from his country, losing himself in sunnier climates: Algeria, Los Angeles, Cairo, New Delhi, even Australia.

The farther he ran from his homeland, the more he was haunted by it; the farther he got from the fog, the more it seemed to invade his art.

"Why?" I asked. He shrugged his shoulders. He expressed himself terribly in Russian. He had come to Crimea to paint but became just another penniless tourist, a lonely, ugly man ignored by the pretty women in the hotels and restaurants.

"Why?" he repeated after me. "I don't know. I left England twelve years ago. My family . . . that's a story . . . and not a very pleasant one. . . . So I travel. When I sell a few paintings, when I feel homesick, I splurge. Otherwise, I live from day to day." He went silent, finished his bottle of water in a swig, and threw it onto the sand.

"I haven't seen the fog for twelve years, but I feel like I live it every day, in my hair, in my mouth, under my skin. This morning, getting out of bed, I walked right into it . . . that gray chill."

He closed his eyes for a moment, letting the Crimean sun warm his face. I knew he was telling the truth.

There are things you can't explain. They live on, inside of us, with a strange persistence. The fog in that Englishman's paintings reminded me of a pond filled with duckweed. There was an odd but undeniable correspondence for me. There were so many landscapes that painted fog could have evoked for me: the rolling plains, kites hovering overhead, the amber rice paddies that ringed the hills in terraces, the pristine whiteness of the beaches of Nha Trang, My Khe, Dai Lanh. . . .

The fog could have reminded me of the road that wound around the mountains in the Northwest: I had followed it one spring, with my friends, before we started college. The road careened and snaked around the precipices, reeling, drunk on its own danger. Along the roadside, purple and white bauhinia flowers spread like a quilt of blossoms over the peaks of the trees, as far as the eye could see. Once, I walked into this forest, plunging myself into its sea of purple flowers. At dusk it was a terrifying, unnerving beauty, like a revelation.

Many landscapes have left their mark on me, but one in particular haunted me like the fog that followed my English painter: a certain vision of duckweed floating on the surface of a pond.

An ordinary pond, like the kind at home. A pond lost in some godforsaken village, in a place where the honking of cars and the whistling of trains is something mysterious, exotic. A place where young women bend like slaves at their husbands' feet. A place where a man whips his wife with a flail if she dares lend a few baskets of grain or a few bricks to relatives in need. A strip of land somewhere in my country, in the 1980s . . .

I was still a child. I followed my mother to a village on the outskirts of Hanoi. I saw an old woman washing rice in a huge pond, filled with clear water. One corner was brimming with Japanese duckweed. Purple flowers bloomed out of this blanket of green, just as the face of a loving woman blooms into mysterious, laughing promises. I gazed at the flowers, spellbound. The old woman finished washing the rice, rinsed the basket, and began to wash her feet. The surface of the pond rippled, sending a shiver through the duckweed. Its purple reflections deepened with the pitching and tossing of the water.

The old woman lifted her head. "Where are you going?"

"To Madame Lai's. My girl just loves duckweed flowers. She had to see them," said my mother, laughing.

"What's so special about them?" The woman shrugged, turning back to her washing.

duckweed = hope for future

Years later, whenever I traveled in the Vietnamese countryside again, I always stopped to contemplate these flowers: in real ponds, in real villages. Ponds just like we had near Hanoi: stagnant, oily bogs flecked with bubbles from rotting algae; murky pools surrounded by a clutter of miserable hovels, ramshackle gardens, and outhouses stinking in the summer sun; the stench of rotting weeds and dried algae washed up on the banks; the mud, the decomposing toads, the dead fish, their scales gone black, their scorched carcasses twisted into arches.

sensory imagery

At the center of these stifling landscapes, on a green carpet of weed, those purple flowers always glistened, radiant in the middle of the filth: the atrocious ornament of a life snuffed out. The water glowed in the light of dusk like the wine served on festival days—wine mixed with the blood of animals just butchered. The air was always heavy, oppressive with the tedium of waiting, the *quoc* bird's shrill, jerky cries shattering the silence. The men stood watch as they lay in waiting, breathless, hanging on the distant whistle of a train.

This purple became an obsession, both a childhood delight and an adolescent nightmare. In my memory, it is at once both the purest balm and the most overpowering poison of my existence.

Chapter *EIGHT*

*T*HE TRAIN PULLED INTO THE STATION. THE MAN WITH the silver-capped teeth opened his satchel and brought out two peaches, offering me one. I thanked him. It was a Bulgarian peach, as big as a child's fist, red-skinned, juicy, and fleshy, the kind of fruit that drew huge lines at the Russian markets as soon as it appeared. Just smelling it in my hand made my mouth water. The traveler had already swallowed half of his peach. "Eat some, little girl, it's very good."

I bit into the peach, its sugary juice filling my mouth. Sweet enough to wake the dead. Out the window, I saw passengers rushing toward the train. On the platform, a couple were embracing. A farewell kiss. The woman was teary. Separation, this ancient pain, perhaps the greatest of all human sadnesses.

The young man on the platform tossed his bundle over his shoulder. She hugged him one last time. Their straw-colored hair mingled, their heads glowing under the lamplight like two silkworm cocoons. A final kiss and they separated. The young woman cast a tall, thin shadow across the cement platform. The man's voice echoed from the window of one of the cars. The woman waved and then started to walk. After about ten steps, she turned around, her face streaming with tears. The train started up. The man's voice was drowned in the wind.

I watched the woman left behind on the platform until the train station blurred behind us. The train streaked through the suburbs, plunging into a landscape of endless, rolling hills. In the half-light of dusk, I could just make out their dark masses of green.

Good-bye. A train whistle, like a cry . . .

No separation could rival the vulgarity of those in my country, at the Noi Bai Airport. The day I left, only one person, lost in a village somewhere beyond the river, cried for me. I thought of Aunt Tam, of her broken heart, as I watched the young people on the platform.

The Noi Bai Airport. It all came back to me: the swarms of people, the suffocating heat. Even worse was the anxiety, the fear that tormented these people as they went through the customs formalities. Their numbed, panicky faces, their hair clammy with sweat, their eyes furtive, darting about impatiently, ferreting everywhere, ready for a last-minute disaster.

Outside, on the other side of a black iron grill, was another crowd, just as anxious, just as sweaty and frightened. These were the parents and friends of those departing. They all waited for deliverance. When all the customs procedures had been completed, when the crowd of travelers had passed through the last security booths and were walking toward the tarmac, you could see, on the faces of those left behind, the relief, the joy, the pride of vicarious success. The vision of a happier future elsewhere, anywhere but here. Smiles of contentment, faces radiant with happiness. Nowhere else in the world does separation bear the hideous face of joy. This was a grotesque face, a deviation from all rules of human nature.

I was alone in the middle of the line of people waiting their turn at customs. I wiped the sweat from my temples, peering over the top of the iron grate. My mother was in the hospital. Aunt Tam was angry with me, so she wouldn't be there. I knew this, but I still looked for her in the crowd. I looked without hoping. I knew that she was crying alone, in her big, empty house on the other side of the river.

My memory drifted back to the day, three years before I had even dreamed of seeing that airport, when my aunt Tam came to stay with us. At the time, I was preparing for the college entrance exams. Hearing of this, Aunt Tam had left her house under the care of Madame Dua for the entire week. She stayed at our house during my examination period, fussing and spoiling me, fixing all of my meals. My mother continued her routine at the market. "Street vendors," Aunt Tam huffed. "You never see them sacrifice a day of business."

At the end of my examination sessions, Aunt Tam returned to the village. Every week, she wrote to ask me about my results, even though I had told her at least three times that it would be a wait of several months. Her expectations terrified me. Fortunately, I passed my exams and was accepted to the university.

The minute she found out, she arrived on our doorstep. Once again, I saw Madame Dua approaching, laden down with hampers of fruit, cakes, ducks, and chickens.

"These are for Hang. She can treat her friends," Aunt

Tam chirped. She pulled a wad of bills from her pocket. "This, this is for traveling. Rest a bit. The week before you leave for the university, I'll be sending someone to call for you. I'm inviting the family and the neighborhood to celebrate your success."

I squirmed at the idea. "Please, my aunt, it's really not worth the trouble."

"You must listen to me."

"But it's ridiculous."

She pouted, her face clouding over. "Your father only had a secondary-school education. You are the first, the only one in the entire Tran family line, to get to the university. This is no small matter. . . . Listen to me."

It was impossible to refuse her, so I said no more. She left right away, Madame Dua dragging the empty hampers behind her. I watched the skinny, hunched back of this strange wizened slip of a woman who had never borne children. I felt like crying.

After I got the examination results, I devoted myself to having a good time with my friends. One of them, the daughter of a high-ranking official in the Ministry of Foreign Affairs, offered to take me on a trip. Her family was well off compared to other officials of the same rank in other ministries. My friend's sister, who was single, also took a few days off to accompany us. We were more than comfortable in terms of our finances, and we visited all the coastal towns of central Vietnam: Nha Trang, Da Nang, Quy Nhon. In the north, we stopped at Sam Son and Bai Chay. Finally, just after Tet, we went to see the mountains in the Northwest. That was the best trip of all. Still, I could barely manage to make a dent in the money Aunt Tam had given me.

Ten days before I was scheduled to leave for the university, a man drove up to our house on a Honda 67: "Is this the home of Madame Que, the one with the daughter named Hang?"

I was busy embroidering a traveling case. The man seemed to speak into the air. I didn't even reply.

"Hey, I'm talking to you." He raised his voice but didn't budge from his motorcycle, which sputtered and popped, spewing smoke into the air.

"I'm asking if this is little Hang's house?"

"Yeah, what do you want?" I replied, wearily.

He looked at me, sideways, through green sunglasses. "Madame Tam sent me. Get ready, miss, I'm supposed to take you over to her place."

He cut the motor and parked the motorcycle in a corner of the courtyard. Without waiting for my invitation, he walked into the house, sat down, and lit up a cigarette. His self-assurance annoyed me. I threw a few clothes into a small suitcase and followed him.

"Drop me off at the market, please."

"At your service."

He tossed his cigarette butt into the courtyard and revved up the motor. The Honda 67 looked like a huge hornet, but it was comfortable all the same. The man dropped me off at the gate to the market and disappeared into a bar for a cup of coffee. "I'll wait for you here. Take your time with your mother. Madame Tam wants you to spend at least a week in the village."

"I'll be back in a quarter of an hour."

I wound my way through the market toward my mother's stall. There wasn't a customer in sight. Two vendors, both women, were getting their white hairs extracted by their daughters. Nearby, a third vendor was dozing. "I'm leaving," I announced to my mother.

"Yes, go ahead," she muttered, still bent over her hamper, fumbling through her peanuts in search of some shriveled seeds for a customer.

Because my aunt Tam had taken me under her protection, and because my mother had already found another object for her affections, a kind of indifference had slipped into our relationship. I hadn't expected this. How could she cease to be my mother? I paused a moment, silent, and then asked her, "You don't have any advice for me?"

She looked up, surprise tinged with irony in her eyes. "Ah, but you have Aunt Tam for that."

I felt sickened, but continued calmly, "I don't feel like going, but I've got to."

"Go ahead. They're probably all waiting for you with some great big feast. I'm not rich enough to . . ."

I looked straight at her. "Don't say that. We've always lived simply but happily together. Is that because of money?"

Avoiding my eyes, she replied. Her voice was cool, neutral. "The past is the past. It's not the same now."

The seeds slipped through her fingers, falling into a tiny plastic basket. She stared at the basket, as if to cut short our conversation. She looked calm, distant. She had the air of a woman in perfect control of herself, so different from the woman I used to accompany to Uncle Chinh's house.

That was how it was between us: I sought her love, while she sought recognition from the Do family; it was a kind of grotesque hide-and-seek. I swallowed my tears. "Well, I'm going. Take care of yourself."

"Yeah, go on now."

I found the man seated at the café, flirting with a plump young woman with a round face and frizzy, permed hair. She looked like a chubby-cheeked children's doll. When he saw me enter, he called out, "Oh, finished already? Didn't even have time to finish my cup of coffee. How much do I owe you, missus?" He brought out a filthy wallet bulging with big bills. The plump young woman shot him a coy sideways glance. "Why, you rich man."

He laughed. "Oh, it's not too bad. See you next time. I've got to complete my mission." Then he turned to me. "Hop on, miss."

I sort of liked him, but his vulgarity still irritated me. I waited until he had revved up the motor before climbing on the back. The man readjusted his green shades, waved goodbye to the young woman, and we took off. Perched behind him like that, I almost suffocated from a wave of nauseating odors: a mixture of gasoline, male sweat, and some cheap local cologne. It was unspeakable. I didn't open my mouth for the whole trip, trying to avoid the stench of him. At first, he tried to start up conversation; when he received only vague grunts from me in reply, he gave up. My silence probably annoyed him—he seemed like the gregarious type.

When we arrived at Aunt Tam's house, he shouted, "Hey there! Boss! Open up now! Your messenger's back!"

I heard a giggle of pleasure from inside; it was Aunt Tam herself behind the door.

"Well, that was quick! I wasn't expecting to see you before nightfall."

The latch clicked, and the door swung open. Aunt Tam pulled me down toward her in a hug.

Her nervous excitement made me laugh.

"So how are you, my aunt?"

"I couldn't be better. I've been waiting for you all day."

She turned toward the man with the green sunglasses.

"Come in for a minute."

"Thanks anyway. I've got to get home, or my tigress will tear me apart. Anyway, you're happy now."

The man kick-started his motorcycle and was off. I was surprised to see him go.

"Why didn't he come in for tea?"

"Come, let's go in first."

Only after she had latched the gate to the house behind her, did she explain. "He's got a mistress about fifteen miles from here. His wife is out of her mind with jealousy. Some days, she even threatens to set herself on fire. So it was better to let him go right home."

She brought my bags inside. The clock struck two. On

the low table, under a domed wicker cover used to keep off the flies, she had set out a meal for us.

"You waited for me to eat?"

"I wasn't hungry. This morning I had potatoes cooked with sesame seeds. I washed it down with some aglaiata tea. Guess it spoiled my appetite. Anyway, now that you're here, I'm hungry. Go wash up. We'll sit down to eat."

She followed me to the well, a clean towel in her hand. It was one of those luxurious, imported towels, decorated with a spray of lilac embroidered onto an immaculate white background. As I plunged the towel into a bronze washbasin she had filled with clean water, a kind of tenderness broke over me. The water erased the tension and the dust of the trip. A clean towel. Cool water. All this at the end of a long journey. I savored the feeling of knowing someone had waited for me. It was sweltering and, from time to time, the cry of a bird echoed in the air. The shadow cast by the wall behind me had already climbed to the third stack of bricks in the courtyard.

"Come, let's sit down to eat," Aunt Tam called to me. When she lifted the cover off the food, I let out a squeal of delight. She had made one of my favorite soups: a mixture of lily buds, puree of crab, and crab eggs. The eggs floated like clouds of spun gold in the middle of the lily buds, translucent from the cooking. There was also a vegetable pâté made from cactus plant and thick slices of fresh soybean loaf.

I gorged myself, which made her happy. From time to time, she even put down her chopsticks just to watch me eat. I had almost finished, but she still nibbled on a second bowl of rice. She ate almost nothing, as if watching me gave her greater pleasure.

For dessert, she brought out two bowls of a homemade pudding made of potato flour and mashed lotus seeds. She had put so many lotus seeds in the paste that it smelled sweet and fragrant even without any vanilla.

As Aunt Tam cleared off our plates and wiped the table, I asked, "So where's Madame Dua?"

"She's gone out to round up some help for me tonight."

She handed me a tiny pillow made of white cotton, keeping the coarser, wicker pillow for herself. "Let's take a little catnap."

The bed she had prepared for me, a strip of amboyna wood, was as cool and smooth as marble. I stretched out and fell asleep in an instant. When I awoke, it was almost nightfall. A pig waiting to be butchered squealed somewhere in the distance. The door to the bedroom was tightly shut, leaving me in an unnatural darkness. But through a tiny window above the door, I saw that the courtyard was still light. I sat up in bed, listening to the pig's cries: a sharp screeching, a few rasping grunts, and then it was all over.

"Enough, I told you that's enough. Gather the rest in that stoneware basin." It was a man's voice, coarse and brutal. After a pause, he went on, "Understand? Next time, you hold it there, exactly there. A bit more blood, and this dish will be good for the garbage can."

"Yes, Father, I understand," a young man's voice replied. It was a butcher training his son.

"Bring me the boiling water, Son. Quickly!"

"How much time do you need to carve it up?" I heard one of the men ask.

"It only takes me twenty minutes," the father barked at him. "You can go ahead and prepare the mortar and pestle. I'll be ready in a second."

"Perfect. The women can start cutting up the scallions and the parsley. We're going to make an unforgettable tripe stew out of this," another man chimed in.

"Oh, yeah, like the last time, for old Toan's memorial service. It still stank of excrement," someone shot back.

The father spoke now. "You are bitter, aren't you? I told you: I was drunk, and so I let the Cuu brothers help me. That was fatal. Everybody knows they'll eat just about anything."

Their voices reverberated and echoed across the courtyard. I opened the door a crack. On a barrel-shaped blue por-

celain stool in the middle of the courtyard, a gas lamp burned
at full flame, casting a halo of light through the curtain of
palms and over the hedge of flowers, a halo that finished in
a sparkle on the fringe of trees.

Next to the kitchen door, a young man was shaving the
butchered pig. His razor glinted in the beam of the lamp. Another young man with just a shadow of a mustache—he
couldn't have been more than seventeen or eighteen—doused
the pig with buckets of boiling water, dumping them over it
at regular intervals. The blade of the first man's razor followed the rhythm of each cascade of water and the pig's black
bristles sheared off to reveal the naked whiteness of its skin.
Next to the two young men, a wooden plank had been
scrubbed and laid out as a carving board.

Two women chopped onions and fragrant herbs, probably
for the blood pudding. Behind them, Madame Dua was roasting peanuts, and to her right, two men were busy cleaning
the mortars and pestles. The granite pestle was my height,
and the mortar was almost a yard high; I had never seen such
huge kitchen tools. They had obviously been borrowed from
a local butcher or a large family used to entertaining hundreds
of guests.

The scene was lively but well ordered, as if all the feverish activity was directed by the iron hand of some invisible
conductor. It wasn't long before I discovered it was Aunt
Tam, crouched on the third step of the landing in the shadow
of the ginseng plant. She was whittling toothpicks from bamboo, hunched over a tiny knife that she flicked methodically,
oblivious to the commotion around her. Yet everything there
seemed to emanate from her orders.

A dull thumping sound: The butcher threw the pig down
onto the carving plank, glanced up, and shouted in an imperious voice, "Knives!"

One of the most handsome of the boys jumped forward,
clutching a whole array of cleavers in his fists. The butcher
rolled up the sleeves of his shirt; then the carving began. He

thrust a blade into the middle of the open carcass to hold it steady and then took out a large square cleaver. The sound of a single penetrating cut, razor sharp, precise, slicing right along the vertebrae. Then a second, and a third, each cut falling exactly in place. In seconds, the pig had been cut into two portions so equal that the Scales of Justice could have found their equilibrium. The butcher looked up from his work. "Bring me the baskets! The nylon cloth!"

The two men, who had been busy with the meat grinding, rushed to his side. The handsome young man with the mustache pulled a nylon cloth out of his wicker basket and unfurled it. The butcher tossed one half of the pig into a huge basket and propped the other on the wood plank. Then he used another knife to cut the meat on the plank into long slabs. Someone looking on let out a whistle of admiration. "That was quick! The meat is still steaming."

The butcher spoke sternly. "To get a good pâté, the meat must still be steaming. Cold meat is only good for the socialist cooperatives." As he spoke, he hacked off an enormous block of meat. "To your mortars! Quickly now!"

He barked his orders as if he imagined himself a general at the front. "Don't forget the fermented fish sauce and the black pepper." The two men grabbed the sides of meat and moved like athletes carrying a trophy.

The butcher continued to carve up the meat, growling occasional advice to his assistants. "Don't be shy. You've got everything in there now." The courtyard resounded with the blows of their pestles.

In front of the kitchen, the women had finished mincing the onions and fragrant herbs. Now, they began to mix the blood pudding, their chopsticks chiming and clinking against the sides of their metal cooking pots as they stirred. Conversation ebbed and flowed as they chatted about their farm work, about quarrels between the president of the commune and the director of the cooperative, about some woman evicted by her mother-in-law who found herself in the street with nothing but her conical straw sun hat and a change of clothes. As they worked, the conversation picked up speed. Night was falling, and everything else went silent as the dinner hour neared an end. Somewhere, a dog barked at someone passing by.

It was that evening that I felt for the first time the emptiness here, silence, and loneliness of the countryside. Everywhere, an indescribable backwardness hung in the air, immaterial yet terrifyingly present: It would be like this for eternity. This backwardness seeped into the stillness here, like the brackish waters of the past: cold, stubborn, a sluggish, liquid sweetness escaping all control, ready at any moment to drown those unable to rise to its surface.

My aunt continued to whittle her toothpicks in the shadow of the ginseng plant. She looked like a statue hunched over like that, her pointy shoulders framing the two sides of her tiny skull. As I watched her, I finally understood: This woman, one of the only human beings dear to me, this silence, this loneliness, this backwardness, were all one; she was my blood, my source, my mooring in this world. No one was closer to me; yet no one could have been stranger. It was through her that I knew the tenderness of this world, and through her too that I was linked to the chains of my past, to the pain of existence. Confusedly, as if through a fog, I saw a vision of my future.

She must have sensed my presence. "You're awake, Hang?" She offered me some of the tripe soup, but I wasn't hungry. I drifted back to the bedroom.

When I awoke again, it was four-thirty the next morning. The sleep made up for my week of late nights: card playing and movies with my friends. My aunt's wicker pillow was still in exactly the same place. She must have stayed up all night.

Dawn was breaking when I wandered out into the courtyard. The gas lamp was still perched on the porcelain stool. The men from the night before had vanished. Their pestles, scrubbed and drying now, were propped up against the flower hedge. The granite mortars had been up-ended, feet in the air, and the carving plank left to drip dry against the wall.

The large hampers were gone, but others filled with meat were piled at the edge of the well. Steam rose from two of the baskets; the pâtés, which were still scalding hot, must have just been strained from their bouillon. On the other side of the flower hedge, near a grove of palms, a fire smoldered between two huge stones, a few sparks flying intermittently.

My aunt was washing the last traces of blood from the stones of the courtyard. When she saw me coming, she said, "Why are you up so early, my child?"

Her sleepless night had left no trace; she looked alert, lucid.

"Don't you ever get any sleep?" I teased her. She just laughed, revealing her stained but strong, regular teeth. "This is nothing. During the harvest season, I stand watch for five or seven days at a stretch. Wash up and come have some breakfast."

I dawdled a bit in the courtyard, but she prodded me on. "Hurry up now, Hang. The cooks will be here any minute. I'm going to be very busy." As I headed toward the kitchen to get some salt to brush my teeth, I noticed Madame Dua curled up on the bamboo couch near the wall, still sound asleep. She hadn't even had the energy to stumble over to her bed in the servants' quarters.

As I stared at her, Aunt Tam started to chuckle. "People are like that. They keep their character for life. She'd drink from dirty paddy water to quench her thirst. When she's hungry, she'll eat a moldy bowl of rice without even noticing it. And when she's sleepy, she'll keel over anywhere, at the foot of a tree, by the side of the road. . . .

"When I was a young woman, Madame Dua had a son. Her husband was a Tho from the high plateaus of Cao Bang, a carpenter who worked for the Nhieu family. He found her pretty, healthy enough, and fell in love with her. The Nhieus accepted his proposal of marriage immediately, even offered to foot the bill for the wedding ceremony. So her husband moved in with his in-laws to work for them. Dua was so fertile that by the end of the first year, she had borne him a son.

"He was a beautiful baby, plump and round as a sweet flour candy. Tho adored the child, doted on it when he wasn't working. But a few years with Dua were enough to try his patience. It has to be said: It would be difficult to find a clumsier woman. If Dua grabbed a bowl of fish sauce, the bowl would break; if she tried to age a plate of pickled cabbage, the cabbage would rot. The day her son turned seven, the husband ran off with the child. Then her parents died, and she had to sell the house to feed herself. So that's her story. Born a rich man's daughter, she'll finish her days as a servant."

"What relation is she to us?"

"Her parents were cousins of your paternal grandmother. So Dua's a third-degree relation. During the land reform, she was elected to the Peasants' Association, but when they realized they couldn't get anything out of her, they sent her back. All through the years of collectivism, she never did earn a full day's wages. Even on that little plot of hers, she could only get a few potatoes. In the end, she survived by begging. Two years ago, she was in such a miserable state that I decided to take her in. After all, a single drop of our own blood, even a hundred times diluted, is worth more than swamp water."

Next to us, Madame Dua dozed on, snoring noisily like a man. Aunt Tam said, "Let's go wash up. She had better sleep her fill—if she doesn't, she's likely to fall into the fire while boiling water."

It was light out in the courtyard now. The fresh, light odor of betel nut permeated the air, mingling with the moist, dewy smell of night. Outside, in a bush near the entrance to the hamlet, a blackbird trilled. Aunt Tam had prepared my breakfast: sticky rice and chopped meat baked in the shape of a hollow cylinder. The meat was the same texture as an ordinary pork pâté, but it had been seasoned with ground cinnamon and pepper, rolled out in a thick crust around a bamboo pole, and then grilled over a wood fire. The meat was light, fragrant, and very crispy, since it had been freshly ground and mixed with a bit of alum to give it that texture. Even the best butcher shops in Hanoi couldn't produce pâtés of this quality. As usual, Aunt Tam ate almost nothing, putting her chopsticks down several times to watch me eat.

We had just finished the meal and were about to have tea when the doorbell started ringing.

"They're here. Clear off the table for me."

She got up to open the door, and three matronly-looking women entered. Like my aunt, they wore almost identical clothes, the same black pajama pants and white shirt, their hair bound back in a tight chignon or a ponytail. Nobody in the countryside wore her hair bound up in the traditional black turban anymore.

"Is it too early, Madame?" they asked.

Aunt Tam let out a laugh. "Of course not. It's already dawn. Come on in." The women crossed the three steps of the landing and entered a room at the left. In the meantime, I had cleared away our bowls and chopsticks. The women set their wicker baskets at the base of the wall and seated themselves around the low table. Aunt Tam brought out a huge tray heaped with bowls of sticky rice, a pork pâté, a pile of white porcelain bowls, ebony chopsticks, and a basket of ripe bananas. "Have some lunch before lending me a hand."

"Oh my, this is a real feast you're offering us," exclaimed one of the women. "*Bon appétit*, sisters. Everywhere else, the host eats before the guests. Only at Aunt Tam's do the guests start first. Let's lift our chopsticks."

They nodded to each other and then turned to my aunt. "Is the banquet for lunch or for dinner?"

"For both. There are going to be a lot of guests. We'll need two services."

"How many dishes and how many soups per guest?"

"Five dishes and five soups."

"So much?"

"I'd be grateful if you would all make your best effort. This is the first time a member of the Tran family, my niece Hang, has made it into the university."

"Why, an aunt like you, there can't be two of a kind in the whole country. Go on, tell us what you have in mind."

"Yes, with your blessing. For each guest, I'd like five plates: white meat pâté, mixed pâté, pâté roll, spring rolls, and roasted meat. And five bowls: asparagus soup, vermicelli soup, soup made from chicken marinated in lotus-seed sauce, vegetable soup, and a chicken curry soup. The meat, the pâtés, the bones for the bouillon—that's all ready. The chickens for the lotus-seed and curry soups are still in their cages. For the dessert at noon, I'd like a sweet mung-bean pudding. For this evening, sweet sticky-rice pudding flavored with rose-apple juice."

"My, this is three times as much food as at any banquet we have ever had in this village," one of the women commented. "Now I know why Duong's wife, as soon as she got up this morning asked her husband if he was invited."

Hearing this, a sickly-looking woman with a scar across her cheek turned to my aunt and hissed, "You invited that bastard Duong?"

"Yes, and all the other important people in this village as well," snapped Aunt Tam. "I have been waiting a long time to give this banquet. I assure you, my money will not be wasted."

"No, but that bastard is planning to take my sister's plot of farmland in the Trai hamlet," said the woman. "My sister is a widow. She's been broke and alone since her husband died. Her son, the one that left for the front, all she's got left of him is a badge for 'meritorious combat.' If Duong takes that plot of land with the persimmon trees from her, she'll have nothing left to feed herself with."

A woman next to her added, "And Duong just married off his eldest daughter. So he wants the plot to set up a household for her and her new husband."

The woman with the scarred cheek went on, "My sister filed a complaint with the township authorities. Not that that will help at all. . . . In any case, I refuse to serve that bastard." She bowed her head.

Aunt Tam spoke without emotion. "I know the whole story. Trust me. You won't have to serve him."

She got up, walked out onto the veranda, and gave a shout: "Madame Dua, are you awake?"

The woman with the scar raised her head now. She seemed calmer. I followed my aunt's movements with my eyes. What force lay hidden in those frail shoulders of hers, what power inspired such trust in her words, such absolute obedience? It was from that moment that I began to look forward to the banquet, to the arrival of this village personality, this man they called "that bastard Duong, vice president."

Chapter *NINE*

A T NOON, THE WHOLE VILLAGE ARRIVED LIKE A RIP-
tide. Dozens of dishes were served and cleared off
in rapid succession. As for me, I played the part of the successful niece. Cousins and other distant kin were all invited,
and I smiled dutifully at everyone. My lips stiffened into a
permanent smile. Playing the role of hostess was not exactly
a rest cure. To smile as many times as I did per hour seemed
to me as exhausting as the wailing we had to do at burials. I
lost my appetite and felt completely drained. At three o'clock,
when I couldn't stand it anymore, I wolfed down a bowl of
green mung-bean pudding and snuck off to the neighbor's
house to take a nap. At nightfall, Aunt Tam sent Madame
Dua to fetch me.

In the living room, the gas lamp hung from a wood
beam, casting its light through all the other rooms, the court-

yard, and even through the flower hedge to the edge of the first row of betel palms. Fortunately, they were already serving dessert—the *che* sweets and the sticky rice. People were raving about the sticky rice.

"A sticky rice flavored with rose-apple juice! Why, it's exquisite."

"You won't find this at any other party."

"Oh, it's nothing special. All you need are lots of beans, sugar and lard, and you have it."

"Are you kidding? I could give you a whole bag of sugar, and you would come up with some disgusting paste. . . . Remember the famous sticky rice you served us at the time of all the construction in the village? A real soup that was . . . You were in the bloom of youth, and I was a budding young—"

"Oh please, will you stop it?"

"He's right. It's not easy to make a good sticky rice with rose apple. After the rice is cleaned, it has to be dried with a hand towel, grain by grain if necessary. And when you mix it with the rose-apple juice, the grains mustn't clump together. And you can't use just any rose apple. You have to pick the fruit with just the right thick red skin and thin spines. To distill the essence, you have to mix the flesh with the finest rice wine. So much for the rice. As for the beans, the preparation is more complicated than you'd think. Once you've shelled them, you have to dry them thoroughly before the salting. And when it's time for the cooking, the lower pot should have a large opening, but the upper pot must be firmly sealed. If there is even the slightest excess of steam, the rice loses all its flavor. No, I'm sorry, to make a dish like this is a real art."

I followed my aunt, threading my way through a hive of distant relatives. Their faces flushed from the wine, they chattered and cackled away, letting out raucous belly laughs. As I wound my way from the courtyard into the house, I dutifully answered the same questions:

"How old are you now?"

"Eighteen already, my, my."

"Which university was that?"

"Ah, the Institute for the Social Sciences? With a diploma like that, why, you must be able to get a job in the civil service!"

We finally arrived at the low, rectangular dining table. Aunt Tam spoke first. "Allow me to introduce my niece, Hang."

They all began to talk at once. I couldn't get a word in edgewise, so I nodded mechanically, greeting them one after the other, moving my lips politely in silence. Aunt Tam began to introduce the guest of honor in a steady, precise voice: "And this is Mr. Duong, vice president of the village. Let's welcome him."

He was barely half my aunt's age. He nodded his head in greeting, his lips twitching to one side.

I tried to start up a conversation. "Have you been leading the village for some time now?"

"For quite some time now, yes."

I was silent, not knowing what more to say. But I had time to examine him at close range. He was a short, pudgy man, with a barrellike waist. A strange ruddy face, neither round nor square, but lobster-colored. Under heavy eyelids, he had the eyes of a viper, a stubby nose, and a scar that ran jagged along his right nostril. His lips protruded in a funny pucker, as if to blow out a fire.

The vice president looked over at Aunt Tam and chuckled. "Here you are at last. Do us the honor of sitting at our table. Have one of your delicious sticky-rice balls, a bit of wine. After all, this is the century of materialism." Pleased with his clever remark, he let out a loud guffaw.

"Thank you. I couldn't eat another thing, but please make yourself at home."

The vice president leaned toward my aunt and gave her

sleeve a little tug. "You don't have to eat, but do sit with us. I have a favor to ask of you later."

"Gladly," Aunt Tam replied smoothly. "Who could refuse a vice president?"

Uncomfortable, he protested, "No. Don't say that. If it got around, it might look bad. Not everyone here would understand your sense of humor."

Aunt Tam was still all smiles. "Why so much circumspection, Mr. Vice President?"

He shook his head. "How could I do otherwise? These days, people stab you in the back without the slightest warning."

"Really? I don't go to meetings, so I'm quite ignorant about all this. Who would want to hurt you?"

He started to laugh, a jerky, nervous laugh. "Oh, there are people, there are always—but why worry yourself about these troubles?"

He narrowed his eyes at her in an ingratiating squint. "In fact, to live like you do is really happiness. The whole village dreams of having this: a nice house, a granary full of rice, money in the bank. Calm, peaceful days far from all the sound and fury."

"I guess I never realized my good fortune. How silly of me. Do have some more wine. We've barely dipped into this bottle."

The other guests raised their hands for mercy. "Enough, enough, we can't keep eating and drinking like this."

Aunt Tam called to the kitchen, "Hey there, could someone come and clear off this table?"

"Coming," a voice shouted back. A woman appeared instantly and began to clear off the table. She had probably arrived that afternoon; I didn't recognize her. Poised and calm, Aunt Tam brought out a thermos of boiled water and some teacups. "I flavored the tea myself with aglaiata flowers. Please, try some."

The vice president roared with laughter. "Well, if you

PARADISE OF THE BLIND

made it, it will find no comparison in this village."

"Please, you flatter me, Mr. Vice President."

Aunt Tam served the tea herself, moving graciously among the guests. It was then that I noticed a young woman, crouched in the opposite corner of the room, her arms hugging her knees to her chest. It was the woman with the scarred cheek. After finishing work in the kitchen, she had hidden herself there to watch the scene.

My aunt continued to serve the tea, pausing to chat politely with each guest. The vice president nodded his head. "Excellent, truly delicious. You really must teach me the recipe. I'll ask my wife to plant a few of these aglaiata bushes."

"You're very kind. How could I claim to teach you?"

He was insistent now. "No, no, I mean this, sincerely, Madame Tam. You know, these days it's rare you find sincere, honest people; bastards abound."

"Now, now. Aren't you really too harsh? I myself find the people in our village extremely kind, rather too malleable. Look at your militia. Now, didn't they just tie up Danh without a warrant for his arrest? Did he put up even the slightest show of resistance?"

The vice president nodded in agreement. "It's true. But he only got what he deserved. He dared to challenge one of our Communist party resolutions. He's lucky I didn't send him straight to prison."

Aunt Tam just laughed softly. "According to the law, it's illegal to imprison a man without a warrant for his arrest. Danh wasn't a robber, and he certainly was no opium trafficker. His only crime was that he insulted you and the party secretary. You didn't even have a warrant for his arrest. The man offered you his wrists; he accepted the ropes you used to bind him. Where else would you find people as obedient as in our village? After something like that, how can you complain about their stubbornness?"

The vice president drew his brow, fuming. "Think about it. Agitators must be silenced immediately, or it will be anarchy. Today, he insults the township party secretary, tomorrow he'll end up—"

He stopped in midsentence, slicing the air with a chop of his hand. "All power is dictatorship. It must be exercised without weakness. The state needs obedience to its authority and its laws."

Aunt Tam, still smiling: "Taste some of my homemade *che* pudding. . . . And do try some of these imported cigarettes. Some friends managed to get them for me." Turning toward the vice president, she spoke slowly, almost in a whisper. "I never did receive any formal political instruction, so I don't know too much about authority or the state laws. But when I was young, my father often told me a story on the subject. If you don't mind, I'd like to tell it."

The men who, according to custom, were seated separately, cheered her on.

One of the elderly guests interrupted them. "Wait, just let me take a smoke first. These moments are rare." He filled the bowl of a water pipe with tobacco and then lit it. As the pipe started to sputter and gurgle, the man tossed back his head and exhaled, blowing the smoke high into the air. Aunt Tam waited, calm and relaxed. Guests playing poker and other card games suddenly abandoned the courtyard to gather again on the veranda. Everyone was listening. The old smoker, sated, nodded his approval to her. "Go on now, tell it."

Aunt Tam set down her cup of tea and composed herself.

"My father told it like this: During the reign of Tu Duc, there was an honest minister from Thai Binh. The common people called him the venerable minister Chinh, and King Tu Duc honored his memory by composing a rhyme:

"No justice in the South without Binh.
"No peace in the North without Chinh.

"One day, the venerable Chinh was assigned to build a network of canals to irrigate the rice paddies throughout the province. The central, grand canal would have to cut across the largest of the townships, which also happened to be Chinh's own.

"As you know, the tradition is that each man accepts, without protest, the passage of the irrigation canal through his land. The slightest wavering by one official, and corruption becomes rampant—so, of course, the wealthy didn't hesitate to bribe civil servants to divert the canal's trajectory through the property of their poorer neighbors, who could only bow their heads in silence.

"After reflecting for a long time, Minister Chinh finally hit on an impartial method for determining the course of the grand canal. At nightfall, he ordered his soldiers to light torches. The beams cast by the torches traced two parallel lines across the rice paddies, and along these lines they placed the markers. The course of the canal was fixed in this manner. No one dared protest, and so the canal was built in a straight line, like a single inky brushstroke.

"But when the canal sliced right through the minister's township, the local dignitaries realized that they would have to dig up the minister's own land and rice paddies, even unearthing the tombs of his ancestors. They hastily proposed a special dispensation and demanded permission to alter the course of the canal.

"But the venerable minister Chinh was firm. 'Since I honor the tombs of my ancestors, others must do likewise. The rule has been established, so let us apply it.

"And the mandarins were forced to obey. But when their shovels hit the tomb of the minister's great-grandfather, a blood-red torrent burst forth. Horrified, the soldiers fled the fields and rushed to tell the minister. Again, the minister only grumbled, 'Woe to those who dare not respect the laws of the state.'

"The mandarins and the soldiers kowtowed before the minister. And once again, they returned to their work on the canal. The canal brought prosperity to the entire province.

"Proverbs, and popular songs celebrated the great public work. In my father's time, even in my grandfather's time, everyone knew this story."

My aunt paused for a moment and laughed. "There you have it. What do you think? How many mandarins of our own can compare with Minister Chinh?"

A murmur of approval rippled through the audience. Everyone wanted to offer his own praise or comment.

The first to speak up was the vice president. "Formidable, these ancestors were. Truly formidable."

But the other guests drowned him out:

"Now there's a mandarin who earned his name."

"That one's worthy of one of the great Chinese classics."

"Madame Tam really does have a prodigious memory. I've heard that story several times but had completely forgotten it. It dates back to the days when my father used to play chess with his grandfather and I was just knee-high. May I ask what astrological sign are you born under, Madame Tam? . . . Ah, the Boar? Well, madame, then I am two years your senior."

Aunt Tam served herself a cup of tea, sipped a mouthful thoughtfully, and then continued, "My parents weren't exactly blessed when they gave birth to me. I'd be good for nothing if it weren't for my memory. My father told us many stories, you know. But I remember the story of the mandarin Tran Binh in great detail."

"Oh, that's a wonderful old story. Please tell it, Madame Tam."

"What a pleasure this evening has been. A sumptuous meal followed by such spellbinding stories."

"This is a blessing from heaven."

The elderly guest seated at my aunt's side chuckled in contentment. "Wait just a moment, I'd like to have another good smoke before you start."

Clucks of irritation rose from the women huddled in the

corner of the room. "How rude! Why not just go home to your wife."

One of the men spoke up, trying to conciliate. "Come on now, don't be so impatient. We're not going to die waiting."

But it was all a ritual. Everyone knew that they would wait patiently while the old man took a drag on his precious water pipe. Only after he had exhaled languidly, savoring the pleasure of the moment, did Aunt Tam's voice rise again:

"When venerable Minister Chinh retired, he decided to return to his childhood home, near the township of Duyen Ha. At the same time, a lesser mandarin, Tran Binh, who came from the same township, had just been promoted to the post of governor.

"The mandarin Tran Binh decided to flaunt his new position by returning to his village in great pomp and circumstance. To escort his luxurious retinue, the mandarin ordered a whole battalion of soldiers to shade his palanquin with huge parasols. The soldiers formed a huge, noisy procession, beating their drums and rattling their swords in the wind.

"But when Tran Binh's soldiers marched into the mandarin's hometown, they came upon a strange sight: In the middle of the road, two porters were carrying a man on a simple hammock, with only a rush mat to protect him from the sun. Incredible as it may seem, it was none other than the famous minister Chinh. Following the ancient moral code of simplicity and discretion, the elderly minister was making his way home to retirement on a simple hammock.

"But Tran Binh's scout took them for commoners and shouted at the porters, exasperated, 'Make way. Quickly now!' Still the two porters forged ahead, oblivious. Furious, the soldier brandished his whip. 'It's an order, understand? Make way for His Excellency!' With a flick of his whip, the soldier thrashed the rush mat to pieces, and it fell away to reveal the elderly minister, who hid his face discreetly behind a silk fan.

"Stunned, the scout whispered to Minister Tran Binh,

'Excellency, this man in the hammock: It's the famous minister Chinh!' Tran Binh blanched and gestured to his soldiers to retreat and sheathe their swords. Humiliated, he prostrated himself at the minister's feet. But the minister's porters passed by without stopping.

"Legend has it that Tran Binh, his vanity wounded, tried to present his apologies to Minister Chinh, begging his pardon for the crime of contempt for authority. Minister Chinh ordered a beating, but at the third blow, his eldest son begged for Tran Binh's release.

"I should mention that this same son had passed the civil-service examination and was eligible to become a mandarin. He was an honest, pious man, and as he was, of course, the son of Minister Chinh, the king had invited him to take up an important post. But Minister Chinh had insisted he decline the post, explaining to his wife, 'Our son is honest and hard-working, but he's a simpleton. We can't possibly entrust him with political power. It would be a disaster for the people.' His wife agreed. The son, of course, obeyed his parents' wishes and stayed in the village, leaving behind any aspirations to glory and power.

"And there are more stories about this mandarin Tran Binh. My father told me many of them. It's been a long time, and I can't remember half of the mandarin's crimes, but the story of his misadventure with the blind singers, why I remember that one as if I'd heard it yesterday. . . ."

My aunt passed and poured herself another cup of tea. The guests watched her thin, ravaged face, fascinated. They waited in religious silence. She looked at no one, and her voice rose again:

"Tran Binh's father was blind. And Tran Binh's only son as well. So Tran Binh posted an announcement in the imperial court which read, 'Generous reward to cure Excellency's father and son.' Six months passed. Finally, a young man from the southern citadel presented himself and proposed a cure.

No one had ever heard of him, but he was talented and had mastered medicine, geography, and palmistry.

"Lo and behold, when taken in twenty doses, his prescriptions actually had a curative effect. Tran Binh's father said, 'I see two Tran Binhs.' The son's vision also improved. As a proof of the treatment's effect, when Tran Binh entered a dark room carrying a candle, his son exclaimed, 'I see two Papa Binhs and two candles.' The mandarin smiled to himself and left the room. The next morning, he summoned the doctor and, after rewarding him with a few coins, asked him to continue the treatment.

"Suspecting nothing, the doctor accepted the money and left for the southern citadel to buy more medication. It was then that he discovered the hoax: The money was counterfeit. He returned to tell the mandarin. But when he did, Tran Binh let out a low, cold guffaw. 'What are you saying? That I, a mandarin in the service of the state, would deal in false currency?' Then he left for his chambers, his hands clasped behind his back.

"The doctor was astounded. He began to reflect on his predicament. Suddenly, he realized that Tran Binh had indeed intended to cheat him of his reward. Since he stood virtually accused of being a counterfeiter, the young doctor had visions of torture and imprisonment. The next morning, he rose before dawn, packed his bags, and waited at the back gate. He melted into a crowd of farmers on their way to the fields, then broke away and headed toward the market, where he knew a family of blind singers who lived in a straw lean-to built for travelers. There was an old man, a couple, and a seven-year-old child. They were all blind and earned just enough money for food by singing. Dawn was breaking, and the family sat around a fire, sharing a potato stew. The doctor greeted them: 'Listen to me carefully, His Excellency the mandarin has commissioned me to summon you to his court. He will entertain very important guests at a huge party today and has requested that you sing for them.

"The elderly blind man trembled with joy. 'What a blessing! Can this be true?' The entire family rushed over to thank the doctor before he departed.

"The blind singers rehearsed their songs and then hobbled toward the mandarin's residence. But soldiers barred their way. The blind singers protested and scuffled with them. Awakened by the racket, Tran Binh demanded an explanation and was told that a group of blind singers waiting outside the gate claimed to have been invited for a dawn ceremony His Excellency was organizing for the town dignitaries. As for what had become of the doctor, Tran Binh was told that he had fled. Tran Binh suddenly saw the humiliating farce he had been subjected to and ordered the doctor's arrest. But the doctor hadn't left a trace. And the poor blind singers, well, they were given a good drubbing and sent away. The doctor from the southern citadel had disappeared, but his curse took hold.

"Deprived of his treatment, Tran Binh's father and son sank back into darkness. Seven years later, the mandarin himself went blind, and though he couldn't even see to walk without a guide, he somehow still managed to play his card games. This dynasty of blind men became a laughingstock for the people. . . ."

"My father used to say that Tran Binh's only real passion was money, that of all the mandarins this country ever had, none surpassed him for his lust for it. Like others of his generation, my father saw Tran Binh's blindness as a sign of heaven's wrath. Anyway, a verse which later became legendary compared him to Pham Thu, an upright mandarin of times past. It went like this:

"With Pham Thu at the helm,
    a man's loincloth was safe.
"But with Tran Binh at the helm,
    even a man's balls will lose their
    hairs."

All eyes in the room were riveted on the lips of my aunt. She had barely finished reciting the second verse when the older men started to hoot and guffaw, slapping their thighs in amusement. The women giggled and clucked in appreciation; but some of them, unable to grasp the classical literary language, just stared about in bewilderment. One of the most brazen asked, "Hey, what are you all laughing about?"

Everyone had a comment. The brazen woman repeated her question: "What does this verse mean? Won't you explain it to us?"

The elderly man near the water pipe snickered, baring a set of blackened, rotting teeth. "Open your ears, woman. The first verse means, under the rule of Pham Thu, the people kept their shirts. The second: Tran Binh had hardly come to power when even your muffs lost their fur."

"Heaven have mercy!" Wild peals of laughter rose in wave after wave from the women, who shrieked and punched each other playfully. Some of them doubled over in tears, shaking with mirth. "You dirty old man."

"Dirty old women yourself! I'm just explaining to you, making up for your lack of education. You should thank me instead of insulting me."

The men were first to see the light. At first they whispered and caught each other's eyes furtively. But then their twinkling eyes and broad grins said it all.

I shot a glance at the corner of the room: The woman with the scar was still there, invisible among the crowd of guests. Her eyes smoldered, bottomless, haunting. I would never forget them.

Vice President Duong laughed along with everyone, his lips stretched into a forced grin that exposed his tiny teeth. His rosy cheeks had gone pale, almost livid. Then, as if he couldn't stand another minute of their laughter, he glanced at his watch and asked in a loud voice, "Now then, Madame Tam, didn't you have some sweets to offer us?"

Aunt Tam, smiling as always: "With pleasure, Mr. Vice

President. What do you fancy you'd like to have?"

He laughed hollowly. "I was just joking, of course. After a meal like that, you won't find space for a swallow's nest in our stomachs. I must be going now."

"But didn't you have something to ask me?"

He avoided the eyes of the other guests. "Some other time."

My aunt smiled encouragingly. "Why wait for another occasion? Let's settle the problem right away." The vice president bowed his head, hesitating for a minute. "I just married off my eldest daughter . . . and . . . well, everyone knows your talent for making noodles . . . and you have that wonderful machine. I wondered if you wouldn't mind teaching her."

"With pleasure. I'll teach Mr. Vice President's daughter and anyone else for that matter. But you should bear in mind that this noodle trade, though it may sound simple, is in fact even more backbreaking than working in the rice paddies. As I recall, your daughter isn't used to getting her hands dirty. During the collectivization campaign, wasn't she the one who worked in the artistic section of the Propaganda Department, and then went off to study in town? And then, when we finally got our private plots, wasn't she living off your salary?"

The vice president flushed crimson. All he could do was nod and bob his head submissively. "Yes, yes, but this time my decision is irreversible. She will live on her own and by the fruit of her own labors . . . and nothing else." He swallowed and looked at his watch again. "My, it's already ten o'clock. I must be going. I have a meeting. Good night, everyone."

Here and there a few of the guests muttered a farewell. He swaggered his squat little body through the crowd toward the door. The courtyard was lit by the beam of a battery-driven lamp. You could hear his footsteps growing fainter as he neared the street. Aunt Tam called out from the house,

"Would someone please open the gate for Mr. Vice President?"

"Coming," yelled back Madame Dua.

A dog barked, and its yapping subsided in the distance. Suddenly, the room exploded with laughter and sarcastic comments from the guests:

"The mud on his face tonight, why, he'll carry that to the grave. Like they say, if you ask for a bit of wind, you get a tempest."

"What are you saying? This village has seen nothing *but* storms!"

"Hey, how would you describe the scene tonight?"

"You're full of hot air. You think a few words put everything in order? Have no illusions about this man. He's capable of plotting against someone because of an evening like this. And he's got the power and the means to do it too. Just you wait—Madame Hai hasn't a prayer of holding onto that plot of hers."

"She's lodged a complaint with the township bureau. But these days, that's like robbing someone in broad daylight. . . ."

"Would you like to bet on it?"

"Why not? What are the stakes?"

"Oh, not much. How about a few pieces of pork and three bottles of rice wine? Careful though, I want the real stuff, understand?"

"Let's all thank our hostess. She's entertained both our stomachs and our souls. We should be going now, so she can put the house back in order."

After the guests retired, Aunt Tam carried the cooks' baskets to the kitchen. She piled each of the hampers full of gifts: one plate of sticky rice flavored with rose-apple juice, one slice of the thin pâté, one slab of the rolled pâté, two pounds of cooked meat, a few bananas. She wrapped each plate meticulously in a banana leaf and packed them herself in the hampers. When the women left, laden down with their heaping baskets, it looked as if they had just returned from a festival day at the local pagoda.

The woman with the scarred cheek turned to my aunt. "Thank you, Sister Tam."

"It's only natural. Who doesn't have a heart? Half the village is outraged by Madame Hai's suffering. Go on now, you take that food home to your children."

My aunt saw the cooks out to the gate. Her help had cleared off the remains of the meal, and they were relaxing now, each savoring a portion of sticky rice and meat. Aunt Tam chatted with them quietly, inquiring about each one's troubles, their families, their news. I watched her birdlike silhouette, the slight shoulders, her flat body floating in her brown *ao dai*. She looked like a little girl.

The last guest finally left. When she latched the door, it was after midnight. The veranda was bathed in fog. She sighed and sat down next to me on one of the steps.

"Tired?"

"You're the one who should be tired. I didn't lift a finger."

She laughed softly. "That's the way it should be. I'm used to it." She squeezed my hand. I felt her bony, gnarled hand next to mine, the roughness of her skin, the warmth of her body. We stayed that way for several minutes, silent, motionless watching as the moon slipped out from behind the shadow of the orange grove, a disk of green jade above the trees.

The train braked, as if to grind to a halt, and then rolled forward again, throwing me and my traveling companion forward in our seats. It finally came to a stop at another station, bathed in neon light, almost deserted. A few passengers slowly boarded the train. They were carrying small bags no larger than makeup kits.

The station was small, but solidly built, with huge blocks

of stone piled about, and rows of lampposts. I had traveled this line many times, but I could never remember the names of the stations, so long, so cacophonic that they seemed to jar with the simplicity of these people. But I will never forget the location and architecture of each station. This one was the ugliest. I don't know why, but each time I stopped here I felt suffocated. These vulgar, anarchic forms seemed threatening, like some omen of future trouble.

The train idled in the station for a long time, undoubtedly conforming to some ironclad rule. Just to kill time, I fished out a handful of butterscotch candies from my pocket and offered some to my traveling companion. He laughed. "My teeth are already rotten, now you offer me candy."

I fidgeted with my candies, waiting for the departure. The train finally started up. One by one the cement blocks disappeared behind us, then the lampposts shaped like upside-down pears, the tubs of flowers, and finally the brambles that lined the platform.

"Only three stations left," said the man, consulting his schedule. "We'll be in Moscow in an hour and forty minutes. Got someone coming to meet you at the station?"

"I dunno. Maybe."

He shrugged. "You poor thing. So no one's coming to meet you?"

I just smiled in reply. He looked at me, skeptical, his eyes narrowing into slits as he tapped his foot. The door opened, and two men entered. One of them was huge and bearlike, with a mop of blond hair. The other was dark, with a bushy black mustache that matched his hair and eyebrows. They looked arrogant. The cabin suddenly stank of vodka. The young men didn't even look at my traveling companion; their eyes darted in my direction:

"Ah," said the darker of the two, leaning over me.

"Have any pre-washed jeans? I'll buy 'em."

"No," I said, shaking my head.

"Pre-washed jeans, even stained ones, I'll buy 'em," he said, as if he hadn't heard me.

"No, I don't have any."

Now, the blond one leaned over me. "Come on, I'll give you one hundred and thirty rubles. They'd give you less in Moscow. At the most, one hundred and fifteen rubles."

"I told you, I don't have any."

The dark one frowned, his mustache twitching. "We're not robbers. We'll pay you. . . . Look." He reeked of alcohol.

I felt faint, and my heart started to pound. "I told you, I don't have any. Are you crazy or what?"

"You don't want to sell us any, is that it?"

His brown eyes glistened with rage. He stuffed his wad of bills back in his pocket and leaned over me, blocking my traveling companion.

"You don't want to sell, is that it? Who would sell this stuff besides you Vietnamese? The last time a girl like you sold me a black market T-shirt, my sister wore it once and it started to fray. On Arbaat Street, only Gypsies and Vietnamese, like you, deal in this stuff. . . ."

My eyes blurred with tears. The man with the silver-capped teeth jumped to his feet. I couldn't make out his gestures, but he must have grabbed the dark one by the collar, because I heard him yell, "Get out of here. Now. Or I'll throw you out."

His voice hammered in my ears, but through my tears he was just a blurry silhouette. I buried myself in Madame Vera's shawl, sobbing helplessly. My traveling companion tapped me gently, awkwardly, on the shoulder, to console me. He crossed his arms and sat in silence, the resigned attitude of someone who had seen his share of life.

I'll never understand why I cried like that. It was the first time I ever allowed myself to cry in front of a stranger. He lit a cigarette. I scrunched up in a corner of the compartment, watching the lampposts outside fly past me like fireflies.

*　　　*　　　*

None of Uncle Chinh's orders shocked me anymore. I felt as if I had seen it all before. In fact, he had begun to direct my life a year earlier, when Madame Vera brought me the first telegram:

COME TO MOSCOW IMMEDIATELY.
HOTEL ROSSIYA. ROOM 607.

All I had to read was "Moscow" to know it was from him. My mother had written me three months earlier to tell me he was in Russia. I even took the same train to Moscow and arrived at the crack of dawn. As I remember, it wasn't snowing yet, but the leaves had turned and they swirled around the passengers, spiraling into the air. I was underdressed, and my teeth chattered as I ran toward a subway station. The streets were deserted. It was early, just before offices opened, and only a few policemen milled around the intersections. I ran, dreaming, impossibly, of hot, sugared tea. Everything was closed, even the state-run collective restaurants and the cheap "buffets." I threw a five-ruble coin into a machine and pushed through a turnstile into the subway station. Once inside the subway car, I was overwhelmed by the heat. I threw myself down on an empty seat, panting. My skin relaxed in the heat. I felt calm again. My head propped against the back of the chair, my eyes closed, I listened to the brakes screech into each station. A few solitary passengers got on, but the car was almost empty. I wasn't lonely, though. I was looking forward to this family reunion, to news of my mother, of my country.

The subway conductor bellowed out the name of each station. That was how I knew to get off. The subway lurched to a halt, and I stepped onto the platform, jumping in place and stamping my feet to keep warm.

The subway exit wasn't very far from Uncle Chinh's hotel. I crossed a garden of graceful willows and plane trees. The grass was yellowed, and the lawn had a sooty cast. A few scruffy pigeons dragged their tails along the cobblestones looking for food. The water in the canal next to the garden stood in a serene, leaden shadow. A man ambled down the edge of the canal, a tall silhouette, his hands in his pockets. He was whistling an old tune, and I followed him, listening dreamily to the song.

I had time to kill. At this hour, the hotel guard would never open the door for me. When the singing man reached the front of the hotel, he raised his head as if to search for a window.

I waited a half hour for them to open the doors. My uncle was waiting for me to arrive in a room on the ground floor. A young man waited beside him, an interpreter for the Vietnamese Embassy. The interpreter had pleaded with the guard for so long that I was permitted to go upstairs. In an exclusive hotel like this, young Vietnamese like myself would usually be taken for street hawkers and shown the door. My uncle lived on the sixth floor on a corridor covered with dark wall-to-wall carpeting. Everyone was asleep, but my uncle spoke to me in a booming voice.

"It's a good thing you came. Otherwise, we would have had to wait all day in that lobby. Thanks, I'll call for you when I need you."

"Careful, Uncle," I whispered. "We're not at home here."

"Oh, right." He shook the interpreter's hand and said good-bye. I saw the young Vietnamese interpreter smile maliciously before disappearing into his room. He lived in the east wing, while my uncle had been assigned to the west.

We walked down the long corridors and crossed a common room. Two young women were knitting. My uncle nudged me and whispered, "Try and sell them a few shirts." I glared at him. He stopped in front of the door to his room.

"Please come in, Niece." Then he locked the door conscientiously behind him.

"You live in a room all by yourself?"

"Yes, my rank has certain privileges."

After reflecting for a moment, he added, "It's more practical too." He glanced out the window and down into the street. Outside, rooftops were just emerging from the milky haze of dawn. He gave another look around.

Reassured, he said, "Give me a hand unwrapping some of these imported goods." He knelt down and clicked open my suitcase. "My, your aunt prepared everything to perfection." He started to unwrap one of the packages. Cadres in my country lived for these moments, for their luxury goods. They were good at this sordid secondhand trade in scarce imports. Some even lived off it. My uncle was no exception. All he cared about was the contents of my suitcase.

"Wait just a moment, Uncle."

He fretted, "But I've got a meeting later. I've got so many things to do."

"We have time. People don't get up so early here."

He seemed a bit worried. "But the interpreter might come at any minute!"

"Don't worry. He doesn't need to come for that kind of thing. He already knows about your shady little import business," I snapped at him.

"Hang, what are you saying?" He had gone white.

"The truth," I replied.

He clenched his jaw. "Bastards."

I said nothing. He ran to the window and flung open the curtains. Who was he looking for in the dawn, over the rooftops of the city? Who could be watching us? He just stood there, shoulders hunched over, perched on the palms of his hands, breathing in deep jerks.

After a moment, he turned to me, his voice softer now. "Come . . . you shouldn't have spoken like that."

I didn't answer.

"Hang, I don't want to depend on help from people outside the family. They could do me in, denounce me, or spread
rumors. . . . Help me."

I felt tired. A deep tiredness. A sharp pain gnawed at my
joints. The muscles in my back tightened, tense with cold and
hunger. Was this shame I felt? The urge to cry? No. I didn't
have any more tears.

I looked at my uncle and spoke softly. "You should have
told me about the family. You could have given me some
news of my mother. You could have made me a cup of tea.
I came thousands of miles to see you."

Stupefied, he stammered a few unintelligible sounds,
made a few awkward gestures, and then moved toward the
refrigerator and opened it: There were piles of little two-coin
rolls, the kind you find in the cheap stand-up cafeterias.

"Thanks anyway, Uncle," I said, getting up. "Please,
open the door for me." I went out, walked down the corridor,
and crossed the common room. The two matrons were still
there, engrossed in their knitting, but I asked them the way
to the cafeteria. At the cafeteria, a few beefy men were devouring slices of ham and cheese. At another table, at the
back of the room, a tall, handsome couple, probably tourists
from some Nordic country, were looking at a map. I bought
a quarter of a chicken, an omelet, and a strawberry tart. The
cold and the hunger subsided. I headed back with a few pieces
of fruit.

At Uncle Chinh's room, a group of men were holding a
meeting. It was his propaganda delegation from Hanoi. The
interpreter was seated by the window, gazing absently into
the street. The others listened, scratching themselves, picking
at pimples on their faces. They all seemed on edge, impatient.
They were probably busy thinking of the goods they had
smuggled in and had to sell off, or those that they needed to
acquire.

Uncle Chinh was hectoring them in a loud voice:

"Comrades, you must behave in an absolutely exemplary

manner while you are in this brother country. Each one of you must show you are capable of perfect organization and discipline.''

I walked out and slumped down to wait in an old, red fake velvet armchair in the foyer. The tawdriness, the humiliation, of all this. I wasn't cold or hungry anymore. This felt more like shame, like a torn wound.

It wasn't just the bitterness or the tears anymore. It was this slow torture, this bottomless sadness. And something else, unutterable: I could see mother, at that moment, tender, smiling. My mother, so close and yet so strange to me.

Chapter *TEN*

IN SPITE OF EVERYTHING SHE STOOD FOR, EVERYTHING I was trying to escape, she was still my mother. And in spite of it all, I loved her. After the banquet at Aunt Tam's, I had left the village, my aunt, and everyone there with a certain nostalgia. When I finally returned to our house in Hanoi, the first time since my mother had kicked me out, I found her combing out her hair.

"Did you miss me?" I asked.

She stared up at me, blinking with emotion. But only for an instant, then she spoke to me in her indifferent voice. "Of course. You're the one who never thinks about anyone else. You must have had some good times."

I hugged her and laughed. "It's true, I didn't think much about anyone . . . except you. I missed you." Then, softly: "No one can replace a mother."

She lowered her head. Perhaps this was the silence of contentment. That evening, she made me a lotus-seed pudding. At night, she slept in my arms.

I had three more days. Then university would start, and this affection would come to an end. While my old friends had drifted off, I had begun to make others. My new university classmates came by the house. New clothes, new books. We argued and calculated endlessly: My education would all be expensive, and here our mothers even worried about the price of a pair of clogs. One of my friends had to go work for a *pho* soup vendor so she could buy a suit and a pair of shoes. She had spent the summer washing dishes, lugging buckets of water.

I was one of the privileged ones. Aunt Tam had given me fabric coupons for everything: khaki, wool, nylon, colored poplin, synthetic fibers mixed with silk. It was enough to clothe me for four years. But my mother insisted on buying me a coupon for a special eggplant-colored cloth with white polka dots that was imported from Japan. She bought it herself on Cotton Tree Street and had a shirt made from it for me in a well-known dress shop.

"Neighbor Loan says this Danish-style shirt is very, very fashionable these days."

"You're so fashion-conscious. I have trouble keeping up with you," I said, giving her a little hug. She laughed, pleased for once. But the shirt was ridiculous with its dots, bows, and garish clasps. I looked as if I had disguised myself as a singer with some Latin American band.

My mother was beside herself. "It's so modern." She had probably just learned this word from her customers, the people who came to her to buy dried bamboo shoots, vermicelli, dried beans, and sugar. When I wore it, my first day of college, the students from the higher grades stared at me, amused: "Who created this little marvel for you?" I said nothing while they exploded in a fit of giggles. I kept wearing that ridiculous shirt just to see my mother smile.

*   *   *

When autumn came, the rain pattered down monotonously on our sheet-metal roof. We were happy like this. At night I watched my mother knit; she was making me a canary-yellow wool jacket for Tet. I buried my head in my books. Life rolled along, softly, peacefully. From the street, from time to time, the sound of the cripple's singing drifted to us:

"Hail autumn with its procession of dead leaves."

But I no longer felt the stab of sadness, the despair that had weighed me down as a child. All I heard now in this song was a vague pity in the middle of the chaos of life, a call for tenderness, protection, the desire to reach out for comfort.

One Sunday, my mother invited me to come with her to Uncle Chinh's. To make her happy, I went along, even after years of absence. Residence K had aged, and the main driveway was now scarred with bumps and potholes. People had tried to repair it with all sorts of materials, as they would have mended an old shirt with rags. The walls, faded dirty gray by rain and wind, were covered with obscene graffiti, and the air was stagnant and oppressively humid. There was something suffocating about that place, with its water pipes, cigarettes, old gasoline fires, burned sawdust, and the stench of the garbage that lay around the houses. Music blared out of the houses into an unspeakable mix, as rock tunes and love songs competed with prewar choruses and theater music. Teenagers, cigarettes dangling from .their mouths, hung about on the stoops and sidewalks, jeering at people as they passed by.

Everything had changed. The guard post at the entrance had disappeared. Someone had torn down the wooden walls; a bamboo pole, the remaining barrier, pointed pathetically toward the sky.

My uncle and aunt were busy plucking a duck when we

arrived. My aunt washed her hands and waddled toward us, smiling, attentive. The boys had grown and, thanks to my mother's gifts of food, were even a bit chubby. "Greet your aunt, children . . . and your cousin Hang."

This time, they didn't wait for their father's prompting to shout a greeting to us. My aunt looked me over. "My, you're filling out now."

Aunt Chinh had gained a bit of weight herself. She was wearing a blue satin suit embroidered with rose vines and a shirt trimmed with copious amounts of lace. She bustled about energetically, preparing tea for us. I noticed the bulge of fat on her thighs and rump as she hurried over to serve us; and I noticed her eyes, which darted furtively in the direction of the hamper of food my mother had set on the floor. Still, I found her more likable now than in the days when she used to sit at her desk, picking her teeth and reading Lenin.

Since our last meeting, I had heard some gossip about her through a friend whose parents worked at the university. My friend's parents had been recruited to teach at the Communist Youth League School for Young Cadres. They were responsible to my aunt Chinh, since she was a senior party member, and they had slaved under her for eight years. They were educated, proud people and couldn't stand the ignorance of their superior. Aunt Chinh was extremely neurotic and often lost her temper for no reason. But how could it have been otherwise? She had only completed two short remedial courses designed "for workers and peasants," and yet she was now the dean of the entire Philosophy Department.

"Have a sip, my niece. And you too, Sister."

She smiled and tapped me on the shoulder, pointing a finger at the cup of tea. When she smiled, her pockmarked face seemed less threatening, so I asked her, "You used to read the *Selected Works of Lenin*. They were brand-new, as I remember. Where are they now?"

"In the chest. I've put them away."

She beamed, proud of her brand-new chest, which still

gave off a strong varnish smell. "If you need them, I'll lend them to you. I've finished my study of Marxism-Leninism. Now I'm analyzing official documents." She interrupted herself suddenly, and said in a different voice, "Let me do that, Sister, please let me." She rushed over to take the packet of sugar out of my mother's hands. The packet had burst, and the sugar had almost spilled out. Aunt Chinh laughed. "We almost spilled that one."

She had forgotten Marx, Lenin, and the official documents, and was now absorbed by a hamper of groceries. She helped my mother pour the sugar into the huge, long-necked glass canisters that people usually used to hold snake liqueur for men or to marinate apricots and plums for women and children. Then she sliced up the meat and the pâtés: one chunk for the cupboard, one for the casserole, one for the platter. Her ruddy cheeks were glistening with sweat. "Look how you spoil the boys. Why, there's enough sugar to last them till the fall. Chinh, have you finished? Try not to spoil that duck's blood custard. It's Sister Que's favorite dish."

She laughed, her eyes puffy with pleasure. My mother laughed too, a sincere, natural laugh. She now had her place in the Do family. She didn't feel abandoned or disdained anymore. This was her mission: to gather, coin by coin, the money necessary to serve the needs of her brother.

The old roof on our hovel still rotted in the same patchy state. The summer seared down on it, numbing our brains with the odor of tar. In autumn, when the rain drummed down relentlessly on the sheet metal, tiny rust holes started to appear. The past still stirred under all those ashes: this jumble of self-sacrifice, duties, generosity and blind obedience. Women like my mother were not terribly farsighted. They lived in the certainties of the moment.

Uncle Chinh raised his voice. "Hang, my niece. Give me a hand serving duck's blood custard."

I obeyed, taking the plate of blood custard from him and putting it down on the tray. The dish looked good: The blood had congealed into a thick gelatin; there wasn't a trace of liquid at the rim; and the surface was sprinkled with fine strips of duck liver, crushed garlic, and peanuts grilled to a perfect golden brown. "Bring those fresh herbs that go with it too," he barked.

I brought the herb platter. Nothing was missing: mint leaves, green onions, cilantro, Vietnamese parsley. "Help yourself to the condiments: Spice it to your own taste," said my uncle, rubbing his hands. "When I was with the Viet Bac underground, the section chief took me under his wing just because of my talent for preparing curdled duck's blood custard."

Aunt Chinh added her own praise. "Nothing's changed. His chief still invites him to make tortoise soup and this blood custard."

"Where's that bottle of liqueur?"

"It's in the chest, in the very back, to the left."

Uncle Chinh opened the chest and fished out a bottle of snake and orange-peel liqueur. The meal was served, as usual, with the windows closed and the blinds drawn. We could eat now. There was steamed duck, duck in ginger sauce, the blood custard, and my mother's pâtés.

Uncle Chinh poured the liqueur: "A toast. To the family!"

Everyone raised their glasses. I raised my own, clinking it with everyone present.

"Eat your fill," my uncle urged us.

This happiness lasted a year. The following year, Uncle Chinh came down with diabetes. A suspicious illness given those miserable times, when each grain of rice was weighed like a pearl, and even common spices seemed as expensive as cinnamon to us. He could only eat very lean meat, without the slightest trace of fat. As a second-rank cadre, he earned a pittance. Although there was prestige in being a Communist official, state salaries were barely enough to live on.

When I went to visit him in the hospital, he sat squatting on his bed, his arms gathered around his knees. His eyes were sunk deep in their sockets, and with that sallow, yellowy skin, he looked like a small bird.

"Where's your mother?" he asked me, watching the door greedily.

"She's gone to try and buy some oranges," I replied.

"Oranges? Why? I'm forbidden to eat fruit."

"My mother thought you could eat fruit."

"Nothing. Nothing," he whined. "The doctor has forbidden everything."

My mother entered and approached her brother's bedside. "You're so pale."

"I'm not dead yet. Stop this crap."

It was the first time I'd heard him swear and speak without the officious tone he liked to use with us. His hands shook, and his eyes darted about, gleaming strangely: He was afraid. My mother bit her lip and looked at him. "What did the doctor say?"

He raised his head to stare at the wall and spoke as if to himself. "I have to avoid everything, even fruit. And I have to take imported American medicine. . . ."

My mother lowered her head. Was she perhaps looking at her flattened, shredded old pair of sandals? After a silence, she sighed and said, "Don't worry. Take care of yourself. I'll find the medication for you." She started to arrange the fruit, the food, and the tonics on his bedside table. After she asked Uncle Chinh's roommates to look after him, she said goodbye to everyone and took me home. On the way back, we didn't speak. Once we arrived at the house, she put away her sack and quoted another one of her proverbs, "Well, like there's no river without a bend, there's no life without its unhappiness. There's no one left in our family. I'm all he's got, you understand?"

I paused for a moment, but in the end, I said, "Do what you have to. Don't worry about me."

Our meals started to shrink by the day. The few slices of roast pork or fried fish disappeared and were replaced by bean curd marinated in tomatoes or pan-fried silkworms. In the end, even these were replaced by small fried dishes marinated with pieces of star fruit, or minuscule, salt-dried sea shrimp. The vegetables went next: cauliflower, green beans, green Chinese cabbage, then cucumbers, each vanishing in turn. Most days, all we ate were cheap greens. In the end, just a bit of minced banana stalk.

"It's really fresh, good for your health. This is a very nourishing vegetable. Wonderful for skin problems."

That was how my mother would justify herself each time she brought home a vegetable that could turn my stomach just looking at it. That winter, Uncle Chinh's illness went from bad to worse. The doses of medicine doubled overnight, and the doctor's demand for "special food supplements" as well. My mother's face was hollow and pinched. It didn't take me long to figure out that she skipped her noon meals while I ate mine at school. Her cheekbones stuck out grotesquely, and the skin on her forehead creased with worry. The freckles on her nostrils and sallow cheeks seemed to expand into huge blotches across her face. She had become dull, ugly.

All we ate now was a bit of pickled white cabbage fried in a spoonful of fat. I'll never forget that dish. We cut the cabbage into tiny cylinders the size of a piece of cane sugar and then cooked it with very salty black beans. To give it taste and create the illusion that we were eating a bit of meat or marinated fish, we seasoned it with a bit of grease. That winter, I ate nothing else. The taste of it will probably follow me to my grave.

And I'll never forget those evenings, when I got out of class and pedaled through the streets, my nose clogged with dust, my stomach clinched in under my belt, rumbling from hunger. Passing the houses of our neighbors, Madame Mieu, Madame Lan, and Mr. Hop, I dreamed of a bit of meat. My knees went weak at a whiff of barbecued pork, its smell assaulting, intoxicating. Nights after my foreign-language classes, I lingered around the *pho* vendor's stall, pretending to stroll, greedily inhaling the odor of this soup. I will never forget the humiliation I felt when I looked away, swallowing my own saliva as I watched a woman sliding chunks of a barbecued pork satay onto a pile of vermicelli.

One night, when I couldn't stand it anymore, I said to my mother, "I don't even have the energy to study. Let's sell one of the rings."

"We can't. They're Aunt Tam's," my mother said, irritated.

I tried to keep calm. "She gave them to me. I need to survive and study before I can wear any ring."

"No," she snapped.

"Mother, I'm hungry," I pleaded, biting back my tears.

She went white and glowered at me. Suddenly, she jumped up, screaming like a madwoman, "No! Shut up! I said NO."

She had never looked so terrifying, never spoken to me like this, with such violence. I said nothing and ran out into the courtyard. I wasn't hungry anymore: The desire for food had been knocked out of me. I waited for her to calm down and tiptoed back into the house to sleep.

I woke up about two in the morning to a freezing cold. The room suddenly seemed immense, and I felt terribly alone. I glanced over at my mother's bed: It was empty, the covers still rolled into a tight ball at the head of the bed. I heard muffled sobbing and recognized the voice, but I sat motionless in the darkness until my eyes got used to the dark. I got up and opened the door soundlessly, slipping out into the courtyard. My mother was in the kitchen, crouched on the floor, her head between her hands. Through the open door, I saw her shoulders shuddering in jerks as she tried to choke back her sobs. From time to time, a brief, rebellious moan escaped her. I stood there for a long time, transfixed. Something inside me yearned to console her, and something else, even stronger, held me back. I saw her and her anger of the previous evening stripped of their brutality. I sensed a reason, a hidden meaning behind my apprehension. It was a force I didn't understand, and it terrified me. I stood there, paralyzed.

Suddenly, I felt the clamminess of the fog in my hair and shivered. I walked back to the house, stretched out on the bed, and listened anxiously for her to return. But she didn't. The night dragged on. From time to time, a sob echoed in my ears like a wave in the distance.

The next morning, the backfire of a motorcycle jolted me awake. The door was open. In the courtyard, a man with a sunburned face straddling a Honda 67. He still wore the same green sunglasses. A smirk flitted at the corners of his mouth.

"Sleeping in? No country boy will marry you," he said, spying me in the doorway. Aunt Tam got down from behind him. I threw a wool jacket over my shoulders and hurried toward her.

She was pale and looked chilled, but she smiled at me. "My dearest niece."

Suddenly, instead of hugging me, she pushed me away from her. "Why Hang, what's happened to you?"

I laughed. "Nothing at all."

In a practiced gesture, she slipped her hands under my vest, pinching my ribs. "Then just how is it that you've become a skeleton?" Her voice was tender, but oddly frantic. I didn't have time to reply. My mother appeared in the doorway, bleary-eyed and puffy, her sullen face anxious and scared. "Did you just arrive? Come on in, Sister."

She turned toward the man on the motorcycle. "Do come

in for a moment." She had a kettle in her hand and had probably just prepared the rice, since I could see steam still curling from the spout. The man declined, nodding his head graciously, and turned to Aunt Tam. "What time should I be here to pick you up?"

"In a half hour. You can go. We've got things to discuss."

The man lifted his glasses off his nose with a callused finger and nodded again to my mother. "Thanks for the invitation. Next time."

That said, he revved up the motorcycle and guided it toward the street. I watched his Mongol-style fur cap with its funny earflaps. The noise of the motorcycle echoed through the tiny courtyard, through the streets, shattering the silence of the neighborhood. By that hour, all the street vendors had packed up and left. All you could hear was the drip-drip from the public fountain.

Aunt Tam took me by the hand, clutching her hamper in the other. My mother, her eyes bloodshot and ringed with huge circles, followed us with her kettle. As she filled the thermos bottle, she called to me, "Bring me that sachet of tea, Hang."

"Where, Mother?"

"Get it from my hamper of goods for the market. I've been too busy to buy any."

I opened the hamper, fishing out a sachet of tea, the kind she used to sell to poor people throughout the year. My mother would never have served this tea before; I could feel the sharp gaze of my aunt bearing down on me, following my every gesture as I prepared it.

She waited patiently until I had finished and my mother had seated herself facing her, and then said, her voice neutral, "Hang is starving. Why haven't you told me about this?"

"I've been busy at the market."

Aunt Tam turned to me. "Why didn't you write me?"

"I asked Mother last night if we could sell a ring so we could eat, but she refused," I replied.

"What do you mean, she refused?"

"Yes, she said it was yours. That I can't just do what I like with it. Her business hasn't been going so well these last few months."

Aunt Tam started to laugh and then turned on my mother. "So you think money is more important to me than a human life? You know very well Hang's going to inherit everything after I'm gone. What use do you think she'll have for gold if she wastes away like this? To decorate her skeleton, perhaps?"

"Of course not. You gave it to her, but I thought she shouldn't sell it without your permission."

"Fine. She has my permission. Bring me the rings and the earrings as well."

"Yes," my mother replied, flushed with anger. She hesitated a moment, then disappeared into her room. We waited for what seemed like a long time. Aunt Tam paced slowly toward the family altar and picked up a photo of my father. She dusted it with her handkerchief and placed it back on the altar. She just stood there, gazing at it intently. Suddenly, I saw it, now, just how much this young man in the faded photo, the carefully parted hair, the shy smile, those finely chiseled ears, the flashing eyes, had resembled her, this tiny emaciated frame of a woman with thin, bony shoulders, sunburned skin and wrinkles that had hardened around her mouth. Perhaps this was what they call the power of blood.

"Sister." It was my mother. She had emerged from her room, deathly pale, her fists clenched tightly around something. Aunt Tam turned toward her calmly and sat down at the table. The tea must have been cold, but she took a sip and asked, "What's the matter?"

My mother, her back hunched, was still standing. She kept one fist clenched, and with the other hand, she leaned against the table stiffly. "I want to tell you that . . . that . . ."

Aunt Tam stared at my mother without speaking. Her eyes were like an interrogator's, razor sharp, icy, as if flooded with black bile. I thought my mother would crumble under the chill of this unblinking gaze. I wanted to rush to her, to support her, but something riveted me to my seat. My mother was still standing, her face ashen. She seemed to struggle violently to finish her sentence.

"The rings . . . I sent them to some friends to start up a business. . . . They promised to share the profits." My mother was lying, and I knew it.

Aunt Tam smiled. "And your cut? What are they giving you each month?"

My mother replied quickly, naturally, "Five percent."

Still smiling, Aunt Tam continued, calmly: "So the interest alone should be enough to buy a few pounds of meat every month. Why's Hang so skinny?"

Again, my mother replied instantly, "It's only been three months since I made the loan. They haven't had time to do anything. They'd have to find a reliable person to bring me the money. Besides, I asked them to capitalize the interest, so I'll get it all in six months. It'll be a respectable sum."

"Where are these people?" pursued Aunt Tam.

"Way down in Minh Hai Province near the southern-most tip. It's a kind of crossroads for people from all over; they went that far to start the business."

I was stupefied. I had never seen this side of my mother, this cleverness. Only the first lie really costs us; after that, everything flows from the same wellspring.

My aunt walked calmly toward the kitchen, returning with the tray we used to serve our daily meals. She placed it on the table and lifted off the wicker fly cover: a bit of pickled cabbage, a bit of cabbage marinated in black-bean sauce—our menu for the last few months. She smiled contemptuously. The skin of her face and hands was purplish, the color of bruises left by the blows from a bamboo cane.

"Please, sit down," said Aunt Tam.

Distraught, my mother obeyed. She kept her head bowed.

"Give me the earrings."

My mother unfurled her fist slowly and a tiny satchel made of blue silk rolled out onto the table. Aunt Tam didn't even bother to open it. She flicked it aside toward the tea with the back of her hand, as if it were some vulgar package of tobacco or a box of matches.

"Madame Que, I have always liked you. Even during our worst moments, during all the unhappiness, the injustice, I have never felt any resentment toward you." Her voice dropped to a cool monotone, like a prayer echoing in a pagoda, infinitely serene. My mother flinched as if she had felt the flick of some invisible whip. Her head drooped lower on her chest, her shoulders caving inward to form a point, as if to protect her from blows to come.

"Do you remember the day you pretended to chase those crabs in order to speak to me?" Her voice was cutting now. "When you were at the edge of the fields, and I was pretending to wash my laundry? I pitied myself, my brother, Ton, even you. We were all victims. How could I hate you? We shared the same fate."

My mother crumpled into a heap on the corner of the table. But the voice continued, cool, unrelenting.

"So many nights I stood watch in those fields. I saw my mother again, I saw Ton again, wandering, miserable. I saw your tears in that blistering summer heat, under the blazing sun. . . . I knew you had loved each other . . . That at least my brother's soul had known the taste of this sweetness. . . ."

She stopped, her gaze lost in memory, then spoke again. "I remember the harvest that year. Every morning, at three o'clock, I got up to cook a potato stew. I ate half and took the other half with me to the rice fields. I even picked for the others. By noon, I would feel tortured by hunger, but I fought it, eating only once. I never stopped picking. Then winter came, and it was unbelievably cold. People were still out tilling their little plots of land, minding their pigs, their chickens. Evenings, they could relax in peace with their families. As for me, I paddled through the fields to spend the night at my aunt's. At eleven o'clock, you could still find me at the millstone, grinding rice flour. I was only allowed to go home after midnight.

"One night, near the guard post by the eastern hamlet, some man jumped on me, pulling me down into the grass at the edge of the road. Maybe I shouldn't have resisted. Maybe I'd have a child to raise now. . . . In any case, I fought for my life. I scratched and kicked and bit the bastard. The place was deserted, so screaming wouldn't have done me any good. What's more, even if someone had heard, who would have come to help me, the daughter of some 'filthy landlord'? They probably would have called me a whore.

"So I fought him off alone. I was young and I resisted with every bone in my body. I bit the bastard's neck, and his blood gushed into my mouth, dirty, kind of salty, and warm, like chicken's blood. And he screamed and let go of me. I grabbed my straw hat and ran off spitting his blood, the salty, nauseating taste of it sticking to the roof of my mouth. When I finally made it home, the rooster had already started crowing the first watch. I dived into the pond to wash the stinking odor of his sweat out of my clothes. By the time I got out of the water, the rooster was crowing the second watch. It was lucky I didn't catch pneumonia. I could have died."

She paused again, placing her gnarled hands on the table: They looked like ancient, tangled roots. I could see her thick, coarse nails scored with deep furrows and her shriveled skin, flecked with age spots. For a moment, she seemed lost, distracted by some faraway vision, and then she started to speak again.

"You remember the 'Rectification of Errors Campaign'? The night the mob of villagers surrounded your family house? They wanted to break down the door. They wanted to be paid in blood."

"Enough. That's enough." My mother's voice was high-pitched and supplicating now. "That's enough. Please, I beg you . . ."

She sobbed, her head slumped onto the table, her body convulsed and shaking. I moved toward her. "Don't cry, please."

My gestures seemed to float around me, hollow and weightless. My mother continued to stammer, choking on her own sobs. "I beg you . . ."

Aunt Tam stopped. Her eyes had sunken into a dull stare. It was as if light and shadow had mixed and frozen into one in these deep amber eyes that gazed out into the misty darkness. She waited for my mother to stop crying before she continued in her monotonous voice:

"In the end, everything comes to light in this world. The needle always emerges from the haystack. Do you think you can hide human actions, day in and day out, as they are revealed to others? Even from my village, I know about your life, see the price you pay. I don't reproach you. We all turn to family. After all, blood runs thick. And this love I feel for my brother, how could I deny it to others? But I want you to understand something clearly: Your brother is my family's mortal enemy. He killed my brother. I forbid you to use my money to feed him."

Aunt Tam raised herself. "From now on, you no longer have the right to honor my brother's memory."

She walked toward our altar, picked up my father's photo, and bound it up carefully in a piece of cloth. Then she unwrapped the contents of her basket and piled it on the table: pâtés, sugar, milk, cakes. Aunt Tam packed my father's photo in the empty basket. "All this is for you, my niece. My money, my sweat, and my tears are not going to go to that assassin."

I didn't dare to speak. I kept my head bowed. My mother

had stopped crying now. She hadn't raised her head once, but she had certainly heard every one of Aunt Tam's words. Just then, something like a firecracker exploded in the courtyard outside. Aunt Tam yelled out the window, "Don't stop the motor. I'm coming."

She took the blue silk packet from the table and slipped it into her pocket. "I'm keeping these earrings for you, my child. This is not the sum total of your inheritance. There are many things. But I don't want them to fall into the hands of others."

She turned her back to me and left without saying goodbye. Out in the courtyard, the man with the green sunglasses touched his hat respectfully and smiled to her. I watched as my aunt, frail and bony, mounted behind him, hugging herself to his back, like a brittle insect squashed against a rock. They left in a cloud of dust.

I went back in the house. My mother lifted her head off the table and looked at me. Her eyes were strange. Puffy and hateful. I tried to speak to her, but she didn't reply. Instead, she slung the bamboo pole she used to carry things to the market with over her shoulder and left without eating.

From that day, things between us degenerated slowly. I didn't know what to do, so I tried everything. But in the end, I was the one who yielded, who compromised. But even my little compromises couldn't bring back the respect that we had once felt for each other.

First, there was her coldness tinged with irony. At mealtimes, she would sulk and eat only the cabbage. When I tried to sneak a few morsels of the meat pâté into her bowl, she tossed them back onto the plate. "Please, I wouldn't think of letting these chopsticks touch someone else's food."

"Listen, Mother. Aunt Tam was angry. She spoke thoughtlessly. Don't be so offended."

She shook her head and let out a mirthless, bitter

chuckle. "Her money, her sweat, her tears. How dare I?"

I forced a laugh myself, trying to appease her. "Look, let's not be absurd, like children. I'm not going to eat any of this if you won't join me."

Her face was stony. Her voice, whiny and contemptuous. "Yes, yes, we should all fortify ourselves, study and succeed. Why, we're fattening the pigs at this very moment. We're just waiting for your blessing to feast with the village, the whole country. . . ."

I tried to joke with her. "Mother, I'm afraid you're the only one patient enough to wait for me to succeed."

"Oh, but that would be too great an honor: How could I be so presumptuous? I mean, compared to your aunt?" And once more, she flicked aside the pâté I had just served her.

Again, I tried to force a smile. "How can I show you I respect you? In my heart, there's only one place for you—the very highest."

"Don't try and flatter me. Put someone else on your altar."

I was nineteen years old. I couldn't stand any more of this and I exploded: "You've given me my life, Mother. But the truth is the truth. This time, you're wrong. You lied to her. I lied to you once in my life. Once. I was seven years old. Remember? You had asked me to buy three ounces of roast pork. I bought two and a half so I could keep the rest of the money. You beat me mercilessly for it. I really suffered for that, I felt so ashamed. You told me never to lie, and since then, I never have."

My mother's face was purple with rage. For a moment, her eyes seemed to swirl wildly, and she raised herself from the table, threw her chopsticks on the floor, and lashed out at me: "Get out. Get out of this house. . . . Go to your aunt."

I got up and gathered my clothes. I took out my bicycle. My mother met me outside and threw Aunt Tam's gifts into a wicker hamper attached to the bicycle's handlebars. "Go. Get out of my sight."

I pedaled toward my high school. The weather was beautiful. Winter was almost over. Already the air felt warmer, and the sky was so blue, so clear, it was eerie. People crisscrossed the streets, weaving their way through the bustle and noise. I cut through the crowd, indifferent, burdened by the weight of my family drama. I asked the high school dean to admit me to the dormitory. He put me with five roommates, including a young Tay minority woman from Lang Son. She was over-weight, chubby-cheeked, and she never stopped gabbing. She helped me put away my things; when night fell, she put on her makeup and went out.

"Don't wait for me. Put up the mosquito netting and sleep. I'll be back late," she said, winking. "My boyfriend is waiting for me at the university, you understand?"

She left in a cloud of cheap local perfume. My other roommates went out too, one by one, leaving me seated on the bed, knees clutched to my chest. I stared at the pale elec-tric lamp suspended from the ceiling; it looked like a malevo-lent orange eye glaring at me in the darkness. Outside, the wind whistled. I wasn't cold, but I couldn't stop shivering. I tried to imagine our house, the lamp above the white porce-lain vase, my bookshelves. I saw the clay pot filled with a few yellow daisies perched on our window ledge. I saw my mother, at that moment, grasping her knees to her chest in the middle of an empty house. I felt the tears trickle down my cheeks, one by one. That's the way it is. There's no dig-nity on this earth for those who live and breathe in misery. I had lost again.

My life as a boarder got off to a good start. The days passed uneventfully. From time to time, an insignificant quar-rel. But I wasn't bitter. Everything always worked out. My friend was nice. She wore her heart on her sleeve and had a sunny disposition. She did poorly at school, though, and I had to tutor her on more than one occasion. Nevertheless, she was quite sought after by the young men, who seemed to swarm around her. Some dedicated poems to her, others wrote songs for her. She numbered the poems and songs, filed them in notebooks, showed them to me once a month. I helped her answer these queries and even composed a few idiotic poems, a few sentimental melodies. Her lovesick men went crazy. In short, we got along well.

As for money, I had no worries. I had barely begun my second week in the dormitory when the man with the green sunglasses appeared again with Aunt Tam in tow. After that, she came to see me every two weeks. Money, food—I had it all in abundance.

In truth, my five roommates and the boys who lived nearby in the dormitory often secretly dipped into my stock, pilfering a bit of oil, a little sugar. Once, the boys got together in front of our door and started tapping their empty tin lunch boxes, and I had to share my casserole of salted pork.

"Hey, Hang, lend me a bowl of fish sauce, will you?"

"Oh, Hang, gimme a spoonful of lard. . . ."

"Gee, Hang, plain white rice sure is hard to swallow. . . ."

"Don't you think you should share some of that fish in brown-sugar sauce? Communism, you know, solidarity and all that."

I was better off than the other students; I didn't have to worry about food or clothes. But I missed my mother. Whatever had happened, she was still my mother. I still loved her. I pieced together tidbits of news through friends: Her business was improving; Uncle Chinh had gotten better and had gone back to work. Once, my mother had fallen ill. Uncle Chinh and his wife had come to visit her. My mother, as she had done before, invited Neighbor Vi, and the others who lived nearby, and served tea, cigarettes, and candies to introduce her brother and sister-in-law. "He's a party cadre, and she's a professor at the Communist Youth League School for Young Cadres," said Neighbor Vi's daughter, recounting my mother's pride at being able to introduce her family to the little people of the neighborhood. I was relieved and happy for her. After all, everyone needs something to be proud of.

All the same, I couldn't seem to dispel my feelings of injustice, humiliation, and loneliness. These people, of whom she was so proud, had torn my family apart. Often, as I sat on a bench in some corner of a dark, empty lecture hall, I dreamed of our leaky roof. I dreamed of the rain drumming down, of the noises and smells of my childhood, the rumors of dawn, the cries and calls, even the insults, the chorus of nagging and bickering that rose over the walls and mixed with the sounds and smells of cooking. I dreamed of the flowering creepers that scaled our tumbledown shacks and ran along the tops of the walls lined with shards of dirty glass. I dreamed of the cripple's rasping voice, crying out to us, a violent chant of hope in this swamp that was our life: I dreamed of a stick of barley sugar.

That year, I was ranked one of the best students in the class. Aunt Tam gave me two dresses made of imported muslin: one a shrimp-colored pink; one a crisp sky blue. Everyone said they made me look younger, prettier. Aunt Tam listened, lost in a dreamy silence, probably plotting how she would create heaven on earth for me. She had replaced my old Vietnamese Reunification bicycle with a new Russian Mifa. Now she wanted to buy me a Peugeot. Fortunately, the man with the sunglasses talked her out of it in time: "I'm no tightwad, but I'm against it. With all the young hoods running around these days, a luxury like that will only cause trouble for her."

She followed his advice, but insisted that I wear a gold chain around my neck: "A man who doesn't drink isn't quite a man. And a woman who doesn't like to pretty herself up a bit isn't quite a woman."

I rarely went out, or into town. I spent my free time in the library, reading, and although I was almost twenty at the time, I refused to see any men. I didn't feel like going for walks, or to the movies, or the circus. So the money piled up. I had planned, when my mother's anger subsided, to use it to repair our roof. It wasn't enough to build a new terrace, but there was at least enough for a new tile roof. But my plans fell through.

It was a spring evening. Drizzle covered the town, and the sun filtered purple through the rain, like smoke. We were in our room, eating watermelon seeds, gossiping about the marriage of the class president, who had just gotten out of the army. He was thirty years old and rather homely, but a good, honest man. Everyone respected him, and even the most arrogant boys and the laziest, cattiest girls accepted his sanctions.

The morning of the wedding, it was still raining, a dense, unrelenting drizzle, and the whole class formed a procession in the rain, splashing through the puddles in the potholes on the main road that led from the train station to his house. He lived in Vinh Phu Village, a poor region with rolling green hills. At his wedding party, he served us nougat, Hai Ha candies, and green tea, a specialty of the region. He even had watermelon seeds from Hanoi. His bride was a country girl with a square back, large, splayed feet, and rosy cheeks. We all felt quite boisterous, and so we stayed to chat until nightfall before heading back to the dormitory. The young married couple rolled up their pants and waded in the mud with us to the train station. They gave us a big sack of watermelon seeds, a packet of *che* cakes flavored with green tea, and some cakes made of potato flour and sticky rice.

We took the overnight train, chatting nonstop, jostling with a horde of fellow travelers who boarded at other stations. We fell asleep at dawn, just before we arrived at the dormitory. Still sleepy, but excited, we got our group together and

193

once again started chatting and munching watermelon seeds. For teenagers like us, love and marriage were inexhaustible topics. Suddenly, one of the girls cried out, "Alert: We're almost out of watermelon seeds." We all shouted at once:

"Refills!"

"Whose turn is it?"

"Ninh. It's Ninh's turn."

"She's already shelled out money three times."

"Hey, Dao Thi Ninh, cough up the money. Your turn to pay the corporal tax!"

"But I don't have a cent on me today. Got lucky."

Dao Thi Ninh was from Hai Phong. She was a heavy girl with sunburned skin and a hooked nose. She stood up in the middle of our group and turned the pockets of her pants and her shirt inside out. The boys turned up their noses, pretending to sneeze from her odor.

Everyone burst out laughing. Conversation flowed even without the watermelon seeds. We turned toward Ninh.

"You little leper. When it's your turn, you're dry."

"It's fate. The angel of prosperity has taken me under her protection," said Ninh, laughing and breaking into a theater dance.

A girl from Hai Hung let out a shrill laugh that rippled through our group. We were in hysterics. Some held their stomachs, and others fell onto the bed. The boys rolled over on their seats, kicking their feet in the air. The wave of giggles went from one person to the next, irrepressible. It took us about ten minutes to calm down.

Ninh turned toward me. "Hey, you little banker in peasant clothing, cough up the money."

"Okay," I said, "but you have to go get the watermelon seeds. I don't feel like it with this rain."

She rolled her eyes threateningly. "Oh, so it's like that, is it? Just because you're rich, you refuse to go?"

"Naturally. Each of us must make her contribution."

The female Hercules grabbed me by the collar, lifting me

off the ground. "Look, there's only one law here, and that's friendship, you hear? Get your raincoat and hightail it. If you want to play feudal lords and ladies, you're off the team."

Of course, she was right. I had let my privileges and Aunt Tam's money go to my head. But even if she hadn't been, no one was ever able to mollify this wild woman. I was annoyed; but I got my raincoat and went out. There was a row of food stalls at the gate to the university, and you could get everything there: bootlegged liquor, snacks, imported milk, sesame candies, or a few lousy handfuls of roast corn.

The university courtyard was muddy, and the streets around the residence were even worse. In the back alleys, a few bricks, a few yellowing tufts of grass, scattered here and there, emerged from the muck. I leapt from one brick to the next, trying not to fall into the mud. Absorbed in these gymnastics, I didn't even notice someone coming to meet me: "Hang!"

The sternness of the voice made me jump. I looked up: It was Neighbor Vi, just a few feet ahead of me, covered from head to toe with a sheet of gray nylon. She plodded through the mud, clutching her makeshift raincoat in one hand and the sandals in the other, her pants rolled up to her crotch.

"I've been looking for you since the market closed."

I studied her face, which was dripping with rain. "It's been a long time since I've been home. What's the matter, Neighbor Vi?"

Instead of replying, she just stared at me and commented absently, "You've gotten taller, Hang, but you haven't grown up yet."

Around her, puddles of mud, a few slabs of earth, a few stone paths, nowhere to shelter us. "Come with me to the gate," I said. "There are some food stands over there."

She mumbled and followed me.

We walked in silence until we reached Madame Nhu's food stall. I knew her well. She stared at me and then scurried over to show us to a bamboo rack at the back of the restaurant where we could hang our raincoats. Even the benches were covered with mud, and I asked her for a handkerchief to wipe them off.

"What would you like, Miss Hang?"

"Green tea, nice and hot, with a mung-bean cake, please."

Madame Nhu served us imported tea from Thailand and green bean cakes on a plate decorated with flowers from Hai Duong. "Please, make yourself at home. Excuse me."

After this burst of politeness, Madame Nhu leaned against the wall with her knees bent and fell asleep again. Neighbor Vi drained her cup in one long swallow; she must have been chilled to the bone.

"Why didn't you come by to see me, before you took off?" she asked me.

"My mother kicked me out. I didn't think of it."

"I was still in the house getting my goods ready for the market. If I'd known, we wouldn't be here."

She sighed. I said nothing. Best to keep quiet and wait. Loneliness had taught me this much. Neighbor Vi swallowed another cup of tea. "Your mother has really suffered for this."

"I have too."

"Yes, but a mother is always a mother."

"I still love her."

"This must be her fate."

"She was the one who kicked me out."

"Yes, I know. But she didn't want to."

"She didn't want to?"

"No, she didn't, but she had to. . . . You see, in life, sometimes, that's the way it is. You'll understand someday, when you've lived a bit more."

I lifted up the cover of the cotton tea cozy and filled Neighbor Vi's cup. She wrapped her hands around the hot cup to warm herself.

I asked her, "Have you sold all your goods?"

"Yes, when the market closed, I gave my hamper to my friends and took the bus right over here to see you."

She emptied her cup and got up. "Go find her, and find her quickly, my child."

"Where?" I asked, surprised.

"Your mother was hit by a car on the way to the market. I didn't hear about it until noon. They took her to the hospital. The doctors had to amputate the leg. She's at the Bach Mai Hospital."

What did I do at that moment? I don't know. I remember how my limbs froze up and hardened, how I collapsed on the pile of plates, bowls, cakes, and fruit. Neighbor Vi lifted me up and paid the bill. She whispered something to Madame Nhu, who grabbed her coat and ran out into the rain. She was back in a moment with a cyclo. We got in, and the cyclo driver pulled his old hat of bamboo leaves down to cover his face, his back curved from the effort he had to exert to pedal the cyclo through the mud. The road was riddled with bumps and deep potholes. I saw sparks with each bump; blades of ice seemed to slice through my spine, paralyzing my body. Neighbor Vi rocked me in her arms, hushing me softly. "That's it, cry. You'll feel better if you cry."

But I couldn't. My throat was like ice. I felt my blood thicken, my eyes blur in the darkness. The rain pounded down on us, a downpour to make heaven and earth change places. The gate to the hospital was deserted. Neighbor Vi had to plead with the guard for a long time before he let us through. Colors . . . rows of beds . . . vacant, sad faces . . . Mother.

"Mother!" The cry freed me, and tears ran down my face, feverish and salty, pouring down my cheeks and under my chin. I felt my veins thaw, the ice melting. "Mother," I whispered.

My mother turned over and held out her hand, smiling through twisted lips. Tears streamed down her sallow, blotchy cheeks. Her thigh, covered with bandages, stopped at the knee.

Chapter ELEVEN

A STRANGE VOICE PIERCED THE FOG. I STRUGGLED TO open my eyes but gave up. A voice repeated, "Wake up, wake up, we're here." A man's hand, rough and callused, touched my shoulder, and I jumped.

"Good morning, little girl, are you feeling better?"

My traveling companion laughed. His pug nose didn't bother me anymore. He gestured to my face, brushing my cheek. "Your eyes are still wet."

The scene from the night before flashed before me: the humiliation, the shame I had felt, confronted by those two young toughs. I had probably relived it in my dream.

The man buckled his suitcases. "Get ready to get off, we've only got two minutes."

Moscow was outside. I recognized the city beyond the window, this familiar station, the train rails, the barriers, the cement platforms in the middle of the iron tracks, even the neon signs. The train officials trudged along in silence. Pigeons were flocking on the roof of a building covered with black marble.

The train siren. Did they bellow like this in every train station in the world? The man squeezed my arm. "Get dressed and hand me those bags."

Without waiting for my reply, he heaved my knapsack onto his shoulders. He looked like a workhorse, muscular and kind. We walked out of the station together, as if we were a father and daughter here to visit the capital. We joined the flow of passengers and, from time to time, the man glanced over at me protectively, as if to reassure me.

It stirred something in me: I had yearned for this protective look so many times, in the searing, dead heat of our summers, on the days when the wind howled and the rain pounded our roof. This time of yearning stretched out almost infinite in my memory, through all the seasons of my youth, was woven into my earliest dreams and illusions. The man took my hand from time to time, squeezing it softly. I glanced at him, grateful.

But the happiness was cut short. We said good-bye in front of the station. He bent over me, his voice low, soothing. "It's a shame, young lady, but I've got to go now. I can't escort you any further."

"Thank you so much. Anyway, I know all the subway stations in this town," I said.

He shook his head, laughing. "You speak Russian better than I do. I come from . . ." It was probably the name of a town I had never heard of. It probably didn't even exist on a map. "Well, good-bye again. Go on. Don't let anyone bully you."

He shook my hand, kissed my head, and quickly crossed the street. Never look back, I thought, even for a second. No happiness can hold; every life, every dream, has its unraveling.

*   *   *

I arrived at the subway station just in time for the second train. There were barely a dozen passengers in the subway car. They were all reading their newspapers and eating their sandwiches. Probably all from the same factory. At the third station, they all got off, leaving me alone in the car. I looked at my reflection in the window. I combed my hair and got out a fried-egg sandwich. After my last experience, I had learned to bring my own provisions. Still, I yearned for a cup of hot tea with a few slices of lemon.

Feeling stronger after the food, I studied the directions to get to Uncle Chinh's address again. Last year, he had come for just a short mission and so he had been lodged in the Hotel Rossiya. This time, he had come for a training session at the Communist Party Cadres School. The Aon School was in the suburbs. What an idea, sending an old man of sixty to school. Another stroke of genius on the part of our leaders, I thought to myself. I remembered his disoriented, distraught look from the previous year and couldn't help smiling.

I had to change subway lines several times to get to Aon. It was the most privileged university in the Soviet Union. No other teaching establishment had so many resources, so much funding. This school provided everything for the students: their studies, their activities, their parties, their government contacts. I knew its reputation and knew that each student had his own room, a luxury unheard of at the lesser universities like Lomonosov. I imagined Uncle Chinh would greet me with a hot, sugared tea. But I was disappointed. He wasn't there.

"Is my uncle, Do Quoc Chinh, in the hospital?" I inquired.

"The hospital? The comrade has just gone out. He left us this message," said the guardian, handing me a piece of cardboard with Vietnamese words scrawled on it: *Come find me at Mr. Khoa's house. He is a researcher at . . .*

I couldn't remember the exact location of the street, but I knew it must be somewhere near Lomonosov University. And I knew that it was probably named after one of Lenin's brothers. I finally stumbled upon a huge gray skyscraper, the kind constructed by the dozen after the Second World War.

The main entrance was just adjacent to a small state grocery store where you could find all the usual household necessities: glasses, forks and spoons, pots, toothpaste, laundry soap, butter. In the middle of this clutter, there was a huge counter stacked with different kinds of wines and beer. The shopkeeper, a beefy old man in a baggy white shirt, strutted around this vast display of glass and foil. A huge crowd was queuing up; some took a cheap bottle of fruit juice, others the more expensive bottles of five-star fruit liqueur.

The man served them and took their money, indifferent. Under his bushy white eyebrows, he had startling blue eyes. His huge, firm hands were blotchy with age spots and veins. I stared at him for a long time. I couldn't decide whether to enter the building. I was tempted to return to the train station and go back home. Uncle Chinh wasn't sick; he had invented the story to get me to come to Moscow. But what if something really had happened to him?

No. My mother would have sent me a telegram. Since her accident, she had retired from the market and opened a small soft-drink-and-snack stand in front of our house. She had the window widened and built a cement ledge in its frame. Every morning, she would lay out a wood plank for her counter. She had already sold off her stock of dry goods, and her savings were gone. All she had left to sell now were boxes of peanuts, sesame-seed candies, cheap tobacco, green bean candies, and a few fried-dough balls, the kind you give to children to get them to stop crying. From time to time, friends would give her a couple of New Year's cakes or a few hemp cakes. Just to round out her business, she kept a pot of tea hot in a padded wicker basket to sell by the glass and installed a water pipe.

For the most part, her customers were all neighbors. After a long day of work at the market, they would come for her New Year's cakes and her sesame candies, if only to wash away the salty aftertaste of a *pho* soup or the sweetness of a *che* pudding. Day after day, her friends managed to scrape up a few old bills to spend at her stand, a way of helping her make ends meet. They came too to chat for a while, ordering a cup of tea just to be sociable. And my mother would gather a few of these filthy bills, putting them aside in her little wicker pocketbook so she could buy a few bowls of rice. For the rest, of course, she had to live off what little money I could send her, by boat or through the post, from my job as an "exported worker" in Russia. My life as a university student had ended that spring evening Neighbor Vi came by to tell me the terrible news.

What was I doing here with Uncle Chinh? Perhaps I would never be free of him. The old shopkeeper paced back and forth in front of me, lumbering about like a bear. His gaze was dull, mournful, and yet somehow those startling blue eyes made him look young. As soon as his customers were served, they left rapidly, in silence. A bus station stood right in front of the shop.

This was such a peaceful city, so different from Hanoi's savage screech of traffic, the jams that used to paralyze the city, from the startling bang of firecrackers, the jeering of drunkards, the fights, the quarrels in the streets. Here, people were silent. They waited in line in silence. They got on and off of buses in silence. Placid, obedient, disciplined.

But there was something sinister about this tranquillity, and order of this existence. It was the peace of a swamp, a far cry from our storms and squalls. Russian culture had bred too many broken dreams. All that was left was the pure, thin air of ideals, too poor to sustain a human life, or its need for creativity and fulfillment. These calm, resigned faces seemed engraved with no more than the memory of a culture that had once contributed milestones to the history of civilization.

The bus pulled into the station. The line of people who had gathered under the wooden signs ascended slowly. No pushing. I had to decide: to get on and head back to the train station, or to go into the building.

A young man burst out of the shop, pushing me aside. He turned around. "Excuse me." In a few leaps, he jumped onto the bus, clutching two bottles of vodka under his arms, a third in one of his pants' pockets. The bus started to pull out of the station.

Too late, I thought. It's fate: I'll have to see him one last time after all. I walked toward the building, but the gate was locked, and I had to walk around it once before finding a service entrance. A crowd of young people were hanging about. They were busy eating ice cream and barely spoke to each other. I could see an ice-cream vendor nearby, in the garden, and a long line in front of his counter. They were mostly Vietnamese, probably students and researchers who lived in the building.

I decided to ask directions from a gray-haired Vietnamese man in a light gray suit; his white shirt was embroidered with Chinese characters. "Excuse me, sir, is there a Mr. Khoa here, a second-year graduate student?"

The man slurped down his final mouthful of ice cream and wiped his lips with a handkerchief before replying, "Which Khoa? The whole building is filled with graduate students. What kind of thesis?"

I couldn't answer. I thought that graduate students working toward a doctorate would be scarce, that they would all know each other. I didn't think to give him Khoa's complete address.

The man watched me curiously. "You must have come very far?"

"Very far."

"That's unfortunate. Here, there's a Khoa in mechanics,

a Khoa in biology, a Khoa in literature. . . . As many Khoas as there are subjects. We tell them apart by their nicknames."

I handed him the address. He read it and then glanced up at me once. There was something strange about his expression. Nothing I could put my finger on, but enough to know something was awry.

"It's Khoa the biologist," he said, nodding. "I can take you there. You have all your papers in order? They're horribly bureaucratic here."

"Thanks. I've got everything."

The man lifted my knapsack, mounted the steps of the staircase, and pushed open the door for me. It was the same architecture everywhere here. We plodded down a corridor that emptied into a living room furnished with a few very austere chairs. A screen of painted tiles and wooden squares separated one living room from another room. To the left, near the guard post, an old man was busy reading, his head buried in a book. Tufts of white hair spilled out of his ears. My guide approached and tapped on the wood screen, but it took three knocks before the old man noticed us. "Ah . . . who's that?" He lifted his head suddenly, his voice gruff and severe, like most Muscovites'. Instead of replying, the man with me said mockingly, without a hint of an accent, "Still buried in your books, old man? Who is it this time?"

The old man closed the book. It was Dostoyevski's novel *The Idiot*.

"Ah, the giant of Russian literature," my guide said unctuously. The old man nodded proudly and motioned to us to pass. He held out a hand to the Vietnamese man with me. They caught each other's gaze, shaking their heads knowingly. I was puzzled; I didn't understand the sudden complicity between these two men.

"This young lady came a long way to see Khoa the biologist. Here are her papers; please stamp them, if you would."

My guide handed my papers to the old man and nodded in my direction. "Come here." The old man watched him, deeply suspicious. He opened a large book and laboriously inscribed my name and registration number in one column. Then he put the notebook away in a drawer and nodded to us to pass.

I bowed slightly. I could feel him staring at my back. I didn't dare turn around to confirm it. We took the elevator and got off at the fourth floor, almost in front of Khoa's door. "This is it," the man said. He looked at me again, a weird gleam in his eye, as if he wanted to say something to me. "Well, mission accomplished. Good-bye now," he said after a moment of hesitation, and extended a hand to me. "And good luck." He turned and disappeared around the corner of the corridor.

I knocked, half expecting to be confronted with a stranger. But it was Uncle Chinh who finally opened the door. "Hang, my niece. I've been waiting for you since last night. Was there a message from me at Aon?"

I entered without a word. I took off my raincoat in silence, and in silence I sat down. "I didn't see anyone. The guard gave me this slip of paper."

"Ah yes, that's right," he said, letting out a sigh of relief. I looked at him. He had a large meat cleaver in his hand, and he wore an apron and a pair of women's house slippers, the Vietnamese kind made for export that the Russians could buy for two rubles. The room's owner was obviously elsewhere. An unmade bed. A pile of rumpled covers. The edge of the bed was soiled, stained with the marks of shoe soles. A poster advertising women's swimwear had been tacked over the head of the bed. The European woman in the photo had wild brown eyes, and she thrust her pelvis forward. At the bottom of the poster, someone had tacked up a snapshot, which had been inscribed: *First winter in Moscow. Thinking of you. Nga.* At the other end of the bed, there was a table piled with books and Russian and Vietnamese academic journals. A record player and a stack of records had been propped between the books and the wall. A few old razors scattered here and there; a dirty handkerchief. A few condoms.

My cheeks burned. I suddenly understood the Vietnamese man's leers and the lewdness in the look the old guard had given me. Uncle Chinh's voice interrupted my thoughts. "What would you like to drink, Hang? Some beer or fruit juice? Or some kvass? We've got a lot of that around here."

"Give me a cup of tea," I replied curtly.

"She really has such simple tastes, the little one," he muttered as he prepared the tea. A cuckoo clock struck eleven-thirty. The cuckoo pointed its beak and let out shrill, exact cries, like a crane. "My God, it's almost time." He set down his cup of tea abruptly. "You drink your tea. Rest a bit. But I've got to get busy. They'll be here any minute."

"What's this all about?"

"They'll be here any minute," he repeated mechanically, and began to mince a chunk of meat. On the electric stove, two burners lit up, red hot. A chicken simmered. Uncle Chinh minced the meat with an expert hand, just like a *pho* soup vendor. He crushed the garlic cloves with the flat side of his cleaver and sprinkled the meat with MSG and salt. Then he cut the potatoes into thin scallops and started to break up a head of cauliflower, slicing it into delicate slivers. The blade came down rapidly, precisely, with a cleverness that few Vietnamese women could equal. Then he carved carrots into leaves, and the celery and the garlic into flower shapes. After he had finished, he placed a skillet on the stove and began to melt the cooking fat. Two minutes later, you could hear it crackling. He tossed the potatoes in.

"What's that for? Fried beef with potatoes? Why did you cut the potatoes into scallops?" I asked.

"What a silly question. It's the only way to get them evenly crispy. With a few vegetables, they'll be a perfect side dish to the fried beef. And this bowl of minced beef, marinated in garlic, that's to sauté with the cauliflower, the garlic, and the celery."

He let the potatoes sizzle, turning them from time to

time. He got a pot out from under the table; it was filled with stuffing for the spring rolls: minced meat, chopped vermicelli, beet root, egg yolk, onions, and pepper. From a drawer below, he pulled out rice-flower wrappers. I gaped at him, amazed, as he stuffed the spring rolls. I couldn't help muttering my admiration. "Such talent. Who taught you all this?"

"No one. You have to learn everything to get by," he grumbled. Suddenly, he went silent. You could hear heavy, clunking footsteps in the hallway outside. Dull thuds. Uncle Chinh froze and listened, attentive. "Here they come." There was banging at the door. "Coming, coming," Uncle Chinh shouted, and then whispered to me, "Go open it."

I hadn't even reached the door when a man shouted, "Hurry up! Are you sleeping or what?" I opened it and slunk off to a corner of the room. A group of men tumbled through the door. One after the other, they put down their packages, their boxes, their knapsacks swollen with goods, before looking up. They looked nervous, on edge. "We're starving. Have you finished, old man?" I was almost sure I had heard that annoyed voice somewhere before; the man, the shortest of the group, had broad shoulders, a wide back, a ruddy face, and a square jaw. He suddenly noticed me and went silent. I felt I knew him from somewhere but couldn't remember from where.

"It's coming. The spring rolls, the fried beef, you should eat those hot," said Uncle Chinh, getting up. "I'd like to introduce my niece, Hang. Mr. Khoa, Mr. Hai, Mr. . . ." They greeted me in turn. The dwarf of the group, Mr. Hai, turned to Uncle Chinh. "Old man, you have no manners. You should have told us we had a lady in our midst."

"All the better. The spectacle of your voraciousness is even richer. All you need is a female presence to transform you all into saints," laughed Khoa, the graduate student.

A tall, handsome young man with a tan replied, "Spare us your sarcasm, brother. None of us claim to be saints. Just men. There are those who like to preach that men and women should keep separate company. We know them all too well. They either end up either rotting away or sleeping around. You break one rule, what's to stop you from the rest?" His mouth twitched into an adorable pout. Then he pulled up a chair and sat down as if he were in his own house.

Khoa laughed uneasily, as if he was trying to shake off the mockery. He ran his hands nervously through his hair a few times. "I'm a man of action. I don't waste time philosophizing."

The tall young man broke into an ironical smirk. "Of course. After you've pawned your science and your wisdom off on us once and for all, you'll throw yourself into the real world. Just as long as you make sure to get *your* piece of the pie. At age fifty, you must feel the years catching up with you. And life is so beautiful, all those women out there, so mysterious, so seductive. . . ."

He laughed, a smirk still flitting at the corners of his mouth. He stared at Khoa, his eyes narrowing to slits. Khoa looked preoccupied, and he stooped down to push some of the goods under the bed.

I couldn't tear myself away from the young man's smile; he reminded me of a character out of the film *The One Hundred and Eight Heroes of Luong Son Bac,* a kind of Robin Hood story adapted from a Chinese classic. This character was called "Yen Thanh the Bohemian" and was renowned for his mastery of the classic arts; he was a musician, a brilliant chess player, a gifted poet, a painter, a martial artist. Tall, handsome, elegant, he moved easily among artists, dancers, even warriors. And always with the same self-assurance and this odd smile, with its mixture of disdain and compassion. It was the smile of a man who could dodge an arrow as easily as he could manipulate pawns on a chessboard, of a man in the prime of youth, glowing with health. It was a mesmerizing smile, and I had never met anyone who so resembled this character.

"Oh my!" Hai, the short one, shouted. "Would you two

stop squabbling? My stomach can't take the famine much longer." Then, turning to me, he said, "And we have to entertain our guest. . . . Has Mr. Chinh given you anything to eat? Probably not, eh? He'd keep a dirty coin in his mouth for a whole day if he thought he could save the price of two meals. . . . Come on, old man, dish it out for us."

"It's ready. We can toast in a minute," Uncle Chinh said. He unrolled a nylon tablecloth and served the meal: a plate of stir-fried beef with cauliflower, carrots, and garlic; a platter of roast beef and fried potatoes; a huge plate of fresh vegetables and garlic marinated in vinegar; a big bowl of spare-erib soup; and, finally, artistically displayed in a small basket of white plastic, the spring rolls. The spicy sauce had been prepared according to a traditional Vietnamese recipe: fermented fish sauce mixed with lime juice, red chili peppers, crushed garlic, a bit of MSG, and a pinch of sugar.

We sat down at the table, and Uncle Chinh distributed the chopsticks, bowls, and glasses among us. He brought out a dozen bottles of beer.

Hai rubbed his hands. "Not bad, not bad at all. After the battle this morning for the salvation of the fatherland and the family, a meal like this is just what's called for. Gentlemen, *bon appétit.* . . .

"Oh, but old man, why are you waiting to open the beer? You're so slow. Watch it, you know; at times like these, a man must specialize. Otherwise, it's extinction. If we had been as slow as you, why we'd never have gotten hold of those twelve electric rice cookers, even before Tet. . . . But forget it. . . . Let's see about these spring rolls now."

He bit into a spring roll, savoring it. The two others didn't move. Uncle Chinh struggled with the beer bottles, pouring hurriedly. I could see his hands shaking. He probably wasn't completely over his old sickness, since he discreetly poured his beer into my glass. The short man had already wolfed down his portion of spring roll. They clinked glasses, and the young man with the tan turned toward me. "To your health."

I raised my glass. "To yours."

"To our glorious combat for the salvation of the fatherland and our family . . ."

Their laughter echoed loud and mocking. The glasses chimed; and as the head dissolved, the beer sparkled a transparent gold, the color of rice fields at harvest time. All I was aware of was a blur of voices as the men emptied their glasses and bent over their plates, critiquing the food:

"Spring rolls are a bit salty today, old man."

"Next time, I'll be more careful."

"The sautéed beef isn't bad. Better than last time."

"Last time it was like a piece of old cow. Tough as leather."

"We warned you, though, Khoa. You should have slipped little Irina at the butcher's some money before placing your order. Why didn't you?"

"Forgot."

"Don't play dumb. You only know how to forget one thing, and that's the names of all the little country wenches who come looking for you. Watch it. Don't try and play tricks with us."

"I didn't have enough money for the taxi."

"Next time, pay in advance. The other day I gave her a bottle of rice wine. Not just any old stuff, either, some very expensive stuff. Look at the results."

"Really? Where did you dig that up?"

"At the embassy, dummy."

I sipped a bit of the beer. Suddenly, I felt the room spin. Everything was a total blur: the bottles, the beer, the glasses, the steam rising off the soup, the flushed faces of the guests. The European model on the poster seemed to taunt me with her gaze. Her hair floated around her face, and her red bathing suit, studded with silver sequins, molded to the curves of her body. The lamp shade cast its glow over the books, and everything started to swirl around me. I felt shivers rising in me and tried to support myself against the table.

"Maybe I will . . ." I heard the voice of the young man with the tan: "She looks sick . . . anemic." His silhouette loomed over me. I felt his hand on my shoulder as he guided me to the bed. I saw the outline of his face moving closer to mine. Suddenly, I recognized him. He and I had met before somewhere. He was from my past. I was sure of it: "Yen Thanh the Bohemian."

I don't know how long I slept. Suddenly, lamplight was in my eyes, the light piercing my eyelids like needles. I buried my head under the covers, but I could still smell the acrid odor of tobacco. I felt heavy-headed, but I didn't feel queasy. I was lucid now, stretched out on the bed, under the covers. I heard the record player purring, the thundering voice of the short, fat one they called Hai:

"So, have we finished the accounts?"

"Yep." It was the tall young one, the Bohemian.

Then the graduate student's voice: "How much do I owe you?"

"One hundred and twenty rubles."

"I'm flat broke. My mother is nagging me. I don't have a ruble on me."

"Stop sulking. I'll give you the credit."

My Bohemian paused for a minute, and then went on, "But for your food, you pay up like the rest of us. For this week, that's twenty-eight rubles a head."

The researcher cried out, "What do you mean? Twenty-eight rubles?"

"Do your own calculations. Eighty-four and a half divided into twenty-eight rubles per person. Of course, I'll pick up the extra half a ruble."

"And Chinh?"

"You're so stupid," he said, his voice cutting. "He works

for us. How could we ask him to chip in for his own keep? Since when is that done?"

Hai laughed contemptuously. "Touché. And you others, usually so eloquent in all matters? You don't even have basic manners, do you? In fact, we should be thinking about paying the old man."

"He's making a claim?" asked Khoa.

"Yes. He'd like to be paid right away," said Hai.

"He'll only believe it when he feels the rubles in the palm of his hand. Come now, gentlemen, two rubles each," said the Bohemian.

"Very good," he continued. "Now we can feast our eyes on the smile of old Chinh. What's he up to now? He finished the dishes a while ago didn't he?"

"He's washing his new Panto sweater with mine."

"Washing? But you have to dry-clean them."

"I know, but he was already washing them in the bathtub when I arrived. It's back to the cleaner's now."

"What a waste."

"The last time, he burned a hole in my sweater with the iron. Pure Italian wool. Ruined. He can't even learn how to cut out slogans for our posters, you know. My elder brother's also studying at Aon University, and he tells me the guy spends all his time sleeping. But he's full of energy when it comes to stockpiling expensive goods to sell later. He's always in the front of the lines for the best-quality merchandise. Cooking is his only talent."

"Hey, that counts for something. It's gotten him protection from his bosses. And he's ended up in the Party leadership."

At that moment, I heard the shuffle of footsteps and the halting voice of my uncle. "My God, it's really difficult to wring these. My arms feel like jelly."

"A fine performance," said the Bohemian with a laugh. "My congratulations. And here is your pay. Do us the honor of accepting it."

Uncle Chinh let out a sound I could only identify as neither a grunt nor a laugh. "You've made progress."

"In what?" asked the Bohemian.

"You haven't put on the dance music yet. It's the first time, since I've known you, that it's been this quiet here. That syncopated stuff makes me dizzy. Why are you so addicted to it? It's as if it were a drug."

"Yes, that's it," said the Bohemian, laughing. "So we're just a bunch of degenerates to you, eh?"

"In my time, no one liked this decadent kind of music," said Uncle Chinh.

The Bohemian spoke up in a faraway voice, as if continuing an inner thought. "In the building where my parents lived, there was this man, he was the deputy director of a factory. About your age. He wore huge baggy trousers, nothing like these tight pants of ours, and one of those high-necked Mao jackets, nothing like our V-neck sweaters or our colorful shirts. He had the reputation of being a strict man. Whenever he opened his mouth, it was always to give us some morality lecture: revolutionary spirit, a sense of discipline, international obligations, civic duty. . . .

"There were six families in the building, none of whom matched his rank or power. He had two daughters and was already a grandfather. His wife went to the market twice a day with a government-paid chauffeur and turned up her nose at the neighbors. One day, after a soccer match, while we were washing ourselves, stark naked, in the courtyard, we heard cries coming from the public bathhouse. One of the boys tried to open the door, but it was locked. But we heard muffled screams coming from the other side, so we climbed a ladder to peek through the air holes on the roof. By craning our necks, we made out the deputy director, naked as a worm, crushing a nine-year-old girl under him. She cried as he got on with his business. We shrieked with laughter. We took turns watching. The little girl squirmed beneath him in pain, but he gagged her with his hand.

"She was mentally ill, the little girl, the orphan of a railroad man. She had already dropped out of elementary school. Her mother lived off a small food-vending business, selling a bit of pickled cabbage and salted squash. Before she went mad, the little girl used to play hide-and-seek with us. She wasn't pretty, but she was sweet and very generous, sharing everything with us, even a mandarin orange or a guava. Suddenly, I felt ashamed, realizing what animals we were. I remembered she was my age, that she was just a little girl, and totally defenseless. I ran to alert her mother, who was busy mincing cabbage. When I told her, she screamed as if someone was killing her, and rushed over with her cleaver still in hand. . . ."

He stopped speaking. The room was so silent I could hear the ticking of the clock's pendulum. After a long pause, the Bohemian continued, his voice harsh now:

"So there you have it, Mr. Chinh. The old child molester had never set foot on a dance floor. Of course, he did like to lecture his workers about how dancing was decadent, how their generation indulged in shameful pleasures, and how everyone should devote himself to the revolution. He had the same worldview as you, the same tastes. Don't get me wrong, I don't mean to insult you. I know you don't have the same vices. But I must say, the resemblance is somewhat troubling."

"How dare you?" said Uncle Chinh, fuming.

"Cool it," the young man said tersely. "There's no need to threaten me. What could you do, anyway? Go to the embassy, all scraping and bowing, and complain? Would you denounce me? You wouldn't be the first. Sit down instead, have a drink, because I've still got something to tell you."

There was a silence, and then he continued, "It's people like him, people like you, who like a bunch of Maoists, chased us down to cut off our 'Imperialist' bell-bottom pants—maybe you were jealous because, with all your revolutionary discipline and responsibility, you didn't dare wear Western-style clothes yourselves. But it wasn't too long before you all wore bell-bottom trousers. You still measure our human dignity with your official hemlines. Millions of young people step in line with your taste. They don't dare deviate an inch from your fashions, or you might accuse them of 'betraying the party,' or of 'selling out the fatherland.'

"I'll never forget, when I was young, seeing my brothers, my sisters, their friends, hauled over and body-searched in the streets like criminals by your kind. I can still see their faces, the way they pleaded, mouthed your slogans. I was just a boy. I hid behind a lamppost, shivering with fear, waiting for my turn. . . . Where does it come from, your need to humiliate us? In the name of what?

"Some wounds never heal. Like the wounds of childhood. I've grown up, but I've kept track of these people, watched them, those who used to terrorize us. Like the deputy director. They never deserved our respect, or our fear. They're just a bunch of illusionists.

"Talented ones, though. They decreed their thousands of rules, their innumerable edicts, each one more draconian than the last. But, in the shadows, they paddled around in the mud, without faith or law.

"You say our dances are decadent. But haven't you done some dancing yourself? Invisible dances, infinitely more decadent than ours?"

Uncle Chinh snapped, "Stop telling stories. There's no such thing as an invisible dance."

The Bohemian sneered. "Oh yes, there is. I've seen it myself a few times. It's the dance of the overlords after they've finished laying out traps for their enemies, after they've pandered to the powers-that-be, as they near their prize: a job with power and all the perks. It's the night before they kill the fatted calf, when they sit sucking at their water pipes, rolling cigarettes, waiting for daybreak. Waiting for their consecration. Their minds, undoubtedly, were dancing at the time.

"We dance with girls. You and your kind dance with your own shadows, pawing the velvet armchairs of your dreams. That's the invisible dance I'm talking about. Now, which is the more decadent?"

"I refuse to speak to you. Under my administration, there were no abuses like this," my uncle sputtered.

"Oh, I'll grant you that. So as long as there aren't any bad trends under 'your administration,' it's okay? And the rest of our history? That's not your concern. What use are you then?" the Bohemian shot back.

Uncle Chinh raised his voice. "This is complete nonsense. We, we . . . our task is ideological education."

There was a loud banging at the door. "Who's there?" said the Bohemian. "Hey, Khoa, you're next to the door, open it."

"I'm busy. I've got to finish this text. Hai, you go see."

"Okay!" said Hai, and I could hear his plodding step. The door squeaked open, and a young Vietnamese woman spoke, her voice hesitant. "Is Mr. Khoa here?"

"What's your name?"

"Chuong . . . from Kiev . . ." she stammered.

"Just a minute," said Hai. I could hear the graduate student whisper, "I'm not here. Tell her to go."

"Right," said Hai, and I could hear his footsteps plodding along again near my bed.

Then the Bohemian spoke. "Just a minute."

Hai stopped. I could hear his breathing near me. "What is it?" Hai asked, surprised.

"Wait," said the Bohemian, and then, snickering: "My, my, Khoa, you do procure your girls easily in the middle of the night."

"What would we do with her? There's no room here. Do you want her around your neck?"

"We'll hang her around yours if it's necessary. You're always so sweet with girls you haven't slept with. Afterward, it's like this. Don't you have any self-respect?"

Khoa let out a derisive laugh and a whistle. "Watch your tongue now. We've got all the time in the world to discuss it later."

"I don't feel like talking. Let her in. Where would she go at this time of night?"

"Who's giving orders? I'm the boss here."

"Of course," said the young man, taunting. "It's your room. Don't forget, though, that I too control certain things. . . . More important things. Certain friends in the right places, certain resources, shall we say, that make our little import–export business possible. Should I say it differently? Or is straight talk all you understand? What's the decision?"

The room went silent again, and I listened to the ticktocking of the clock. Then a dull voice; it was Khoa, the student's: "All right. Hai, let her in."

Hai shuffled toward the door again and then came back. "She's gone."

"Run after her. She's probably still in the entryway," snapped the Bohemian. And Hai was off again. I could hear him open the door and then plod down the corridor. No one spoke. There was a long pause, and then I heard his plodding approach the door again.

"Disappeared. I missed the elevator. I asked the guard post, and they said she had just taken her papers back. I ran out into the street, but there wasn't a shadow. She must have jumped in the last bus."

No one spoke. Finally, Hai broke the silence:

"Come on, gentlemen, to bed. A difficult battle awaits us tomorrow. Let's indulge ourselves a bit, while there's still time. Exams are coming up, and we'll have to hit the books." He yawned loudly. "My God. To think that back home they think Russia is a kind of paradise. . . . What a dog's life."

When I woke up the next morning, the room was deserted. As I groped around, I pushed over some object in the dark.

"Awake already?" asked the young man, peeking out of the bathroom. His face and hair were still dripping wet. I felt disoriented, but I still was sure I recognized him from somewhere. He was wearing a checked shirt and a pair of corduroy jeans. He watched me, grinning. "Check your memory. See if you've met me somewhere already."

"How did you know?"

"Witchcraft. More precisely, I push the limits of my intuition. Have you placed me?"

"No. I give up."

He laughed. "Terrible memory you've got. The first day of university classes. You were wearing a purple shirt with funny bows and clasps. And a pair of clogs."

"Ah, I remember now." I laughed. He was one of the students who teased me ("Who made this marvel for you?") when I wore the shirt my mother had bought for me. At the time, he was as lanky as a reed.

He said he had been a history student preparing to come to Russia.

"Are you still studying?"

"Naturally. It's our only way out. And there's the duty to the family. And you? Why did you abandon your studies?"

"My mother lost a leg in an accident, so I dropped out. I've got to make a living."

"What's your job?"

"I'm a textile worker."

He shook his head. "How do you stand the cold here with that skeleton of yours? It's not easy to earn a living in this country."

"I don't have a choice."

He rubbed his hair dry with his towel, his gaze wandered off somewhere, distant. He had hazelnut eyes and a dreamlike air about him. Suddenly, he let out his breath. "And Mr. Chinh, what's your relation to him?"

"He's my uncle, my mother's brother."

"Oh, I see." He shrugged.

I said nothing.

"So you've come to pay him a visit? You don't look too well yourself."

"I just got out of the hospital about a week ago. He summoned me here by telegram."

"What did it say?"

"Oh, something like, 'Very ill. Come immediately.'"

He grinned contemptuously. I could see him again as Yen Thanh the Bohemian. He wound the bath towel around the back of a chair, straddled it, and stared at me. "Do you know why he made you come?"

I said nothing, my eyes questioning.

"He's preparing his trunks full of imported goods for the next boat. And to send them, you have to speak Russian and have lots of money. Your uncle has serious deficiencies in both areas." He paused, pensive, and then continued, "With this kind of man, you don't need the eyes of a lynx to read his heart. . . . But still I can't quite believe it. Calling on a frail young woman like you . . ."

The clock struck nine. The Bohemian continued, "He's gone to buy some groceries. He'll be back soon." And he produced a packet of bills and handed them to me. "Here."

I stepped back. "No. How dare you?"

His lips curled back into a smile. "Don't misunderstand me. . . . Listen to me first: Don't stay here in the suburbs with your uncle. The work isn't easy. We're going to have to bribe some people to get anywhere with this imported-goods racket. You're white as a ghost, you know. You can't have much money saved up. . . . When he asks you for help, give him this money. Tell him you've got to get back to your textile job, that you can't stay long. Here's my contribution toward his little shipping venture."

I shook my head. "No, he'll never accept this."

But he was firm. "Don't be so sure. Take it. You'll see. He'll be here any minute."

He turned and walked away. I stuffed the money under the pillow. The Bohemian started to make me a cup of warm milk. He dropped in a few vitamin tablets and handed it to me. "Drink this."

I took the cup but didn't dare thank him, uneasy about the emptiness of words. I felt the warmth spread through my body, beads of sweat gathering at my temples. I plunged back under the covers. He was probably still shaving when Uncle Chinh came back to the apartment and dumped his groceries on the floor. "Is my niece awake?"

"No, not yet."

"That's strange. She took several aspirin, but she should be up by now."

"You expect to cure her with a few aspirin? She needs decent food. A germ culture couldn't survive on her diet."

"Yes, yes. I'll make her a noodle soup."

I could hear the Bohemian putting something away and saying, "I'm off. Be back around one." After the door slammed behind him, I got out of bed. Uncle Chinh was delighted. "Ah, you recovered. Would you like to eat?"

I shook my head.

"Fine. Then we'll eat at noon."

"When do your courses start up again?" I asked him.

"Tomorrow."

"Why did you order me to come here?"

He stammered something and edged closer to me. "I've got to go back to Vietnam. Just two weeks left. You're here for a bit longer. You've got time to sort out your finances. I need your help."

I said nothing. He struggled to continue. "When I left, your mother said that if I had any trouble, I could count on you. You speak Russian fluently and, and . . . I don't understand a thing."

I remained silent, but he continued, lowering his voice, "Everything is ready. The trunks are sealed. But the most difficult part is the shipping."

Suddenly, I felt weary of all this, wanted to get it over with quickly. I pulled the wad of bills out from under the pillow. "Here, take it."

He looked at me, uneasy. "How much is it? How did you get this?"

"Take it all," I said. "I haven't counted it."

He took the bills from me and counted them. One hundred and thirty-four. He separated them out into piles, first the fifties, then the twenties, the tens, the fives, the ones. He was absorbed with this, transported. I could see his face clearly now, the curving chin, the arch of his eyebrows, his drooping eyelids, the straight edge of his nose. These traits were so familiar to me, right from the beginning, from our very first meeting. I still remember how I had liked him instantly, how happy I was.

That was another time. But his face was still the mirror image of my mother's.

I stayed with my mother in Hanoi for a whole week after her accident. I woke up early the day I finally decided to go tell Uncle Chinh the news. After I had done all my mother's washing and prepared her some hot milk, I carefully arranged the fruit, the cakes, and all my toiletries on her bedside table. Then I asked her roommates at the Bach Mai Hospital to look after her while I went to find my uncle. My mother had asked me to go immediately, from the very first day of her hospitalization. But I had always managed to put it off.

"Today it's Sunday. You're sure to find them at home."

"Yes, Mother. Don't worry. It's too early. It's only six A.M. They like to sleep in."

My mother went silent, but I had read the impatience in her eyes. I procrastinated and only left the house at six-thirty that evening. Even then, I kept finding excuses to delay the visit. I went to the public gardens and bought a plate of sticky rice. Then I stopped by a park where some traveling circus from the South was performing a cycle feat. I went in and watched it. It was after nine when I finally arrived at Uncle Chinh's house. He was repairing a rabbit hutch and smiled at me. "Ah, it's you, Hang. Where's your mother?"

"She's had an accident."

"Nothing serious?"

"They had to amputate the leg."

"One or both of them?"

"One."

"She's lucky. Yesterday there was an accident with some boy in Trieu Viet Van Street. They had to cut both his legs off. That's where it all leads, these traffic violations. When will they finally bring these people to law and order? . . . Come, let me wash up."

I followed into the house and watched as Uncle Chinh put away the pliers, the hammer, wire, and nails. I watched him as he washed his hands. Aunt Chinh was in the room next to us. Hearing us, she poked her head out. "Ah, my niece. Where's your mother?"

I didn't have time to reply. Uncle Chinh shouted over his shoulder to her, "She's had an accident. They had to amputate a leg."

Her expression froze, and her eyes widened. "Really?"

There was a pause, and then she said, "Sit down here with your uncle. I've got to find an old wool sweater for little Tu." She disappeared into the room.

Uncle Chinh had finished washing his hands, and he sat down facing me. "Which hospital is she in?"

"It's the Bach Mai Hospital. She wanted me to come and tell you last Wednesday, but I've been very busy."

He said nothing. I just stared at their living room. It had become more opulent. Where they once had the buffet table, they now had a brand-new Saratov refrigerator. On the chest, a nineteen-inch Japanese television was hidden discreetly under a flowery dustcover. After a silence, Uncle Chinh yelled to his wife, "Thanh!"

"What is it?" echoed a voice from the adjoining room.

"Come in here a minute. We've got to talk."

"Go ahead and talk. I'm busy. I've got to find that sweater for Tu."

"We've got to send some money to Sister Que. What can we offer?"

"But you know we've already run through this month's salary for meals at the cafeteria, the soap, the MSG powder, the tire for the bicycle, and those two aluminum pans."

"What about our savings account?"

"You're such a bureaucrat, honestly! It's a fixed deposit. We can't take the money out for five years. As for the interest, we've got to wait for the seventh of each month."

"Can't we borrow some?"

"Absolutely not. We have never borrowed money from anyone."

Uncle Chinh sighed, muttering something between his teeth. "Can we sell something?" His voice was tense, almost choked. But Aunt Chinh heard it. She rushed into the room, clutching a small red sweater, the kind once donated in the name of the "anti-imperialist struggle." She stared at her husband anxiously. "What do you want to sell?"

Uncle Chinh muttered, "I was just wondering, you know. . . ."

"The Saratov is mine. I paid for that refrigerator with my study-grant money while I was in the Soviet Union. In this house, only the television is yours. Sell it if you like. But try and explain that to the boys."

I drifted off in silence; the couple, lost in their calculations, probably didn't even notice my departure. When my mother saw me walk into the hospital room, she smiled. "Back already?"

It was a beautiful smile. Even on that sallow, sunken face. Her eyes caught mine, impatient, emotional, like the eyes of a dog in search of approval. I felt a tearing inside me and turned away from her. "So, my girl?" she repeated.

223

"Uncle Chinh is away on a mission, Mother."

"Oh? Somewhere far away?" she asked, still beaming.

"Very far."

"I thought so. Yesterday, on the radio, they said there was some ideological education delegation coming from the Soviet Union, to exchange ideas between the two parties. Your uncle must have had to take them down South somewhere."

"Yes, that's it," I replied.

I awoke with a jolt to the sound of Uncle Chinh's voice.

"Wake up, Hang. I've fixed you a bowl of noodles. Eat, it'll give you some strength."

I clutched the covers, fearful that he would rip them away from me. "I'm not hungry. Let me sleep." I felt myself melt into the warm shadow of the covers. A peace washed over me, drowning the clamor of voices. My mind emptied, and I drifted off.

The next morning, the Bohemian offered to drive me to the station instead of Uncle Chinh. I accepted immediately. Somehow, this was not quite right for a single young woman, I thought to myself. But I didn't have the strength to tolerate Uncle Chinh's presence.

The Bohemian bought me a train ticket and some food for the trip; he even got a pass so he could see me off on the platform. Like the man who guided me to the biologist's apartment, he spoke flawless Russian. With his handsome face and impeccable accent, he drew stares from the Russian women. Some just glanced at him furtively, others stared brazenly; I giggled, but he just kept walking, oblivious. As we stood side by side, waiting for the train, I realized that he must have only been a few years older than I was. When the moment came to say good-bye, as I heard the train approach the station, I shook his hand. "Thanks, thanks very much, for everything."

"Hey, not all at once. Save something for next time," he said, his eyes glinting with just a hint of mischief. I laughed. "Any message for your uncle?" he asked.

"No," I said, hesitating, and then: "When did he start working for you?"

"A few months ago. Before that, we had another guy. When he left, he introduced us to your uncle. They were friends. I believe the Marxists here would call this networking among pals 'scientific organization.'"

I shook my head. "I still can't quite believe it. Yesterday, everything happened just like you said it would."

He swept a strand of hair off his face. "Little Sister, you must understand, even if it hurts. Your uncle is like a lot of people I've known. They've worn themselves out trying to re-create heaven on earth. But their intelligence wasn't up to it. They don't know what their heaven is made of, let alone how to get there. When they woke up, they had just enough time to grab a few crumbs of real life, to scramble for it in the mud, to make a profit—at any price. They are their own tragedy. Ours, as well."

The train pulled all the way into the station. He shook my hand and lifted my bag up into the car. I sat down near a window. He remained on the platform as the train pulled out. I watched him blur and disappear in the steam that had formed on my window.

The ride back to the province where I lived seemed interminable. As the train shuttled along monotonously, I fell into its rhythm. Lights dimmed, snuffing the towns out into the night. A forest of poplars stood shimmering, branches bent over lazily, swaying in a silvery reflection. The sky and the earth seemed huge, yawning open like a mirror to the shifting, uncertain colors of autumn. Pine forests swallowed up the poplars, willows replacing the pines.

I watched this procession of the Russian land, with its trees, its dense symphonies of color, of burnished gold melting into bronze. To me, autumn was a unique, foreign kind of beauty. Soon, it would be winter, and snow, endless snow.

I remember my first winter in Russia. The bitter cold that singed my ears, crept into my gloves, tightened around my body like a vise. I can still see the road to the textile factory, the deep banks of snow heaped up in front of the bus stations. I remember the exhaustion, the hours hunched over the machines, trudging back to the residence, in the snow, numb with cold, still shaking from the jolt of the machines, choking on the smoke and the dust.

After days like that, our evening meal was like a benediction. We calculated the price of everything—butter, cheese, meat—leaving ourselves just enough to keep going, to keep from falling on our faces in the snow. The rest was always for our families.

The train hummed along, rocking me gently. I wrapped my shoulders with Madame Vera's shawl, propping my head against the back of the seat. Next to me sat a Russian woman bundled in a white coat, her eyes closed.

She must have been about forty, a faded beauty whose face was already scored with wrinkles. She was elegant, but there was something bereft about her. She probably lives alone, I thought to myself, like so many women today. Her silence agreed with me. So we sat there, side by side, without speaking. We watched the countryside, sinking deeper into our shared silence.

I woke up just after midnight. The woman had changed clothes. When she boarded the train, she had worn a simple gray-checked blouse; now, she wore a red satin dress with a lace collar that fanned out around her neck and abundant breasts. She had spread out a white embroidered handkerchief on her knees, and was just biting into a huge cheese-and-tripe sandwich.

"Would you like to join me?" she said, as she saw me straighten up in my seat.

"Thank you, I've brought some food along."

I rolled up Madame Vera's shawl, tucked it back into my knapsack, and headed for the toilets. The tap on the sink dripped, the trace of some previous passenger. I washed my face and changed into a gray-and-white suit. It was smart, though a bit outdated. At least it was comfortable, better than that Russian woman's fashionable but rumpled affair. I noticed the dust, inevitable on a train, even the most modern. I took a glance in the mirror. Sleep had perked me up. I washed my hands and face and headed back to the compartment to get out the food the Bohemian had packed for me.

Perhaps the memory of our university days had inspired him: I unpacked a sandwich and a tin of tiny cakes decorated with a picture of chocolate mushrooms. The cakes, which were shaped like cabbages, were an extravagance for "exported workers" like us. I spread the food onto the table and bit into the sandwich, offering the cakes to my companion. She stretched out a delicate hand and selected one. I detected a look of surprise. I could tell she was scrutinizing me. She must have been wondering how I could afford such delicacies.

I ate in silence, nervously gathering the crumbs on the edge of a piece of paper. We sat there for a while, munching on the cakes in silence. Then she opened a detective novel, and I turned to the window again, pressing my nose up against the glass. When we arrived, we wished each other luck and went our separate ways.

It was about two-thirty in the afternoon. I suddenly remembered Madame Vera. For my friends, the Bohemian's goodies would suffice, but for Madame Vera, I wanted a gift. I wandered through the stores, finally deciding on a 10-ruble bottle of cognac. That was about all I could afford; I knew that women of a certain age, when they were alone, often turned to the bottle.

I did some shopping and then headed for a nearby park.

Just beyond the park, there was a bus station that would take me directly to the dormitory for textile workers. It was a modest park compared to those in most Russian towns, but there was something strange about it. It was in such a state of neglect that it looked as if the gardeners had abandoned themselves to drink. The trees, the grass, the flowers, the shrubs, everything grew helter-skelter. The foliage on the trees was so dense and untrimmed that it hung down in huge green umbrellas. Vines wrapped themselves around the tree trunks, and tufts of grass pushed their way through the pebbled paths. Clumps of moss and ferns invaded pink-and-white marble tubs that had once brimmed with red flowers.

I cut across the garden, admiring the wildness of the place. We came here often on Sunday afternoons, my friends and I, spreading ourselves out on the benches overgrown with weeds to snack on lamb kebabs and drink Kvass.

A group of young people strolled by. I noticed them turn their attention to a kiosk, under a tree, that sold gifts and souvenirs. Everyone watched them with an odd mixture of curiosity and respect. A young Russian couple stopped talking to stare in their direction. Some of the men, less discreet, gaped at them wide-eyed. Suddenly, I too was curious, and stopped to watch.

This group of young Japanese—three boys and two girls—stood chatting on the cobblestone courtyard in front of the kiosk. They must have been about my age. The tallest of the boys had just come out of the kiosk. He shrugged his shoulders; apparently, there wasn't much of interest to them in that old kiosk. The young man must have been almost six feet tall, an above-average height, even for a Westerner. He had an aquiline nose, but his eyes were Asian. The other two boys weren't as tall, but they looked almost identical both in size and facial features. All three wore white jackets and silky gray ties.

They reminded me of 1950s film posters advertising karate masters. They were handsome in a funny sort of way.

The two girls weren't as pretty. They wore the same short skirts and jackets, the same bobbed haircut, the same rhinestone bracelets, the same café-au-lait-colored handbags. They exuded confidence and ignored the other people milling around them. They seemed almost accustomed to being stared at, watched with envy. They spoke in hushed tones, their almond-shaped eyes sparkling as they laughed. They had smooth, healthy skin, the glow of well-nourished people.

Japanese: The name alone was like a certificate of respectability, a passport that opened all the doors in the world to them. Just like that.

What did these people have that we didn't have? Hundreds of faces rose in my memory: those of my friends, people of my generation, faces gnawed with worry, shattered faces, twisted, ravaged, sooty, frantic faces.

Our faces were always taut, lean with fear. The fear that we might not be able to pay for food, or not send it in time, the fear of learning that an aging father or mother had passed away while waiting for our miserable subsidies; the fear that some embassy official just might not . . .

We had darting, calculating faces: You had to think of everything, weigh everything. All the time.

You had to think to survive, to feed your loved ones, to hustle for a day's wages sharecropping or sweeping on a train. You had to think too of the life that stretched out ahead, the pain that still waited for you, of a future as obscure and unfathomable as sea fog.

Who could fail to notice these faces in the street among the others so certain of their happiness, their freedom?

Or faces like mine: to be twenty years old and see wrinkles forming on your forehead, dark circles of misery welling under your eyes. Desperate, soulful eyes. To have the eyes of a wild animal, darting about, razor sharp, ready to quarrel over goods at a shop counter or scuffle in a line for food. And there was the shame, the self-loathing, in the mirror of another's gaze. Life as one endless humiliation.

I watched the Japanese furtively. What was it? What did they have that we didn't? If it is true that we are born again, passing from one life to the next, then in a previous existence, surely, they were like us. Their intelligence, their perseverance—these are qualities we Asians have in no short supply. All this generation had was a bit of luck. Luck to have been born in peacetime, in a real house, in the right place, under a real roof . . .

I stared down at a patch of thorny bushes covered with purple flowers: I had reached the end of the path. I walked down a wooden staircase with sloping steps worn away by passing feet. At the bottom of the stair, a small paved road led to the bus station. A line of passengers was already forming.

When I finally arrived at the residence, I hurried to the living room to find Madame Vera. She was knitting. I watched her needles dance through her fingers: She seemed to be making a sweater. I greeted her cheerfully, getting out the bottle of cognac.

"Thanks, Madame Vera. I would have died of cold without your shawl. Here's a little something. . . ." I said, waiting for a smile to light her face. But she just shook her head sadly.

"Poor girl, you really don't have much luck, do you?" She pulled a drawer open and handed me a telegram. The paper had been folded four times:

DEAREST HANG, COME HOME. AUNT TAM DYING.

No name. The Hanoi Post Office stamp. The Moscow Post Office stamp. The name of our town. I felt like collapsing right there, to sleep forever and never wake up. I looked down at the smooth old oak floor, the traces of thousands, of tens of thousands of steps. I would spread myself out and they would cover me with a sheet and it would all be over.

Madame Vera peered at me over the rim of her glasses. This time it was an old woman's look, a sympathetic, understanding look. I remembered the calm, rosy faces of the Japanese I had met in the garden, the tumble of green, the path, the flowering bushes, the pigeons perched on the pink-and-white tubs. I felt a hole boring itself in my chest, but I smiled weakly. "Thanks, Madame Vera, I'll just go up to my room."

I returned her shawl and then climbed the stairs. Our room was deserted. My roommates must have still been at the factory. That poor pug-nosed girl as well. I changed my clothes. Instead of getting into bed, I went to the bathroom to wash my face and then returned to my desk. The clean sheets on my bed looked inviting, but I resisted. Since I hadn't collapsed in front of Madame Vera, I didn't have the right to anymore. In life, you break at the moment of surrender. Afterward, you just go on.

Outside, the wind had subsided. The trees loomed silently now. I opened the window, and a gust of fresh air swept through the room. A final sliver of sun, a slight breeze. It was the beginning of autumn, the golden Russian autumn. I would have to leave without seeing it again. Perhaps I was only meant to admire its beauty once. I thought of the bureaucratic formalities I would face at my embassy in Moscow to get an exit visa. It would be two weeks, at the very earliest, before I could leave. The trees in Moscow hadn't even begun to change color.

I expected to wait two weeks, but in the end it took only ten days. Once again, the Bohemian came to my rescue. I avoided meeting my uncle in Moscow by staying with an acquaintance, one of my roommates' cousins. My hostess was a young woman who had come to Moscow on a cultural-exchange program. Now, she eked out a living as a typist for a publisher. She lived in an old, windowless room, but it was comfortable enough.

I ran back and forth all day to the embassy, taking care of my papers for the exit visa. At night, I slept on the living-room sofa. On the fourth day, I wandered aimlessly through the streets. My battle for exit papers was going badly. Our embassy seemed to me like a labyrinth conceived for the sole purpose of torturing its citizens, especially a provincial like me.

I realized, suddenly, that it was my hostess's birthday. I should have bought flowers, chocolate, or imported perfume. I had totally forgotten. At this hour, only the peasant market was open. Absorbed in my thoughts, I didn't even notice the man who had crossed the street to meet me.

"Little Sister?"

I couldn't help myself. "The Bohemian . . ." I muttered.

"What did you say?"

I laughed, explaining the nickname I had given him. He also laughed, and as his gaze fixed on me, I glimpsed a tenderness that both pleased and confused me. Could he be interested in me, the pale little skeleton?

The Bohemian took me to a farmer's market, and I bought fruit and flowers. By coincidence, he was a close friend of the woman I was staying with and had been invited to her birthday party. In the course of the evening, I recounted my ordeal at the Vietnamese embassy.

The Bohemian had a good laugh. "You'll never learn, Little Sister. Come on, let's see your papers."

He took my dossier, and three days later he came back with a plane ticket. "It leaves the day after tomorrow. The flight's at eleven forty-five . . . and I'm taking you to do some shopping. Make a list. And don't be so polite with me."

I had never met a man so gentle and yet so firm. He had helped me. This was the first time in my life I had accepted help from someone outside my family. With him, my problems seemed to melt into thin air.

My Bohemian saw me off at the airport. The sight of his confident, youthful smile beaming at me through a window at customs stayed with me, the last image in this chapter of my life as an "exported worker."

The pilot announced the takeoff. One of my compatriots seated next to me fidgeted and rummaged about, thoroughly absorbed in arranging his precious cargo. All foreign goods: light bulbs, Chinese thermos bottles, fake crystal whiskey tumblers, gourmet foods, apples. His face was drenched in sweat. The back of his shirt collar stood on end. His tie was twisted upside down. He continued ferreting, stacking his purchases, scribbling sums on pieces of paper, oblivious to me.

I stuffed cotton balls in my ears, buckled my seat belt, and closed my eyes. I slept through the whole trip, an endless, exhausting sleep, dreams and images colliding in my brain. But beyond all this, beyond all dreaming and all thought, lay one, insistent fear: Would Aunt Tam have the patience to wait for me?

Two days, one night, and many plane changes later, we landed in Hanoi. As I expected, no one was waiting for me at Noi Bai Airport. The bus from the airport dropped me in front of "Little Lake" in the center of the city. From there, I got a cyclo home.

I found my mother dozing behind her counter, a shelf spread with New Year's cakes, some hemp cakes, and a few overripe bananas. Her wooden leg sat detached beside her. Seeing me, she made a movement, as if to jump up to meet me, but remembering, she slumped back.

We closed the shop early. That evening the house was invaded by visitors, who came, as usual, whenever there was any news. Many came to ask me to help them find their child a place in one of the programs to "export" Vietnamese textile workers.

My mother prepared two huge pots of tea, which she served with raisins and the Gold Key hard candies I had brought from Moscow. The candies were a success, thanks to the Bohemian, who knew what Russian treats would appeal to Vietnamese palates. Conversation was lively, cheery, reminding me of the warmth and familial atmosphere of our hardworking suburb. But something was missing for me: Fuzzy White and the cripple's song.

"So he doesn't sing anymore, Madame Mieu's son?" I asked.

"Oh, don't worry." Neighbor Vi grimaced. "He's probably just busy playing cards with the kids. He'll start up again before too long."

"And Fuzzy White?"

The sticky-rice vendor laughed and shook her head. "Fuzzy White again? What is it with the kids in this neighborhood? My son writes me all the way from Germany asking about this dog. Madame Hoan's son, the one who was patrolling the border with China, came home on leave the other day; the first question he asks me is about this dog! And now Hang . . . Fuzzy White died last winter. Oh, he had nothing to complain about. At that age, if he'd been a man, they would have canonized him."

Everyone laughed. And the cripple broke in, belting out his song in a cracked voice:

"Hail autumn and its procession of dead leaves!"

"You see?"

I lowered my head and looked away, moved, though I was still laughing. It had taken time to grow up, to leave this place, finally to understand this song, the refrains that had haunted our miserable little streets for as long as I could remember. This same voice, this same unchanging sadness. A life snuffed out, aborted, without a whisper of a dream. It was a life unlived, a vegetable existence suckled on rubbish heaps and water lilies, fed on the brackish surface of a bog. You survived life here, but you never really lived it.

> "The poplars on the hill have withered
> The white fog lifts now
> But the one I am waiting for has yet to come. . . ."

The cripple yelled this. It wasn't a song. It was the cry of a crooked heart. a wounded beast.

"Hang, go see if the water's boiling, dear."

I jumped up and went into the kitchen. The kettle was already sputtering. I filled the thermos bottle and prepared a second tea service. The conversation bubbled along, rising and falling with the women's laughter.

"Bring some more raisins as well," shouted my mother.

I grabbed a packet of raisins and emptied them into a dish. By chance, the evening before my departure from Moscow, we had found these special seedless raisins, with hardly any grit. Everyone preferred them to the candies.

"What a feast!" said an old man with a lovely drawl who had been a cook for the French consulate. "It's been ages since I've tasted . . . You'll excuse me, but these aren't nearly as good as real French yellow raisins."

Peeved, Neighbor Vi shot back, "Really, how would we know the taste to compare them? For us, even these raisins are a delicacy."

"It was just for your edification," huffed the old man. Neighbor Vi had already turned toward my mother to gossip with her about a quarrel that had taken place in Hang Bac Street that morning.

Suddenly, the lights flickered out.

"Why are they cutting off the electricity at this hour?"

"Hey, you know, with the part-time power-plant workers we've got in this country—"

"Now don't be unfair. The cables are rotten. Our country doesn't have the money to replace them."

"Oh really? I can tell your son works at the power plant. You're just defending him. Let's drop it. Have some raisins, and then let's leave Hang and her mother in peace."

I lit an oil lamp. The guests said good-bye, each departing with a fistful of raisins or a few hard candies. The clock struck ten as I latched the door. My mother smoothed my hair, sweeping it off my face. "Leave it all. I'll clean up tomorrow. Let's sleep."

Mother hugged me and started to catch me up on various family news. Then it was my turn to tell her about my life in the strange foreign land.

"Does the snow look like the ice in Mr. Loan's refrigerator?" she asked.

"Almost. I've bought you a refrigerator. A real Minsk."

"So you mean we can make ice in the summer and sell red bean ice pops?"

"Of course."

"Was it really that cold? They say that over there the roads are all covered with this ice. I would never survive it."

"You get used to it. But older people have a hard time. I used to see them slip and fall in the snow on their way to the grocery stores. It always made me think of you."

My mother pulled up a shirttail to wipe her eyes. "You suffered so much. All because of me."

I held her in my arms and rocked her as if she were a little sister. In truth, she seemed to me as tiny and as fragile as a child. We stayed pressed against each other, and I felt happy that we had buried the bitterness, that she was here, close to me, that I could again love her. I heard the clock ticking softly, and from time to time, a lizard clucked its tongue somewhere in the darkness. The night lamp on the table looked like a burning ember, glowing from time to time. I gave her a final squeeze and a soft pat on the back.

"Yes, sleep, my child," she said, turning to me.

I eased her down onto the mat from my arms; as I tucked her in, she asked, "Do you ever see Uncle Chinh, over there?"

I felt choked with anger, as if a wave of heat was burning through my chest, rising to my brain. It felt like a moment of madness. I wanted to scream, to smash something, to escape the stench of this wretched roof once and for all. But I only pretended to yawn. "It's time to sleep, Mother. I've got to leave early tomorrow."

I thought I would explode, but my mother said nothing. The chasm between us yawned open again. I didn't sleep at all that night. I just lay on the bed. My mother tossed about and then began to snore.

I hated her snoring. It was so simple. Perhaps it was just that, its simplicity, that struck me as grotesque. About four o'clock in the morning, I heard Neighbor Vi's voice on the other side of the wall: "Light the fire for me, will you." I got up immediately, packed my knapsack, and left a note for my mother on the table: *Going back to the village. Not sure when I will be back. Take care of yourself.*

I should have stayed longer with her. Even a day more would have been enough. But as I closed the door behind me, I felt no remorse. I took a deep breath. An unfamiliar silhouette moved toward me: It was an old blind man. He was tall, with ragged clothes and a cloth sack slung over his shoulder. As he walked, he tapped the sidewalk with a cane. He looked like a beggar, I thought to myself.

Just as I opened my mouth to speak, he raised his voice: "Who goes there?"

"Where are *you* going, sir?"

"I'm looking for my daughter. Is there someone named Nhi on this street?"

I thought for a moment. "There's no one on this street with that name. As for the rest of the neighborhood, I wouldn't know. Try asking someone further on."

"Yes, yes, I'll ask."

He spoke with his head held high, which made him look slightly arrogant. He spoke loudly, very differently from the sad, halting voices of the other blind men I had known.

"You just go along your way . . . don't worry. I'll find mine. I've come here alone, all the way from my village in another province. I don't have time for your pity."

He tossed his head back and continued to walk, feeling his way down the road, tapping his cane on the dirt.

I watched him for a moment and then went on my way. He wouldn't have accepted my help. His daughter had probably fled the village after some scandal, an illicit love, an arranged marriage. . . . Perhaps she had even become pregnant before the wedding. Was he looking for her out of love or to vent his anger? . . . She, at least, had a father. I thought of my own, a stranger, one of love's phantoms. Was he wandering here somewhere along these shadowy roads, a ghost looking for the daughter he had brought into the world, of whose suffering he knew nothing?

I started to hurry. A clock struck five o'clock, and I listened to the morning calls, to the women rinsing the rice, splashing water as they drew buckets from the wells, roosters crowing to announce the dawn. At the corner of the street, an old cyclo driver was sleeping, his mouth open. I called to him, and he awoke with a twitch, straightening his body.

"Where do you want to go?"

"The bus station for the provinces."

The cyclo driver tried to focus his bleary eyes, still puffy with sleep. "Get in."

He stretched, rotating his waist, and I heard his joints crack. He jumped up onto the driver's seat, and the roads seemed to fly past me. I fretted to myself. Had Aunt Tam waited for me?

"Could you go a bit faster, sir?"

"I'm doing my best, miss. Even the young cabbies can't compete with me," he grumbled.

"It's just that . . . it's very urgent," I pleaded with him.

PARADISE OF THE BLIND

He grunted again. "Impossible. I guarantee you'll get the first bus. What more do you want?"

I said no more and just waited. The roads whirred by, and I counted the time left, ticking it off intersection by intersection. The cyclo driver was right: We arrived before the bus station opened. A few travelers were milling about. A half hour later, the bus arrived. I gave the driver a bill worth five times the price of the trip, and he gave me a seat at the front of the bus.

Luck smiled on me again that day: A legion of cyclo drivers were loitering by the market. I recognized one of them; he was the man who drove us the time I returned to the village with my mother. He had aged, and I looked at him, unsure that he was indeed the same man.

"Could you take me to the river?"

"Of course."

Seeing my worried look, he said, "I do it five times a day. Get in, please."

Patches of sweat spread across the man's shirt, plastering it to his back. As the wind swept his pungent odor in my direction, I wondered when it had last been washed. I recognized this place: the old road bordered with stretches of white sand; the arc of the humpbacked wooden bridges; a tiny stream. And from time to time, the familiar shape of an old cotton tree on a grassy knoll; the crazy patchwork of rice paddies, canals, bogs, and fields overrun with weeds.

Nothing had changed. This was still my past. It had been an evening like this when I "returned" to my village for the first time, when I had a mother I could still run to, who would hide me in her arms. I had been happy, confident. I had yet to meet Aunt Tam. I had created my own world in the space of a voyage, under the sail of a boat. Everything seemed precious to me then: the mended sail; the ferryman's distant gaze; the old woman with the baskets of potatoes. This was my corner of the earth, my own paradise etched into the final evening of my childhood. The lapping of waves, a sunset glowing violet over the horizon, a bleached-out mayfly shell floating on the surface of the water. And I had my mother then, the magical, unique paradise of childhood.

"We're here," said the driver, jumping down from his seat. He wiped his brow. "Please pay now, miss."

I settled the bill and walked slowly toward the pier. The big old stone there had disappeared. A huge cement sewer pipe stood in its place. Travelers must have used it as a bench while waiting for the ferry. The cement was smooth and shiny. I looked around for the old boat with the white sail, but all I could see was a motorboat leaving the other bank of the river. In less than ten minutes, it was purring in front of me. The old ferryman who once steered the boat for us wasn't there anymore, but his boat was. It had been equipped with an outboard motor; a teenage boy stood at the helm. Passengers boarded one by one over a wooden bridge. I was the last to get on. The boat's new captain wore jeans and a checked shirt. He even had the long hair of a popular film star. "Pay your fares now, please!"

Times had changed: Now, you paid in advance. The passengers had all come prepared with small change; I had to break one of my bills. After the captain had collected the fares, he started the motor. We reached the opposite bank in no time.

Aunt Tam had waited. I felt it even as I knocked on her door. I felt my heartbeat quicken and my head spin. All around was silence. Like the silence of an abandoned temple. I clenched my fists and knocked harder.

"I'm here, I'm here. . . ."

I heard the dull click of the latch, and I pushed in the door.

"It's you," said Madame Dua. "She's been waiting for you."

"Where is she?"

"In her room."

I leapt over the threshold, slid past Madame Dua, and crossed into my aunt's room. All the windows—and there were more here than in any other house in our village—had been flung open. Aunt Tam always liked the sun, lots of light. She was stretched out, her head propped on a wicker pillow. She seemed to be asleep. I let out a gasp. "Aunt . . ."

Her eyes fluttered open, her gaze floating for a moment. She stared at me intently.

"I've come back, my aunt."

She was silent, those wide, stony eyes of hers fixed on me, dead level. Then the tears started to flow.

"Hang . . . So this is what you've become, my child, a skeleton? At your age. My poor niece . . . selling yourself like a coolie abroad."

She coughed, and her frail shoulders and flattened chest jerked backward. Her cheekbones stuck out like points, islands lost in her sunken face. The tears rolled slowly down her cheeks into these hollow, dry sockets. The hand that patted my back fell onto the bed. She was exhausted, but her eyes still flashed like coals.

She spoke to me, her voice feeble but lucid. "Your mother . . . I detest her . . . sacrificing the fruit of her own womb like this."

I didn't dare speak. I stroked her hands. "Please. Try not to talk too much. You're weak. Rest."

But she couldn't stop herself. "I hate her . . . and her bastard of a brother too . . . They . . ."

I rubbed her shoulder lightly, trying to console her. "Please, for me . . . don't tire yourself. Rest."

She clenched her jaw and stared into the air, hatred glinting in her eyes like shards of ice. I shuddered. Her face seemed to cave in, her eyes dull and flickering. She shuddered again, letting out another cough:

"Hang, come here."

I knelt down and bent my face toward hers. She raised

a wizened hand, placing it on my shoulder. When her hand touched my shoulder, she let out another shuddering cough.

"Poor child."

Her eyes clouded over, focusing only intermittently now. I thought I saw a thread of light somewhere in the depths of these immense, shadowy orbits. I felt my heart twist. Would she regret this war with my mother, this lifelong struggle that only I would pay for?

She murmured something. "Hang . . . I love you." She caressed my hair. "I love you, do you know that?"

I gave her hand a squeeze. It was weightless, dry as an autumn leaf ready to fall. "I know, my aunt, be calm."

Her voice faded in and out, but she was lucid. "I waited for you . . . had to see you again."

"I'm back now, and I'm going to take care of you. You're going to get better," I said, bending over her.

But she wasn't listening to me. She stared ahead vacantly. She didn't believe it anymore. "You're all that's left to me . . . all I have in the world . . . I wanted you to be happy. . . . Once, I loved your father . . . like I love you. Carried him on my back. Fed him while my mother picked rice . . . he's dead now . . . wandering somewhere out there . . . in the night."

She shivered and closed her eyes. I squeezed her hand and felt her bony, shrunken body brush against my own. Love, compassion, the fragile bonds of the flesh. So this was grief. I felt my heart contract, and I heard myself murmur, "Yes, he must be out there somewhere."

She continued mumbling, her eyes closed. I watched the fluttering of her lashes. "It was so cold . . . then he left . . . I wanted to protect you, to raise you . . . and now it's me that's caused you this unhappiness. . . this suffering. . . . Are you angry with me, Hang?"

Her tiny body shivered again. When she coughed, tears ran off the edges of her hollowed temples. I hugged her close. "Don't say anything more, Aunt. Sleep now."

She must not have heard me. "Go find Madame Dua. Tell her to boil some water for my bath."

I ran into the courtyard, where Madame Dua was squatted down, separating grains of millet to cook a special dish for my return. "Please, boil some water for my aunt's bath."

She looked up, surprised. "What? I just bathed her yesterday."

She scurried into the house. "Madame, you must have forgotten. I already bathed you yesterday."

Aunt Tam opened her eyes.

"I have forgotten nothing," she said in a stern voice. "Boil the water because I ask you to and don't ask questions . . . don't forget to put in lots of herbs."

"Fine."

Madame Dua disappeared into the kitchen.

"Close the shutters," Aunt Tam ordered me.

I closed them, and as I sat down on the side of the bed, she pulled something out from under the pillow and dropped it into my hand. After a moment, I recognized the two keys tied to a blue satin ribbon.

"The bronze key is to the big linen chest. You'll find money for the ceremonies of the third day and enough for the forty-ninth day. The nickel key opens the trunk I've hidden behind the chest. You'll find the jewelry I bought you and a map to the place in the garden where I buried your inheritance. You'll see."

She had closed her eyes. I smoothed the hair around her face.

The lines and wrinkles of her face had slackened. She seemed calmer now, and her breathing was feeble but regular. She drifted off.

I went to see Madame Dua in the kitchen. "How long has she been sick?"

"More than four months now."

"Who sent me the telegram?"

"Mr. Tam. The man who brought you on the motorcycle, the last time."

"What's wrong with her?"

"I don't know. The doctors, they all come scurrying over here like bunch of granary rats. Traditional doctors. Western-style doctors. No one knows why she's sick. She just wastes away, that's all."

"What does she eat?"

"Nothing now. At the beginning, she still ate rice. By the second month, all she could swallow was gruel. By the third, only milk. Sometimes a green mung-bean puree. For the last few weeks, nothing but ginseng infusions. She vomits up everything."

"She seems so lucid."

"Very lucid. And obsessed with cleanliness. I bathe her every other day. She can't stand a single fly in her bedroom."

"Thank you, Madame Dua. You've worked very hard."

"You get used to it. And then, without her, I would have been reduced to begging. . . . The water's boiling."

"I'll bathe her," I said, going off to prepare the bath. I didn't believe in all the ceremonies and the superstitions here in the village, but Aunt Tam was dying, and I had to respect her whims. She had woken up, and she let me bathe her. I myself was weak, but she was so light I lifted her like a feather. The air in the room was sweet with the scent of herbs. She made Madame Dua change the matting and the covers regularly, so nothing smelled of sickness. I dressed her in an *ao dai* of white silk, one that she had apparently never worn and that I had found in the linen chest, stuffed under a pile of clothes.

"This is crazy, my aunt. What were you saving this *ao dai* for? In this weather, pastel colors are so refreshing."

She said nothing, just smiled at me, a ray of sadness in her eyes. Perhaps nostalgia at the thought of summer.

*　　　*　　　*

That night, the house was crowded with neighbors and relatives. Everyone in the village had heard of my return. I asked Madame Dua to prepare a casserole of green mung-bean pudding and millet cake for the guests. People chatted loudly, oblivious to the dying woman who agonized on the other side of a thin wooden screen. About nine o'clock, the man in the green sunglasses made his entrance.

"Is she better, miss?"

"She's asleep."

"Good!"

He spoke in a thundering voice. "The other day I had to drive all the way to Hanoi to get that telegram to you quickly."

"I thank you for it."

He seated himself. "Madame Dua, what about my portion of that pudding? You weren't planning on depriving me, were you?"

"Here . . . how could I even consider such a thing?"

She left to serve up the pudding. She must have received a lot of visitors lately; her language had improved. I told her, "I don't seem to see Vice President Duong."

The guests roared with laughter.

"He's taking a walk—in hell."

I was puzzled, so the man hurried to explain:

"The vice president never abandoned his designs on Madame Hai's little plot of land. She was the elder sister of that woman with the scar, you know, the one who used to help us out in the kitchen. The vice president rallied all the local authorities to his side. They hadn't even finished all the formalities when he seized the land and started building a house. He'd even bribed the construction bosses to bring him scarce materials from the township capital. Trucks dumped the cement at his doorstep. Within a few weeks, the vice president managed to raise a three-room house in the middle of her grove of persimmon trees. He bragged about it to everyone.

"Madame Hai lost everything. At night she wandered

like a madwoman around the bog near the temple. At dusk, she would go to the Ha hamlet, to the cemetery for the war dead, and spent the night near her dead son's tomb. He was killed at Tay Ninh. Three years ago, a friend brought back his ashes.

"At first, her sisters took turns trying to console her. But in the end, she resigned herself, and they stopped watching her. They're all very close, that family, and they pitched in to support her.

"As with everything in life, we ended up forgetting. No one thought about the incident anymore. But then, one evening, right after Tet, the vice president was out feeding his dogs. Unfortunately for him, the gate to the house was unlocked that day; his son, who had gone out to play soccer, had forgotten to pull the latch. Madame Hai slipped into the courtyard, slinking toward him like a shadow. She pulled a hammer out of her *ao dai* and whacked him smack on the skull. He dropped dead on the spot. It was a blacksmith's hammer. Even a horse wouldn't have survived a blow like that.

"Then Madame Hai entered the house, doused the walls with gasoline, set fire to it, and hanged herself. By the time the neighbors ran over, flames were soaring over the house, eating it from the inside. All they could do was watch the spectacle. Her body dangled from a rope until the fire ate through it."

I shuddered and felt my eyes go blank. The man started to wolf down the rest of the pudding. The other guests chatted for a few minutes and then left. The man whispered to me, "Would you mind seeing me off? I've got something to discuss with you." I walked him to the gate.

"My son told me you were coming this evening."

"Who's your son?" I said, surprised.

"He's the boat pilot, on the river. He'll be fifteen this year. He's a clever one too. Sooner or later, I've got to think about his future. He'll choose a wife soon, have children.

Then he'll need a house, furniture. Miss, you're going to inherit this house. If you don't want to live here, please give me the option."

He paused for a moment, and then went on, "Whatever you might think, I've always been a friend to your aunt. You don't have to worry about the price. I'm up to it."

"I can't think about it now. Please, leave me alone." I said nothing more, hoping he would go.

He muttered something and stalked off. I felt my legs go weak and had to lean against a wall.

Madame Dua rushed to my side. "Careful, you look like you're going to faint. I'll lock up; you get some rest."

I went in and collapsed onto the bed, fully clothed. I felt myself falling, drifting. It was morning before I awoke. I rushed into Aunt Tam's room. She had probably been awake for hours. She was staring at the door when I pushed it open.

"I must have been exhausted. Why didn't you ask Madame Dua to wake me?"

She just shook her head and held out her hand to me. I clasped it in mine; it was cold, light as a puff of cotton, with veins like tiny webs that vanished under the pallor of her skin.

"Comb my hair, will you."

I picked out a comb and gently began to fix her hair. It had lost its suppleness and was dry and coarse, like leaves of rush. Her skin was translucent and stuck to her skull. With her head wizened like that, she looked almost inhuman, like a ghostly marionette. Not a single louse, no dandruff. Aunt Tam had lived her whole life in the countryside, yet I had never met such a clean woman.

I finished combing her hair and began to braid it. She shook her head.

"No, no braids. Looks too Chinese. Do me a chignon."

I wound her hair into a tiny bun. There was barely enough hair to form a garlic clove, but she seemed happy with it.

Sitting next to her on the bed, I shivered as her spidery body brushed against mine. It was as if I had received an electric shock, a deep, soundless cry of the flesh, like a wave spanning the distance between our two bodies, erasing all borders between us. For a moment, I ached to pass through her, to send her some of my energy, some of my youth.

"When . . ." she whispered. "When I am dead . . . stay here . . . keep this house . . . the altar to our ancestors . . . remember to think of replacing the orange trees . . . and . . ."

Then, welling up from her eyes, those bottomless pools, came something like a reflection in water; a liquid mirror of the silhouette of trees; the lush green of bamboo; the drunken shiver of the betel palms; the shadow of a rooftop; the slow-moving whiteness of clouds. It was a reflection in miniature of the world she had created.

This was her legacy to me, I thought. Its price was a life deprived of youth and love, a victory born of the renunciation of existence.

"Stay here . . . under the roof of the ancestors."

"Try not to speak anymore," I pleaded with her. "Sip a bit of ginseng. Get your strength back. I'm going to take care of you now."

She couldn't hear me anymore. She stared off into the distance, chasing her own intermittent thoughts, a jumble of words, jerky breaths sucked between whitened lips. I watched her inhale violently and close her eyes. She opened them again, and they flashed briefly, a passion still burning.

She seized my arm, rasping in short breaths. "I don't owe anything . . . to anyone in this village. After the funeral . . . those who owe me . . . you cancel their debts . . . you'll remember?"

I promised. She closed her eyes, sucking each breath painfully now. I opened the only closed window to let some more air into the room.. The sky was the purest of blues. A palm tree swayed and rustled gently outside the window, spreading its nutty perfume through the room.

Her nostrils pulsed softly. "Hang. I love you. Poor fatherless child . . ."

Now, I was the one sobbing. "Hush, my aunt, you're frightening me."

I felt the space of the room swirl around me. I didn't recognize this house anymore, this garden, this hamlet. Everything around me seemed to float, detached in the middle of those crazy reeds. My aunt, this tiny shell of a woman, had been my only refuge on this earth. When she disappeared, there would be no one left to protect me.

She coughed and muttered something. "Poor child . . . I . . . can't . . . anything."

I gripped her shoulders. She opened her eyes again, slowly. She looked at me; then she rotated her head painfully toward the open window. "What color is the sky?"

I didn't understand and bent closer. "What did you say?"

"Outside . . . the color of the sky," she repeated.

"It's blue. There's even some sun."

"I've seen a sky in flames. I'm going now," she whispered.

"What?" I cried out.

A pale smile flitted across her lips.

"I've seen hell." She closed her lips and became quiet. I waited. A long time. Then I slipped out into the courtyard. She had fallen off to sleep. That afternoon, around two o'clock, I returned to her room to make a ginseng tea for her. When I opened the door, I smelled a strange, nauseating odor; she had defecated. A few minuscule balls of black excrement. At three-thirty, she stopped breathing.

I don't really remember how I organized the funeral. When the neighbors heard of her death, they flocked to the house. The man with the green sunglasses too. He was very efficient. Everyone helped me; and they found a coffin made of a thick, precious wood, a real luxury in those days. I dressed my aunt in a silk *ao dai* the yellowy color of chicken fat. When I got out some makeup from my knapsack to mask her face, the women of the village pressed around me.

"She's beautiful, Madame Tam. . . . Never seen her this beautiful."

Aunt Tam was beautiful. Few women could boast such fine features. The makeup masked the ravages of time on her skin, the lividness of her lips; her face radiated something almost like the glow of youth. I wrapped her hair in a black turban and slipped her feet into a pair of white shoes. According to southern custom, I scattered white rose petals on her chest and sprinkled special tea leaves from the Thai Nguyen region around her body.

The day of her funeral, I wore a traditional white linen mourning dress and a straw hat. Bowing to custom, I carried a cane and walked backward toward her grave. It was an act that should have been performed by her eldest son.

I was indifferent to the sacred in all this, and I still don't believe in the cults and rites. But the affection between two human beings is something I will always hold sacred.

We drenched her tomb in white flowers. Distant relatives combed the region to gather frangipani, jasmine, peonies, lotus, daisies, and camellias. That evening, everyone gathered at the house for the funeral banquet. The group of women, the ones who had always come, prepared the meal. The woman with the scar on her face had almost wasted away from grief, and as her face shrank, the scar seemed to have widened and spread across it.

The women saw to everything, organizing and preparing without the slightest urging from me. So, in the end, I thanked Madame Dua and told her she could go home.

Madame Dua protested, "I can't leave you alone here . . ." I shook my head, telling her not to worry. She fretted and then slowly rejoined the others making their way to the gate.

*　　　*　　　*

It was suppertime in the village. I was alone in the cemetery. Or rather, I went alone to this netherworld of the dead, this wild knoll scattered with tombstones. A path twisted and wound through a welter of tombs—some new, others old beyond recognition.

It was a shambles, a chaos of wood and stone grave markers. Pineapple bushes and hedges of rattan grew wild around the edge of the cemetery, and the neglected tombs were smothered by weeds and wild flowers. The villagers avoided burying their dead near the corners overrun by pineapple and rattan, fearful that this wild foliage might hamper their journey through the Kingdom of Shadows. The boys who minded the water buffalo didn't dare set foot here.

Aunt Tam's grave was the only one covered with flowers. The others were decorated with just a few incense sticks, already bent over by the wind. Nuggets made of gold leaf—the fake currency offered to the dead for their voyage through the next world—rotted where they had been scattered between the tombs. For my aunt's funeral, we had also burned gold-leaf nuggets and the "hell money" made of paper. The villagers urged me to do this, saying, "She lived magnificently, so she must die in style." They praised my piety and the splendor of the burial. I listened, satisfied. Now, I stood alone before this grave strewn with white flowers.

It was a mild day, the air balmy. Everything here seemed tatty and neglected. To me, it was all so phony, so ephemeral. My aunt was gone now. Gone forever. And there had been no reprieve. She had taken with her all the tenderness left me, all that remained of my father's love. And with her passing, she had also sealed my life's most insistent mystery.

According to tradition, I had to arrange three memorial ceremonies; on the third day, the forty-ninth day, and the hundredth day. I decided to stay in the village until the end of the last ceremony, so I asked an acquaintance to inform my mother. Furious, my mother sent back a message: "May she stay three years if it pleases her." I didn't respond. Life had taught me the value of silence. Instead, I concentrated on organizing the ceremonies.

For each one, I had to provide at least thirty dishes for the guests alone. If I counted the food for the cooks and the food to give the guests to take with them, I would need at least one hundred dishes. The money my aunt had left me in cash wasn't enough. She hadn't foreseen the speed at which the currency had devalued. Eventually, I would be forced to sell a few of her jewels and some furniture.

Starting from the day of the funeral, visitors descended on the house almost every day. They were the nouveaux riches of the village: the tax inspector; the director of the state grocery store; the second party secretary; the former president of the local commune and his successor; the pork butcher; the "boss" of the cow barrows the villagers used as cyclos; and two families supported by their overseas relatives.

They all came to see if they could buy something: the house, the low table of amboyna wood encrusted with mother-of-pearl, the rosewood chest, the mahogany chest, the wooden tea chest carved with vines and fruit bats.

I realized then what incredible effort my aunt had put into amassing this fortune: the ornamental pond in the garden; the hedges of flowers; the bronze incense-holder, the candelabras. She had managed to amass every object, every gem, needed to satisfy a rich peasant's ideal of beauty.

After the ceremony of the forty-ninth day, I opened the trunk she had hidden behind the rosewood chest. Its thick lid was bound in brass, which made it terribly heavy. Inside, I found a layer of Chinese velvet, and under it, a layer of oilcloth printed with a red flower motif. I gasped when I lifted off the final layer of covering: There was a Western-style wedding dress of white tulle; a white hat decorated with fake pearls; a pair of white gloves; a white cloth rose for the bride's hair; a gladiola, the symbol of longevity, to adorn the bouquet the bridegroom offered to his new wife.

I pulled that dress aside: below was another wedding dress, a traditional white *ao dai* embroidered with sequins, a pair of white satin trousers, ornate hair combs dripping with fake pearls. Underneath this, I found more *ao dai* of brocade, satin, and silk, all of them richly embroidered with flowers, phoenixes, and Chinese characters. Some were embroidered on the surface, but others had been elaborately hemstitched. There were also a few dried-out tubes of lipstick, two bottles of perfume, a box of Thai Swallow powder, a rotten Coty base makeup, and an entire sampling of the beauty products that had been fashionable thirty years ago.

At the very bottom of the trunk, I found a wooden box about twelve inches long and wide. I pryed open the lid: Inside was a parcel of red silk, tightly folded. I unfurled it. In it was another packet that I again unfurled to reveal a cotton puff flecked with gold leaf. Inside the puff, she had coiled a gold chain hung with a tiny heart-shaped pendant. There was also a pair of gold earrings, the ones Aunt Tam had reclaimed from my mother. Under the jewelry, I found a piece of paper folded four times. It was schoolchildren's paper, the kind we used to practice penmanship. I stared at the lines written in her careful, old-fashioned hand:

> For my niece Hang: three steps from the left wall of the kitchen, two and a half steps from the first palm trunk—starting from the pond—buried under four feet of earth. Don't forget to unearth it on a moonlit night; the shadow of the trees will shield you from prying eyes.

Underneath this, an awkwardly drawn map and a crooked compass star in the middle of her landmarks: the pond, the kitchen wall, the palms. The line was clumsy but determined.

I imagined my aunt writing these lines on another night, decades earlier, when she slept beneath the trees, a knife under
the nape of her neck, hands folded on her stomach, dreaming
of this vengeance. My aunt was beautiful, and with those vel-
vety eyes, she must have . . .

For a long time, I knelt there, gazing at the wedding
dresses, the glittering *ao dai*, the tubes of lipstick, the face
powder. Desires locked in the secret embrace of an old trunk.
When I buried her coffin, I had unlocked another, this one,
which held her dreams and her youth. And now I closed it.

Chapter TWELVE

I FELT NUMB THE WHOLE DAY. THAT EVENING, BEFORE DIN-
ner, I asked Madame Dua to watch the house while I
walked to the cemetery. It was still light out. The boys minding the water buffalo chased each other through the rice fields,
racing down the furrows. Alongside the road, young girls
teased each other, giggling and chattering. I lit some incense
sticks. The white flowers had wilted and scattered with the
wind. I placed a few peonies on the grave and sat there in
silence, watching the endless fields of rice paddy drenched in
the glow of sunset. So often I longed for this landscape when
I lived in Russia. Now, it seemed to crush me, this moment
of sweetness after the sweltering humidity of the day. The
water rippled on the surface of the rice paddies, mirroring
each ray of sunset. The grass, the reeds—everything was cop-

pery and golden. The wing of a bird shot across my field of vision.

How many times, huddled behind my shutters, watching the hallucinatory whiteness of the Russian snow, had I dreamed of these fields, of their greenness warming to gold at dusk, shivering under a caress of wind. I would remember the cry of birds at dawn, the shadow cast by swans as they floated, regal and serene across the rice paddies, the rustle of bamboo. But that beauty, welling up from nostalgia, existed only in my memory.

A screech owl cried, making me jump. I got up from the ground; it was time to go home. Not a shadow anywhere. Above me, birds darted about, swooping and diving. I followed a path that snaked through the graves; about two hundred yards farther I rejoined the road to the village. I listened to the croaking of the bullfrogs. Lights flicked on here and there. Above the croaking, the shrill hum of toads. In the distance, the chimes from a pagoda jangled in the wind.

Madame Dua was waiting for me at the door. "There's someone here to see you."

I felt my body tense with anger. "If he's here to buy something, I'm not selling."

A man with a horsey face stepped out of the shadows. "Miss . . ."

"I'm not selling a thing. Everything here stays exactly as it is until the ceremony of the hundredth day."

"But I'm not buying furniture."

"What do you want?"

"Look, I know you need money to organize the hundred-days ceremony in honor of your aunt."

"That's none of your business."

"Miss, listen to me. . . ." He laughed now, baring a set of chalky white teeth. They looked like dried pork bones in the middle of this shadowy face.

". . . If you want to keep the furniture, you'll have to sell the gold. I know what gold from Kim Thanh's is worth.

Sell it to me. I'll pay you more than you'll ever get from the others."

Was he some kind of local witch doctor? For a moment, I was confused, distraught. Then I thought of an excuse to refuse him. "Later. It's almost dark, and I can't find the certificates now."

He replied smoothly, "Madame Tam's gold doesn't need a guarantee. I'll buy it from you right now."

Then, after hesitating a moment, he added, "There's no need to be afraid. I'm no swindler. I need this for my daughter's dowry."

That said, he climbed up our landing and entered the house. Resigned now, I followed him.

He got what he came for and left, the odor of his dirty hair hanging in the air behind him. From the veranda, I watched him go. Madame Dua pulled the latch. But I could still see him, standing there in the shadow of the door. Fear rose in me: This man was like a shade the color of night, a specter born of this same greenness.

And I saw the pond again, the stagnant water, stinking, bloodied by the sunset. I saw the men, as they shuffled their cards feverishly, throwing them down in piles on the mats of woven rush. I saw my village, this cesspool of ambition, all the laughter and tears that had drowned in these bamboo groves, and then, in the middle of a blazing inferno, I saw it again: the vision of a woman twisting from the end of a rope.

This man's appearance only made things clearer for me, helped me recognize what had suffocated me. He wasn't guilty of anything: His ugliness was only a cipher, the key to my own despair. I saw his horsey face again. No marks, colorless eyes, lips like . . . Somewhere in my heart, though, I was grateful to him.

I heard Madame Dua yawn and call to me, "Come on in now. The fog's rolling in. You'll catch cold. You city girls aren't made for this climate."

A full moon shone through the dark crown of the trees.

A few stars shimmered. I stood there motionless, staring at them. Never in my life had I felt, with such sharpness, the passing of time. Like watching the tail of a comet plummet and disappear into nothingness. Like the span of my life.

Comets extinguish themselves, but memory refuses to die, and "hell's money" has no value in the market of life. Forgive me, my aunt: I'm going to sell this house and leave all this behind. We can honor the wishes of the dead with a few flowers on a grave somewhere. I can't squander my life tending these faded flowers, these shadows, the legacy of past crimes.

The full moon had slipped out from behind the crown of the trees. It was at its zenith. The stars quivered. I sat down, cupping my chin in my hands, and dreamed of different worlds, of the cool shade of a university auditorium, of a distant port where a plane could land and take off. . . .

TONE OCCURS HERE

A Glossary of
VIETNAMESE
FOOD and
CULTURAL
TERMS

The majority of the terms in this glossary are words for food or special rituals related to food preparation, eating, and drinking. Nostalgia for the foods, fruits, herbs, and exotic street markets of Vietnam occupies a major place in the soul of the overseas Vietnamese.

ALUM (*hàn the*): A mineral that resembles rock sugar, which is used in Vietnamese cooking to make foods crunchy and to add texture to meat dishes.

ANCESTORS' ALTAR (*bàn thò tô' tiên*): A family shrine constructed on a shelf or in a corner in the central room of the Vietnamese family home. This in-house memorial is decorated with candlesticks, fresh flowers, fruit, incense, decorative scrolls, and stone tablets engraved with the last four generations of ancestors. On special occasions, the living offer special foods to the spirits if the dead.

ÁO DÀI: The traditional Vietnamese national dress for women. The *áo dài* (pronounced "ow zai") is a full-length, high-necked tunic that is slit to the waist and worn over white or black silk pants.

BEAN CURD (*dậu phụ*): A spongy white curd made from pressed soybeans. High in protein, bean curd has a milky flavor and is somewhat like cheese in texture.

BETEL (*trầu*): Similar to chewing tobacco, betel is actually a mixture of several ingredients. The "chew" is made by rolling bits of areca palm nut and lime paste into a leaf. Like smoking for Vietnamese men, chewing betel is a favorite pastime for Vietnamese peasant women after a long day in the fields. Chewing betel is a mild stimulant and appetite suppressant and stains the mouth and teeth a startling, crimson red.

BLOOD PUDDING (*dồi*): Like the English blood pudding or the French *boudin*, this is a kind of sausage made from cooked blood. However, another dish, Curdled Duck's Blood Custard (*tiết canh*), is a fresh-tasting gelatinous custard made from uncooked, congealed duck's or pig's blood.

CHE SWEET PUDDING (*chè*): The name for a variety of sweet dessert dishes which, depending on the length of the cooking time, can take the form of either a sweet pudding or a sticky rice cake. One popular version, which resembles a tapioca pudding, is made of coconut milk, ripe bananas, and arrowroot vermicelli; it is served hot and topped with crushed, toasted sesame seeds or peanuts.

CYCLO (*xích lô*): A three-wheeled pedal-driven vehicle. A popular form of local transport in Vietnam, cyclos look very much like large tricycles with a double seat in front of their handlebars. The word *cyclo* is probably of French origin, from *cyclo-pousse*.

FERMENTED FISH SAUCE (*nước mắm*): A strong-smelling, amber-colored sauce made from fresh fish which are salted and layered in wooden barrels to ferment. This salty sauce is as essential to Vietnamese cooking as soy sauce is to Chinese cuisine. The fishy flavor is the base for the spicy fish sauce which is used as a dip for spring rolls and which takes the place of salt on the Vietnamese table.

FIVE-SPICE MIXTURE (*ngũ vị hương*): A coffee-colored curry made of ground star anise, cinnamon, cloves, fen-

nel, and peppercorns; this important spice mixture, used
for flavoring meats, is a result of Chinese influence.

FRAGRANT HERBS (*quế, rau thòm, tiá tô*, and *húng*): The
Vietnamese, in contrast to their northern neighbors, the
Chinese, use a large variety of uncooked fresh herbs,
wild mints, and local varieties of basil and parsley in
their cuisine. A huge, gaily decorated vegetable and herb
platter is often the centerpiece of a Vietnamese meal and
can include raw bean sprouts, sliced green bananas, cu-
cumber slices, lettuce leaves, wedges of lime, and sprigs
of mint, basil, and coriander. The Vietnamese use their
hands to shred these greens into soups or to wrap their
crispy spring rolls.

FRUITS Many of the fruits mentioned in the novel are native
to Southeast Asia and difficult to find in the United
States. CUSTARD APPLE (*mãng cầu* or *na*) is also
known in English as cinnamon apple or sugar apple.
KAKI fruit is also referred to in English as persimmon.
STARFRUIT (*khế*), a fist-sized yellow fruit that has the
shape of an elongated star (also called the carambola), is
extremely succulent and its flesh has a refreshing strawberry taste.

GINGER ROOT (*gùng*): A gnarled, but highly fragrant root
whose yellowish flesh is minced into fine strips and used
to flavor meat dishes. Pungent and somewhat prickly in
flavor.

GINSENG (*cú nhân sâm*): An aromatic root widely used as
a tonic in Vietnam and other Asian cultures like Japan
and Korea. The root of the ginseng has an eerie, almost
human shape; when it is sipped as a tea, it is believed
to have great medicinal and restorative powers, including
longevity.

HAMLET (*xóm, thôn*): The basic unit of a Vietnamese village, which consists of several hamlets surrounded by a protective bamboo hedge.

LILY BUDS (*lý*): The dried, reddish-brown buds of the lily have a delicate but lemony taste and are used to flavor soups and to give them a crunchy texture.

LOTUS (*sen*): An enormous waterborne lily of which the roots, seeds, and jade-green leaves are all edible. For the Vietnamese, the lotus is not only a delicacy, but an important symbolic flower. It has come to symbolize both purity and the Buddhist belief in universal redemption, since it grows from the filthy depths to lift its bloom to the sunlight, just as men must lift themselves above the muddy waters of the world toward enlightenment. The Vietnamese use lotus in a variety of ways; the leaves are used to wrap sticky rice sweets and New Year's cakes, the stamens of the flower are mixed with tea to give it a special scent, and the seeds are boiled into a sugary dessert soup or glazed and eaten as a kind of candy.

MUNG BEANS (*đậu xanh*): Small, yellowish-green dried beans which are used to provide bean sprouts for salads. Dried mung beans are often boiled and used to fill sweet festival cakes and as a condiment for sticky rice. Mungbean cakes (*chè đậu xanh*), actually a well-cooked variety of che dessert, are moist patties of sticky rice filled with sweetened, mashed mung beans.

MUÒNG MINORITY: A large ethnic minority in Vietnam, they live to the west and to the south of Hanoi in Hoa Binh and Thanh Hoa. The Muong, who reside in long houses set on stilts, are known for their expertise in farming. Despite the government's collectivization of

land, they have been allowed to maintain private owner-
ship of their lands.

NEW YEAR'S CAKES (*bánh trung*): These plump, fist-sized
moist rice squares are a traditional Tet Lunar New Year
delicacy. Although referred to as "cakes," they are actually salty rather than sweet. Made of a dense mixture of
sticky rice stuffed with meat and mung beans, the *banh
trung* are individually wrapped in banana leaves, which
stain them a greenish color. The cakes are then boiled in
huge vats over a low flame for six to ten hours. The
Vietnamese traditionally prepare hundreds of these cakes
at a time.

PÂTÉ (*chá*): A loaf made of finely ground meat, usually pork,
wrapped in a banana leaf. Although called a "pâté," a
cha resembles a meat loaf more than the looser French-
style pâté. In Vietnam, pâtés are made by special butch-
ers rather than at home, since these delicacies require
special ingredients and hours of pounding with a heavy
stone mortar and pestle. There are three basic kinds of
pâtés—boiled, fried, and cinnamon-flavored. Cactus-
plant pâté, however, is made from the leaves of a succulent, spineless variety of cactus. Vietnamese pâtés are a
versatile food and are served both hot and cold, as an
appetizer or as a sandwich on French bread, a taste the
Vietnamese acquired during the French colonial period
of their history.

PHỞ or "HANOI SOUP" (*phở bò hà nội*): Perhaps Vietnam's
most popular dish, *phở* is a hearty northern noodle soup
made of oxtail and seasoned with cinnamon sticks, fresh
ginger, and star anise, a licorice-tasting spice whose eight
pods form a kind of star. The exotic, beefy fragrance of
this soup has great sentimental value for the Vietnamese.

PICKLED VEGETABLES (*dua muố*): A staple vegetable dish and condiment, usually made from chunks of Chinese cabbage that are soaked in salt and left to ferment in clay jars for three to four days. Similar to Korean *kim chee* in pungency.

ROSE-APPLE JUICE (*gâc*): An extract made from the juice of the *gac*, a red fruit whose seeds are cooked with sticky rice to bring out its crimson stain. This Red Rice (*xôi gấc*), described as Aunt Tam's specialty in the novel, is served at weddings, banquets, and festive occasions.

SILKWORMS (*nhọng*): The larvae of the silkworm plucked from inside the silk chrysalis and fried with onions or steamed in water. Each silkworm is the size of a baby's finger.

SOUPS (*canh*): Vietnamese soups are huge, steaming creations that can serve as a full meal. Eaten at all hours of the day but especially at breakfast, Vietnamese soups are so popular that they are sold on the street by special vendors. Like an ice-cream vendor, the Vietnamese soup man pushes a cart filled with steaming vats of soup and attracts customers by tapping two bamboo sticks together.

SPRING ROLLS (*chá giò*): A bite-sized fried rice-flour wrapper stuffed with pork, vermicelli, chopped onion, shrimp, and mushrooms. They are smaller and crispier than the Chinese egg roll. The Vietnamese ritual is to eat these as finger food by wrapping them in herbs and lettuce and dipping them in spicy fish sauce.

STICKY RICE (*xôi*): A long-grain, glutinous rice that is soaked for several hours before cooking. Used more than plain rice, this "sweet" or "sticky" rice is often flavored

with coconut milk and is one of the staples of the Vietnamese peasant diet. A key ingredient in both sweet and
salty dishes.

SUGARY RICE-FLOUR BALLS (*bánh trôi*): A moist, sphere-
shaped sweet made from sticky-rice flour which is filled
with melted brown sugar candy or treacle.

TARO ROOT (*khoai lang*): A starchy, potato-shaped root
which is boiled, mashed, and used as a filling in both
sweet and salty dishes.

TEAS (*trà* or *uống chè*): The essential ritual in Vietnamese
hospitality, tea is served before and after meals, but
never during them. Traditionally, tea is prepared every
morning and then kept warm all day in a padded wicker
basket, ready to serve to guests. A favorite, traditional
specialty, "fragrant teas" are made by adding flowers—jasmine, rose, aglaïata (*chè ngâu*), chrysanthemum,
and lotus stamens. In Vietnamese culture, tea drinking
is associated with the appreciation of literature, poetry,
and storytelling, and a favorite adult pastime is to invite
friends to share a few cups of strong tea served from
a miniature clay pot into tiny, thimble-sized cups. The
cheapest tea, *voi*, or "poor man's tea," is in fact not tea
at all, but a substitute, much like chicory is for coffee.

TET (*Tết*): The celebration of the Lunar New Year or
Tet—which means the first day of spring between the
harvest and the planting seasons—is both Vietnam's
most important national holiday and the centerpiece of
its culture of ancestor worship. On the night of the first
moon, the household god returns to heaven to make a
report on the family's behavior. Everything is prepared
for the judgment of the family on this first night; the
graves of the ancestors are cleaned and the family altar

is decorated with offerings of food and wine in hopes that the spirits of the dead will return to bless the celebrations and the harvest.

VERMICELLI NOODLES (*bún*): Round white rice noodles. The Vietnamese like to eat big heaps of these noodles cold and topped with barbecued meats, or chopped and mixed in the stuffing for their spring rolls. There are two other basic types of Vietnamese noodles: flat, white rice-noodle "sticks" for *pho* soup, and yellow wheat noodles used for salads and dishes.

VIET MINH: The resistance front against the French formed by Ho Chi Minh in 1941.

WATERMELON SEEDS (*hạt dua*): A popular, inexpensive snack food, these seeds are dyed red and roasted over a wood fire, which gives them a smoky taste. The Vietnamese love to eat all kinds of dried, salted seeds, which they neatly crack between their teeth to extract the meat.

WINE (*ruọu*): Vietnam produces over a hundred varieties of wines or liqueurs, many of them made from distilled and fermented rice or fruits and sometimes flavored with flowers. "Viperine" or snake liqueur (*ruọu rắn*) is a special clear vodkalike drink for men; the flavor is said to come from a small viper that is inserted in the bottle, but which is probably left there for visual effect.

A Note About the Author

I N 1987, ONE YEAR BEFORE THIS NOVEL APPEARED, THE Vietnamese Communist party called on writers and journalists to shake off the stiff, official Marxist style that had been imposed on them and encouraged them to reassert their traditional role as social critics. In this atmosphere of political openness and questioning, many Vietnamese writers and intellectuals responded with literary works, films, novels, and theatrical works that openly or implicitly criticized the excesses of the Party by satirizing bureaucracy, ideology, and official corruption.

Duong Thu Huong was one of the first writers to speak out. In her essays, short stories, and poems, but especially in her trilogy of novels, *Beyond Illusions* (1987), *Fragments of Lost Life* (1989), and *Paradise of the Blind* (1988)—all stories about the sorrows and disillusionment of average Vietnamese people—Duong denounced, in simple, direct language, the dehumanization of her country.

Honest and self-critical, at the time a veteran Communist party member herself, Duong was in a unique and unassailable position to criticize the Party. The novels she wrote during this period were enormously popular in Vietnam—100,000 copies of *Beyond Illusions* were sold and 40,000 of *Paradise of the Blind* before it was suddenly banned and withdrawn from circulation. Encouraged by widespread popular support for her ideas, Duong became an outspoken participant in public debates appealing for democratic political reform and respect for human rights.

At the age of 20, Duong Thu Huong had left for the northern Vietnamese front as the leader of a Communist youth brigade to the heavily bombarded 17th Parallel, which partitioned the country. In 1979, Duong was one of the first women to volunteer for the northern frontier battle when China launched its attack on Vietnam. After decades of activism, Duong became increasingly disillusioned with the Vietnamese Communist party, and in the 1980s, driven by a deep need to bear witness to Vietnam's political and spiritual chaos, she distinguished herself not only as a writer, but as a fearless and charismatic orator.

But in 1989, faced with the spread of democratic movements in Eastern Europe, China, and Burma, conservative Vietnamese party officials suddenly brought this brief period of political liberalization to a halt. Both the popular appeal and the directness of Duong Thu Huong's writing terrified the regime, which feared the spread of her political ideas, in particular, her support for multiparty democracy. At the time, writers were forbidden even to use the word *pluralism*. In July of that same year Duong was expelled from the Party, and on April 13, 1991, she was arrested and imprisoned without trial on trumped-up charges of having ties with "reactionary" foreign organizations and having smuggled "secret documents" out of the country. She was almost immediately recognized as a political prisoner by PEN, Amnesty International and other human rights organizations. After spending seven months in prison, Duong was released in November 1991.

Duong Thu Huong is no fanatical anti-Communist pamphleteer, nor does she dwell solely on the wounds caused by Vietnam's past political struggles. Like American writer and Vietnam veteran Tim O'Brien (*The Things They Carried*), Duong Thu Huong is in the position of having been both a participant and a witness to Vietnam's tragedy. Her most recent novel, *Untitled* (1990), a soldier's story, questions the human cost of Vietnam's long war with the United States and explores the sensitive subject of her country's deep disillusionment with the nature of heroism itself.

The daughter of a schoolteacher mother and a tailor father, Duong herself defies categorization. Oddly—despite the fact that she has been a professional screenwriter for years—Duong rarely describes herself as a writer. "I never intended to write. It just happened, because of the pain," she told French journalist Michele Manceaux shortly before her arrest. As a Vietnamese woman, as a mother, as a veteran of war, as a former Communist party member, and now as an independent citizen, the power of Duong Thu Huong's voice lies in its honesty and its call to individual conscience and responsibility.